I0580231

Born of Darkness

By Dawn Wilton

This is a work of fiction. Names, characters, places and events are all fictitious and are the product of the Author's imagination. Any resemblance to actual persons, living or dead, locations or events are entirely coincidental.

Born of Darkness Copyright © 2024 by Dawn Wilton

All Rights Reserved. No part of this book may be reproduced or used in any manner without written permission of the copyright owner except for the use of quotations in a book review.

Cover art Created with the help of Bing AI Image Generator

Fan email can be received at dawnwilton@aol.com

For Meri and Lynda. Thank you both so much for being my friends.

For whomever reads this—because I love to read too.

Prologue

It was raining and dark as the darkest pitch outside. The rain came down in sheets, sluicing down and soaking anything it touched. And through that rainstorm, a single figure was stumbling, blinded by the water and the dark. Her body shook with each step she took as she sought shelter.

There was a loud CRACK somewhere in the darkness! Perothia turned and was blinded by a sudden blast of white light that lit up the forest and the wasteland beyond it like a beacon! She swore and stumbled, stunned by the surge of magical power and bright white light! Disoriented, Perothia grasped for something and fell, slid down a shelf of rock that she'd been trying to avoid. She tumbled down, down, down a long way into a dark hole! Bam! Perothia hit her head and lay there, groaning and stunned.

"Lost, are we, Little Bird?" a deep, sultry voice echoed in the dark. Perothia looked around, seeing nothing in the pitch-black dark of the cave.

"Not lost…just lost my footing in the dark," she replied, grumbling a bit as she tried to sit up and felt her head spin! She lay back and waited for things to stop spinning. A haughty laugh came from the shadows, echoing around her and adding to her disorientation!

"It wasn't the dark that made you lose your footing, Little Bird. You felt it just as I did. Someone has cast a very powerful spell nearby. And that power glows in my senses like a beacon in the dark. You feel it, too, don't you, Little Bird?" That silken, sultry voice echoed in her ears, in Perothia's head and heart.

"Yes, I feel it. I also feel like that rock nearly cracked my skull open," she groaned as she rolled onto her side and pushed herself up to sit, feeling her world still spinning like a top. She grasped her head, hearing her blood pounding in her ears. A crash of lightning somewhere outside blossomed. Thunder boomed, making her heart beat harder. Even that brief flash of light did nothing more than to stun her further and made the darkness of the cave even more oppressive.

"Easy, Little Bird. There's no rush to go anywhere in this storm."

"I'm half-frozen and I can't see anything. I'm soaked! I'll die if I don't get warm soon," Perothia snapped, wishing with all her heart that she'd stayed with her former Master, who had been teaching her magic. She now rued that decision as she felt with shaking fingers, seeking a bit of wood or rocks or something that she could use to build a fire! At least at her old Master's, she'd been fed and warm, if held back a bit in the arts she'd wished to learn. In the end she had left because she knew he was deliberately not teaching her the spells she so desperately wanted to know. Spells that would have given her more power, more strength to take power from others. Perothia's teeth chattered as she wrapped her arms around herself, trying to warm up though there was no fire, nothing but that thick, cold blanket of darkness about her.

"Perhaps we can come to an arrangement then, Little Bird. I will give you immortality. No more fear of death or dying and as much power as any decent mage…could ever wish for," the voice purred into her ear before she felt a small gust of wind as someone stepped around her again, circling her like a shark circles its prey.

"What's the price?"

"You will serve me and help me to remake this rotten core of a world," the source of the deep sultry voice was before her now, but she still couldn't see who was speaking to her.

"And just who are you?"

"Oh, I doubt you'd know me. I'm nobody really…I'm just…." A light flared, nearly blinding her again as a green fire suddenly sparked into life, revealing a very tall figure with cloven feet and large twisted red horns. The figure turned to regard her, then he laughed softly, the charming sound sending a chill down Perothia's spine. "I'm just the Destruction God." He held out one large, black hand to her. "Come, Little Bird. Let's discuss our deal…Alyra."

Perothia hesitated, looking up at him as she considered his offer. *I do want more power, but is it worth it to serve him?* She considered it another moment or two more, weighing the odds of her getting such a source of power such as the one that now glowed out in the wasteland at the center of the forest. *Perhaps I can become powerful enough to overcome him and take his place with time,* she thought as she took his hand. Power surged into her, white hot and making her body quake as it surged through her veins! Ice cold surged in the fire's wake, making her shiver and her teeth chatter all over again!

"Our deal is struck! Be remade, Perothia, into Alyra…my Servant!" the God of Destruction cried as her body shook from the magical changes being made to it!

Perothia screamed as she felt the magic burning through her! Fire and ice surged through her, making the world spin and everything burn and freeze all at once. Her body changed, hair growing long and black. Tattoos blossomed over her body as the magic raced through her veins. The pain swelled and grew to a horrible crescendo and

Perothia passed out as the Destruction God's laugh chased her into the Darkness of blissful oblivion.

*   *   *

Perothia woke, feeling every inch of her body aching. She was surrounded by Darkness and yet she could still see! She reached out, touching a shadow…and watched in amazement as her hand seemed to melt into it like butter melts into hot potatoes.

"What is this?" she asked out loud, her voice shaking with each word. She felt as weak as a newborn kitten, and felt as though she had so little strength…why was she so weak?

"Your new gift. One that I gave you," the Destruction God's voice rang out as his hand reached out from that same shadow and drew her into it. His arm curled about her waist as he pulled her to him. "Easy, Alyra. You're still adjusting to your new…state."

"New…state?" she asked numbly, not remembering much at first.

"Immortality and power…beyond your wildest imagination," the God purred against her ear as he turned her around and let her see the new world around her.

The Realm of Shadows.

Chapter One

Sunlight was streaming through the white marble-lined window in the library as Ezra Coren, Sorceress of Ammora Castle, walked in. She stretched, feeling her growing belly jump as the baby decided to kick. The movement caused her linen tunic to flutter over her loose leggings. Ezra chuckled and ran a hand over her growing belly as she paused to look out over the ocean of green that had replaced the wasteland outside of Ammora.

"A thousand years of nothing living out there and now I have to get used to this new view," Ezra murmured to herself as she moved up the ladder to climb out through that tall window and onto the balcony behind the parapets. Standing above the left side of the Unicorn's horn that made up part of Ammora's front wall, Ezra stretched again and rested her hands against the smooth white marble. A small, cool breeze washed over her as she gazed out as she thought about how her life had again changed.

Ezra had become the Sorceress of Ammora as the result of her refusing to leave her husband Bael's side during the End of Days Spell. It had been cast by the Wizard's Council of Axrealia in response to a vision of Axrealia being swallowed by a dark cloud and every person in the world dying within it. To save their world, the Council sacrificed themselves to give Ammora their power and to fuse into a single living being. That being was Baelios, the Spirit of the Council, who preferred to only be visible when he was alone with Ezra or when there was a great need for his presence. Because Ezra interfered, Bael changed the spell and saved her life by changing her from a simple mortal warrior into an immortal mage.

It also made for some drawbacks. Ammora was alive and did odd things on its own at times. Like changing the layout of its interior during an attack or just randomly because the Castle itself wanted a change. Being surrounded by wasteland and the dead forest had made Ezra yearn for living things. Animals, plants, insects and birds had all been such rare occurrences for so long, she had ached for the sight of anything beyond the wasteland dying outside of Ammora.

Until now. Ezra had cast a spell two months ago, changing the wasteland and dead forest into a living plethora of trees, flowers, moss and various other plants. The mercenary company that had come to live here was building a beautiful city outside of Ammora as well and new farms were being incorporated just outside of it. Ezra was still getting used to it.

"You'll never know any different, my dear," she said to the child within her belly as the baby again stretched and kicked. Ezra had reached the seventh month of pregnancy and found herself talking to the baby more and more with each passing day.

"Of course, she won't, Ezra. How are you feeling today?" Baelios asked as he suddenly appeared next to her. Ezra was used to this happening every day, multiple times a day, and didn't startle at his sudden appearance. Ezra chuckled. She had had a thousand years of course to get used to Baelios popping in and out of existence beside her.

"Checking up on me, hm? I'm feeling all right. Tired and restless, but otherwise I'm fine. How are you feeling now that our power has been doubled by the Orb of Eithal?" she asked as she turned to the translucent Spirit. He had blue skin and orange eyes and blonde hair. Otherwise, he looked just like Bael had, though his voice changed at times when each member of the Wizard's Council took their turn to talk through him.

"Stronger and able to stay solid for as long as I wish. I try not to waste the Orb's power like that, but there are times when it feels so good it's almost as if We were all alive again," Baelios replied with a rather large and happy smile.

"Good. I'm glad. Please go ahead and use it for being solid when you feel the need, Baelios. I know you've missed being able to touch and do things just as much as I missed the smell of wet grass," Ezra replied as she turned her ice blue eyes to look out again on that sea of green below.

"Quite true. And speaking of being able to touch and do things…when are you and Derik going to make your relationship more…formal?" Baelios asked in that teasing manner that Bael used to adopt when bringing up a subject he knew Ezra didn't want to discuss.

"When we're ready. When everyone else stops pushing us into it! When we can do it before the Goddess between the two of us. I…I've had a large wedding, as you know, Baelios. I really don't want another one," she replied, feeling uncomfortable at the thought of a large wedding for everyone to see.

"No Priest?"

"No. Priests aren't necessary, if you recall from what I told Bael of my upbringing."

"It might be necessary for Derik."

"He hasn't insisted on it. He's waiting until we've had a chance to finish settling."

"Settling from what?"

"From that damned business with Juktis! That partner is still out there, and she is far more dangerous than he was."

"Juktis was bad enough. Is she—"

"She's either the Darkness or she's working with it. I'm not sure which and I'd rather not give her time to find another partner to use against us. The next one might be worse than the last."

"How're you going to find her?" Bael asked, his tone a little sterner but not scolding…yet.

"I don't know yet, Baelios. Juktis hid himself very well, but she's in some cave somewhere. And I have no idea where to begin looking for it," Ezra admitted, feeling overwhelmed by the task at hand. "Besides, with a baby on the way and Eve insisting that I don't travel unnecessarily, it makes it that much harder to go looking for her." Ezra ran her fingers through her long silver hair, which she had left loose this morning on purpose as she had been having headaches the past couple of weeks.

"True, though we do have time on our side. With Juktis gone, she won't be coming for us directly yet," Baelios was quick to point out.

"That's the trick. Finding her before she comes knocking on our doorstep," Ezra replied as she turned to go back inside to have her breakfast and to get to work. "It's time I took another trip through the Astral to try to find traces of her."

"You've done that three times this week—"

"Sooner or later, I must pick up her trail. It's the only option I have now, Baelios. Just watch my back while I look, okay?" she asked as she made her way down the staircase and back into the library.

"All right, but you'd better make it a quick trip this time, Ezra. I have a feeling that something is coming."

"I've had that feeling too, but it's not the baby and we're not expecting anyone."

"That's what troubles me," Baelios replied dryly as he left her to her breakfast and her own musings.

Kayla was, thus far, having another quiet day.

"Nothing to do…again. Gods the caves can be so boring, and Mother won't even let me go out for a decent swim lately!" she muttered in frustration, lazing at the side of the pool where the cave was filled with more air than water, and resting her long smooth tail against a rock. There was a small hole in the ceiling here and it let sunlight through, and it never failed to fascinate Kayla at how it caused rainbows to dance in the water here.

Not that it improved her mood…much.

Ousran, her childhood friend, swam up, looking like the catfish that had stolen the biggest treat from a shark.

"Hey, Kayla, what're you up to?"

"Nothing, as usual. Mother has me bogged down with duties," Kayla replied, flicking her blue and green tail with the golden fins in frustration. "She keeps saying that I need to learn how to run a pod if

I'm going to be a Queen someday…like I want to run a pod! I really don't, I just want to go out, swim and just be…."

"Normal?" Ousran replied with an understanding look, her own purple and red tail flashing a bit in the sunlight as she flicked her long red hair back out of her eyes. They had been friends since they had been babies, as Ousran's Mother was Queen Felati's handmaiden. Having a Queen for a mother was not easy at all, particularly when they were immortal!

"Yeah. She doesn't get that I just don't want to be in charge of my own pod someday. I just want to swim and relax and just…. just…be me!"

"Well, you were born a princess and one who is going to change someday, Kayla. But that doesn't mean we can't have some fun now, before you change," Ousran replied with that big smile and mischief dancing in her blue eyes as she stretched out her own tail and flicking her purple tipped fins playfully, making a little tidal wave that splashed Kayla.

"What kind of fun?" Kayla asked, instantly interested of course. She was bored and tired of being bored….and tired of nothing but duty, duty and more duty!

"I know a ship graveyard that is fun to play in. Granted, it's where your mother has decreed we're not supposed to go, but…"

"Where is it? How long will it take to get there, and can we be back before supper?" Kayla asked, excitement bubbling up at the thought of being able to play in a bunch of sunken ships. Granted, she was a teenager, but she hadn't seen a sunken ship…ever!

"Yes, yes, and yes…but we'll have to take breathers—"

"Oh, that's not a problem. Let's go!" Kayla said excitedly, grabbing Ousran's hand and diving to swim towards her chambers. She had two breathers already in her room for long journeys, in case her mother needed her to go with her to the Dragon's Keep.

Time to have a little fun, Kayla thought as they prepared for their little adventure.

After all, there was no harm in having a little adventure, was there?

Ezra was sitting on her throne, relaxing. She closed her eyes, allowing her thoughts to drift before she began to cast herself into the Astral plane. Spreading her invisible wings, she lifted herself and began to fly, looking for tell-tale traces of dark magic.

The traces she looked for would be subtle, nearly invisible, but Ezra began the search anyway.

She left traces on the falcon she had hurt. Thank the Goddess for bringing the poor creature back from the dead. But she's left very few traces anywhere else. Still, there must be something I can use to track her, Ezra thought as her astral body soared over the ground at a speed that no creature could physically accomplish.

Ezra searched and searched, seeing nothing. No traces could be seen or sensed no matter where she flew, not even around the Fortress, which now belonged to Jarod. Jarod's twin brother, Juktis, had tried to take Ammora Castle with the thought of conquering Axrealia and destroying it. Juktis had also raped Ezra, impregnating her with an immortal child in the bargain. Ezra, Jarod, and two other immortal mages had imprisoned Juktis within the Orb of Eithal. The Orb was now part of Ammora, rooted into a pedestal within the main Power chamber of the Castle.

Ezra used that power now that was tied within her to the Castle and her body. She used it in vain, looking for the traces that might lead her back to Juktis' partner.

And found nothing. Nothing close by, nothing within a moon's travel from the Castle.

But, to the East, she sensed something. A tension. Something out of balance.

What is that? She wondered as she watched what seemed to be a storm in the distance. Ezra tried to go towards it, but she felt the tug on her astral form. Something was calling her back. But it wasn't Baelios.

The call was from The Castle itself. With a sigh, Ezra rushed back to her body within Ammora. When it called, there was always a reason. And those reasons were rarely pleasant. Ezra flew back gracefully on her invisible wings and dove back into her body as easily as if she were diving into water.

She opened her eyes and breathed slowly, taking stock of herself and her surroundings.

::Baelios, the Castle--;:

::I felt the summons too, Ezra. It's coming from the Orb beneath the Castle.::

::Why would the Orb be summoning us?:: Ezra asked him telepathically, puzzled at the sudden call from Ammora.

::Your guess is as good as mine,:: Baelios replied heavily as Ezra rose and began to walk down the long steps of the dais to go to her workroom.

Each step echoed ominously as Ezra walked through the halls to her workroom, then through the workroom itself to the new back door. The door had appeared, along with the corridor down into the bowels of the Castle itself, after the Battle of the Fortress. She passed through the long hall through the warm incubation chamber, where a Dragon's egg rested in a nest. Each day, she and Baelios had been checking on it to make sure it was still in good health and had not rolled while it waited to be born. Dragons, like reptiles, attached to the inside of their shell and would hatch when the air left within the egg began to run out. Thus far, the egg showed no signs of hatching, but it was still pristine and white and glowing with a faint magical energy.

Beyond the incubation chamber, the hall continued to a door. No mortal could pass through it for it contained the source of Ammora's, and Ezra's, power. And in the center of the room was a pedestal with a large milky white orb atop it. Roots grew from the pedestal and twined around this orb, drawing its power into the Castle's Power Source, augmenting it and adding its power to the Orb as well.

Ezra moved to this Orb, letting the door close behind her even as Baelios moved silently through it to join her beside it.

"The Orb of Eithal…why in the hell is it summoning us?" Ezra asked, looking at its smooth surface. Within, she could sense that angry and dark presence that was Juktis. "I hate coming here. I avoid it as much as I can because I don't want to see him in it," she admitted to Baelios, resting one hand against her belly. The baby was squirming and kicking, sensing her distress.

"I'm not a fan either, but let's see what it wants, hm?" Baelios suggested, his voice sounding deeper and with a sense of fire and brimstone glowing in his eyes for just a moment. Ezra sensed that this was the half-Dragon Wizard speaking instead of Bael and just took a breath. That member of the Wizard's Council had a rather pragmatic and straight-forward way of looking at things. Ezra reminded herself, again, to not get short with Baelios as he couldn't help how he spoke to her at times like this.

Ezra just took a moment to breathe, then stared into the surface of the Orb, letting her thoughts drift away until she could reach out and touch it with a clear mind.

It had an odd sense of time, but she sensed what it was sensing. Like a storm in the distance yet so far off it was barely felt. It was like a faint smell of rain on the wind, yet it was drawing closer with every moment. Ezra felt a tug, leading east, before the Orb released her altogether, leaving her to puzzle it out for herself as she came back to her own thoughts.

"What did it show you?"

"A storm in the distance. But it's not a true storm. I think it's her…she's up to something but the Orb is only sensing a piece of it. And it's East, far away but I couldn't get more than that," Ezra admitted.

"Pretty vague, but maybe it's magical? It might not even be her," Baelios suggested, his voice becoming more like her first husband, Bael's, again.

"Too true, but I'll have to investigate it either way. And with the baby due within the next three months, it's going to be hard, Baelios."

"Use your resources. Ask Lady Reanalia. She'll help you, I'm sure of it."

"I might just do that. I'd ask Lord Faorir, but he made it plain that he doesn't wish to be bothered for anything less than a full-out war. Even then, he'd rather be left alone. And Lord Jarod…"

"You still don't trust him, do you?"

"No, I don't. But can you blame me?"

"Of course not. He might still be of some help, though."

"I'll consider it," Ezra sighed, feeling the room spin for a moment.

"You should rest. You're entitled to it."

"I might be entitled to it, but you know as well as I do that my duties—"

"That was before the baby. Come on. Time to go to your Chambers and have a good rest, Ezra," Baelios insisted as he became solid again and began to help her back up the stairs. Dizzy as she was, Ezra didn't argue. Even as he helped her to lay down and removed her boots for her, Ezra still didn't have the energy to argue with him.

One didn't argue with a Ghost, after all. Ghosts tended to win the argument.

Derik was out on the training grounds with Captain Lita's troops. Since the battle, he had gotten into the habit of training with them daily and learning new skills. Including how to use one of the laser guns that they had sported during the battle.

Now he was dodging stun-bolts from Aeryn's latest toy. Rolling over his shoulders and up to his feet, he popped up behind a barricade only to have to duck again!

"Thank the Gods we got these new training grounds built. But damn it, Aeryn, isn't it time to call it a day?" he called as he tried to get a glimpse at where Aeryn was hiding so he could get a clear shot.

"Nah, you're just out of shape, Derik! Eve said you needed a good workout!" Aeryn called back from the left side of the barricade. Derik popped up again and fired back, managing to surprise Aeryn enough that he dropped his laser pistol.

"Ha!" Derik cried as he saw Aeryn finally surrender.

"Don't be an ass about it now! Good job, Derik. Let's go get a drink and cool off, hm?" Aeryn laughed as they gathered up their fallen weapons and made their way out so the next pair could square off. "How's the Sorceress feeling these days? And when are you two getting married?"

"Oh, soon enough. The Sorceress doesn't want to be pressured into a big wedding is all."

"Why not? She *is* the ruler here, after all." Aeryn pointed out, giving Derik a bit of an odd look.

"Well, if you tell her that, she'll just say that the city is ruled by the Council, not by her. And that she has no intention of ruling anything because her responsibilities are too many as it is," Derik shrugged as they hung their weapons on the weapons rack and headed back towards the back entrance and into the castle. Derik had made sure that there was a local brew-master now and he had procured enough barrels to hold the troops for a few months, so long as they came to the castle to have it with their meals. "Besides, with the baby due in another couple of months, I doubt we'd have time to plan a big wedding."

"Never say never, my friend. What if she insists on a private ceremony?"

"I don't care one way or the other. I love her. I'd rather not have a spectacle either. Spectacles invite trouble, especially around here," Derik pointed out as they emerged from the cool tunnel and headed towards the maze of corridors that would lead to the kitchen. Every person in the city and in the castle now knew these corridors by heart. Though Derik had seen the corridors change before his eyes and take the lives of intruders, the mercenaries here weren't in any immediate danger. So long as you didn't intend harm towards the Castle or it's Sorceress, the Castle was content to allow them to explore within reason. Certain doors only opened for Ezra, as Derik had also seen with his own eyes. For the mercenaries, it was a little inconvenient. But the mercenaries had learned to live with the minor inconveniences in exchange for having their own real homes in the city.

It was a luxury, as Derik knew all too well, that few mercenaries ever got a chance to see in their own lifetimes. It was a luxury that Derik had once been close to earning for himself, but fate had seen to it that his last job was anything but savory.

Derik shoved the memory of Juktis and that fiasco away as he poured two ales for himself and Aeryn while Aeryn grabbed a couple of platters filled with food and they headed to a table.

"Yeah well, things have been quiet since that last battle at the Fortress. The warriors are starting to get a little restless, but you didn't hear that from me," Aeryn said as they settled and accepted his drink from Derik.

"I know the feeling. I'm feeling restless too. It's like a storm on the horizon that I can't see, but something big is going to happen soon. Things have been far too quiet, particularly with that mysterious partner out there somewhere. The Sorceress has been searching for her since we got home, but she still hasn't figured out where that woman went."

"Too bad. I was hoping to exact a little revenge on that wench for what she did to Mara."

"I think we'd all like to. That woman's up to no good and only the Gods know what she'll do next," Derik replied as he studied briefly what was on his plate before tucking into it.

"No kidding. I just hope that we find that partner of his soon and get rid of her," Aeryn raised his ale before taking a long pull from the tankard.

A horn sounded, one loud long note.

"Visitors?" Derik mused as he waited to see if two more short blows would come next. That would signal attackers, a common signal that armies and mercenaries both agreed should be universal. But one long note would signal visitors.

The two shorter notes never sounded, so Derik rose, leaving his meal half-eaten.

"Duty calls it seems," he said to Aeryn before he drained his ale.

"Aye. I'm comin', just a moment to finish my ale," Aeryn said as he took two more hurried bites, drained his ale and rose to follow Derik to the kitchen to drop off their plates. Then they both hurried to the Entrance Hall to greet their guests.

"Ezra, wake up. There are visitors outside," Baelios murmured into her ear as Ezra dozed. She turned over and rubbed her eyes, blinking sleep out of them as she looked up at the Spirit of the Council.

"Who is it?" she asked sleepily, trying to find some semblance of thought.

"A diplomatic party from one of the further cities. I'm unsure as to which one though…but the interesting thing is it's composed of both Forest Elves and Dark Elves."

"I thought those two tribes hated each other," Ezra said as she pushed herself up to sitting, then forced herself to rise reluctantly from the soft mattress.

"They do, but it seems something has forced them to put aside their differences."

"Must be something serious then. Those two have been at each other's throats with little thought other than eliminating the other for centuries," Ezra mused as she began to straighten herself up with a little magic.

"Careful, you've done too much magically already today, Ezra," Baelios warned, alarm written on his near-transparent features.

"Yes, yes, I know. But duty calls and I'm not going to go out looking like I just rolled out of bed."

"You did just roll out of bed," Baelios said, almost teasingly. Ezra sighed, threw up her hands and headed out the door to go to the throne room.

"They don't know that," she called back over her shoulder as she hurried along, walking brisky back towards the Entrance Hall.

*   *   *

"So, how long have these people been missing, Ambassador Suiadan?" Derik asked as he wondered where in the hells that Ezra was. Normally, Ezra would have beaten him to the Entrance Hall, but thus far there was no sign of her arrival, which was very odd in and of itself. The tall, regal looking raven-haired Forest Elf stopped his careful observation of the hall to look back at Derik as they waited. Aeryn, luckily, was standing with him, in case things got ugly.

"Four days. A storm took them. Some sort of magical tornado and we demand that you give us our brethren back—"

"And what about my Queen and my sisters?" Ambassador Talice demanded. She was nearly as tall as the Elf ambassador, but where Suiadan's skin was fair, hers was nearly as black as night. Long white hair was bound back in a long, severe braid that hung down her back. "They have been missing almost as long as his people have and were also taken by a magical storm! No storm could develop down our caves unless you sent it!"

"We had nothing to do with it. As you can see, there is some debate as to who has who, Sir—" Ambassador Suidan began.

"Derik. The Sorceress should…ah, here she is now. Shall we proceed to the throne room, and you can both tell your stories to her? She might be able to help you to locate your people," Derik suggested, trying to gently steer them that way.

"Greetings and please forgive my tardiness. I was working in my Chambers. How can I help you both?" Ezra asked, falling into step with them as they began to walk.

"It seems magical storms have kidnapped several members of each of their societies, Sorceress,--" Derik started.

"The Dark Elves have taken—"

"No, the Forest Elves have—"

"Please! Please…let's not blindly accuse anyone, Ambassadors. Why don't you each tell me your tales and we'll see what I can do to help you to find your people," Ezra paused mid-step to breathe then continued to walk on towards the throne room.

"Sorceress, are you--?"

"I'm fine, Derik. It's just a very strong kick from the baby," Ezra replied softly. Derik gently grasped her elbow and put an arm around her back as they walked, trying to give her what support he could.

Ezra paused as they walked towards the throne room with the Forest Elf and Dark Elf Ambassadors. She felt a tight squeeze about her belly and back. Turning to Derik, she tried to reassure him, but it was plainly written on his face that he was worried about her and the baby.

::Baelios, could you quietly go tell Eve to please come to the throne room after the Ambassadors have left? I don't think I'm in labor yet, but--::

::No need to explain. I'll go tell her now, Ezra. We'll be there shortly,:: Baelios replied telepathically as Ezra used her magic to teleport herself up to the throne. With the pressure off her back and legs, Ezra was able to relax and look back to her guests with a semblance of her usual dignity.

"Ambassadors, why don't you tell me your tales…one at a time. Ambassador Talice, why don't you begin," Ezra suggested gently.

"Very well. It happened five days ago," the Dark Elf woman replied. Ezra briefly looked over her black and white armor, her weapons which were sheathed and settled in to listen. "We were in our caves, preparing for a celebration to honor our Goddess, the Spider Queen. A large storm cloud appeared in our caves. Fog rolled in, thunder *boomed*…and when the maelstrom finished blowing itself out, our Queen, her consort and seven of our highest priestesses were all missing. The Forest Elves *must* have—"

"Now now. Just the facts that we know for now, please. Let's not accuse each other. I can tell you that I would never send a storm to kidnap people, and I have never heard of the Forest Elves having such a power either. Ambassador Suiadan, what is your tale?"

The green and brown male Ambassador of the Forest Elves straightened his fine tunic. Ezra couldn't see any weapons on him. She did sense that he might have some hidden somewhere on his person. Which she could understand, knowing how dangerous their world was at times.

"We were also preparing a celebration on the same day. We were preparing to honor our God, the Lord of the Forest and Wilderness, when a storm broke out over our forest. Wind blew so hard it knocked some of our oldest trees to the ground! Fog *rolled* in, thunder boomed all around us and when it cleared, our King and his Consort were missing. As were our most revered priests. The Dark Elves—"

"Again, we are not going to accuse anyone of this deed. So, on the same day, you both had a storm appear out of nowhere and when it cleared, your people were missing?" Ezra asked just to get it clearly in her mind.

"Yes, Sorceress," both Suiadan and Talice replied at once, giving each other a look as they realized they had each echoed the other. Ezra gave a slow nod and held out her hands. Lightning leaped from her fingers upon her command to strike the Marble floor. Where the lightning struck, a large pool of water appeared and Ezra held out her hands, letting the magic flow through her and into the pool.

I'll need to be careful with this spell, but they'll need to see as I see. Goddess, please help me to find the truth! Ezra prayed silently as she worked. Energy poured through her from the Castle, into her and into the spell. Her hands began to glow, and the water below began to glow an eerie blue. Images sprung forth into her mind's eye, which then showed on the surface of the pool she had summoned.

Ghostly images of Dark Elves, Forest Elves, Mermaids and Dragons as well as humans floated over the surface of the water, all in cages of one sort or another. Ezra focused, trying to get an image of what was beyond them, but the only thing that she could see was plain brick walls…chains…and dark shadows.

Nothing that could tell her where they were. Nothing that would help her to locate them at all.

The energy of the spell suddenly flared, and Ezra lost her control over it and the pool flared briefly with light before the water settled and the images vanished.

"I'm sorry…that is all that I could see with this spell. But as you saw…yours are not the only people who are missing. Someone else has taken all of those we saw."

"Yes, but who is it?" the impatient Ambassador Talice demanded to know as she adjusted her armor about herself. A telltale sign, Ezra realized, that the Ambassador wasn't used to wearing such accoutrements.

"I don't know yet, Ambassador Talice. But I assure you, I will find out. Derik, could you escort our guests to their rooms? They've had a long journey and until we find the answers they seek,o I will not turn them away empty-handed."

Derik bowed. "Of course, Sorceress. Ambassadors, if you'll follow me, I'll show you to your rooms and give you a tour of the Castle." Aeryn also gave her a salute and a grin as he turned to go with Derik to escort their guests.

"Is that all she's going to do?" Ambassador Suiadan demanded as they began to walk away.

"Of course not! The Sorceress will continue to look for your people and the others who are missing," Derik reassured them both as they left the throne room. Ezra sighed and rubbed her eyes, feeling drained and still feeling pain as her belly continued to squeeze tightly about her womb.

::Baelios, is Eve--?::

::On the way, Ezra. Breathe and relax. I saw what you saw, and I'll take up the search while you rest. I'm not limited except by what the Castle has for energy and since we added the Orb...I can try to extend my reach over as much of Axrealia as I can. Don't worry,:: Baelios replied telepathically just as Eve walked into the throne room.

"The Spirit said you're having contractions?" Eve asked as she hurried up the stairs to Ezra's side.

"I think they might be, yes. My duties are calling, and I can't concentrate as well with my middle tensing up painfully every few minutes."

"Okay, let me take a quick peek," Eve replied as she began to go into trance. "Are you upset about anything?"

"Only everything. There are people missing from all over Axrealia. Captain Lita keeps asking when we're having a big ceremony...and my main priority to find Juktis' partner keeps getting waylaid. And the baby isn't due for two more months...ow!" Ezra winced as she took a long deep breath and tried to relax.

"Ah...practice contractions. You need to calm down. When you get upset, you'll feel like you're going into labor, but it's just your body practicing for the main event. I'll walk you to your chambers. Why don't you take a little rest and do something relaxing?" Eve suggested as she helped Ezra up and off the deep seat of the throne. With Eve's help, Ezra managed to make it down those stairs safely and she gave a nod.

"My nap was interrupted by our unexpected visitors earlier. I think a rest is in order," Ezra admitted, feeling so weary that it was a wonder that she was still standing.

"Good choice. Let's get you tucked in," Eve said as they began to make their way down the winding maze of hallways.

Chapter Two

Getting out of the Mermaid caves wasn't as easy as Kayla had thought it would be. Guards, of course, were at all the entrances and exits that the entire pod tended to use daily, and they all knew who Kayla was.

::How're we gonna get out?:: Kayla asked Ousran softly mind to mind, studying the guards over by the side entrance to the caves.

::Hm…You're going to have to wear a disguise, I think. Or we're going to have to take a secret way out,:: Ousran sent back, studying the guard with a hint of a smile. ::There's entrances and exits that you royals don't use, and that most of us commoners do sometimes when we need to take care of something for the pod.::

::Like what?::

::Oh it's small though, just to warn you. But there's a couple of smaller exits over on the eastern side of the caves…but it's dry so you'll have to transform for a few minutes. Once we're on the other side…there's a nice big wet pool to get into and swim out through,:: Ousran replied, still looking like the catfish that had stolen the treat from the shark. And all too pleased about it.

::Better than trying to disguise this. Let's go,:: Kayla sent back and motioning for Ousran to lead the way.

Ousran surged ahead and headed for the servants' section of the caves.

Ousran stretched as she dried herself off, feeling her body transform into that of a human teenager. She stretched, then pulled on a long skirt that she had stored here earlier and a linen top and handed the same to Kayla as Kayla transformed. Kayla looked like an Elf when she changed, complete with pointed ears, but this was part of the reason why she was immortal. With such magical blood from two species running through her veins, it made it possible to be the rarest sort of Mermaid possible…a Queen or a King. Queens were born with blue tails that would eventually change color and turn white with flecks of gold. And the change was already beginning to start for Kayla as her fins were already changing into a gold color. Kings were born with orange tails that slowly changed to white and silver. When a pair was side by side, they looked magnificent.

Ousran's tail would never change like that, not that she minded.

I wouldn't want Kayla's place for all the pearls in the Ocean! It's not fair how many duties the Queen piles on her, but…I know that it's because she'll be leading a new pod someday. Maybe she'll be kinder to her own children, Ousran thought wistfully as Kayla finished changing and they began to walk with their breathers tucked into satchels on their backs for the side entrance.

Slipping through the narrow space wasn't terribly hard for two teens and Ousran giggled as she heard Kayla gasp in awe at the sight of the chamber beyond.

Stalactites hung from the ceiling, looking wet and dark though they had various colors laced throughout them. Formations that clung just to the ceiling that looked like curled pieces of bacon in all sorts of hues added to the beauty of the wild cave. And the pool below was beautiful with wild algae and seaweed, and gorgeous flowers of the sea.

It was as wild a cave as anyone saw as the others were well tended and gardened in the water. But no one had touched this ever as the servants enjoyed the wild beauty that was part of their ocean environment.

"What do you think?" Ousran asked her best friend, watching her face with excitement now dancing in her own blue eyes.

"It's the most beautiful thing I've ever seen in our caves," Kayla whispered back, clearly in awe.

"It gets better. Just wait until you see the ship graveyard!" Ousran replied as she undressed and slipped into the pool, instantly transforming back into her mermaid form and taking her breather out of its satchel. She began to strap it on as Kayla eagerly hurried to catch up with her friend.

Ousran then led the way from the pool through the underwater exit out and into the wild Ocean.

Ezra rubbed her eyes as she regarded Lady Reanalia in the mirror. A simple spell, using the mirror to communicate with others. Ezra still felt amazed whenever she received an answer and tried not to show how worried she was.

"I have the Drow Ambassador and the Forest Elf Ambassador here, Reanalia. They both have people missing," Ezra began immediately, not wishing to beat about the bush.

"Huh…I've had complaints from a nearby city that they have about a dozen people missing. Three other villages and cities sent me scrolls today saying the same," Reanalia replied with a puzzled look on her face. Her long red hair was loose, accentuating her long face and her green eyes sparkled as they regarded each other. "Any idea who's doing it?"

"A mage of some sort. They've been using magical storms to snatch people. Beyond that, I haven't a clue. I'd say it might be our quarry, but it could be any dark mage with an axe to grind," Ezra replied, feeling frustrated at what little they had to go on."

"Lovely. Would you like a hand in the search? Elves, particularly Dark Elves, are not known for their patience."

"I'd love some help. The closer I get to my due date, the more of a strain using magic is. I'd prefer to find out who is behind all of this and take care of them before the baby comes," Ezra admitted.

"I'm on the way. I should be there by tomorrow morning," Reanalia replied with a reassuring smile.

"Bless you, Reanalia. I'll be waiting for your arrival," Ezra replied before she closed the spell down and collapsed back into her chair, feeling tired all over again.

::At least that is a little good news. Since Lady Reanalia is coming, she might be able to take over parts of this puzzle so that you don't have to strain yourself--:: Baelios whispered into her mind.

::Baelios, I'm not straining myself. The baby is a drain on my resources. The Orb's energy being added to the castle has helped—:: Ezra retorted.

::But you're struggling to do your daily duties. You can delegate--::

::I can, but I'm trying not to. We all have our own jobs here. My first responsibility is to Ammora and keeping Axrealia safe. And if people are getting kidnapped from their own homes, in front of crowds…then no one is safe. I'm asking Reanalia for help because I don't have a choice. I need someone to…ah!:: Ezra felt another sharp squeeze about her middle and found herself gasping for air and grasping the chair's arms with an intensity that left her knuckles white!

::Ezra, I'll get--::

::I'm fine. I'm fine, I promise. It was just another practice contraction,:: Ezra sent back hastily, relaxing and breathing as she had been taught to do by Eve.

The journey wasn't very long. Just long enough to need a breather, but not so long that Kayla wouldn't make it home in time for the evening meal with her mother's court.

As they made it over the crest to look down at the ship graveyard, a flood of excitement washed through Kayla's veins.

::Race ya!:: Ousran sent telepathically before she darted away with a telepathic laugh.

Kayla laughed taking chase! The blue and green mermaid with the long golden fins and very long purple hair dove head-first down amongst the sunken ships under the water, chasing her friend, Ousran, amongst the tattered sails and ropes.

::Ousran, wait up!:: Kayla called, her mental voice laughing as she tried, in vain, to catch up to her red and purple friend.

::You can't catch me, Kayla! C'mon, slow-poke!:: Ousran laughed in Kayla's mind as she ducked and dodged around sharks and down into a hatch in a ship itself.

::No fair!:: Kayla called, trying to follow as quickly as she could.

They dashed and swam through the various rooms of the ship and came out through a large hole in the side.

Then drew up short as a dark cloud appeared in the water!

::What is that?:: Ousran asked in wonder, having never seen such a thing happen before. It was like a perfect storm cloud, suspended in the water before them.

::Magic. Go, quickly!:: Kayla called, pulling her friend away from it. She'd heard her mother discussing a phenomenon exactly like this. A storm cloud in the water wasn't possible!

Ousran didn't argue. Hearing the fear in her friend's mental voice, she turned and swam straight up and back towards the reef, going over the boats they had just played in.

Kayla tried to do the same, but something grasped her by her long, beautiful tail. She looked over her shoulder in absolute terror as she struggled to try to get away from it and saw a dark tentacle pulling her into the cloud.

Kayla screamed, struggling in vain as she was pulled into the cloud…

And into nothing but Darkness.

Ousran turned, hearing her friend's mental scream and watched in horror as Kayla was drawn into the storm cloud by a long black tentacle!

Oh Gods, what have I done? Ousran thought in horror, seeing the cloud disappear suddenly as if it had never been. The teenager hesitated, unsure of what to do at first. Then she remembered her duty. *I must tell the Queen…we must get Kayla back!* Ousran thought as she turned and put on as big a burst of speed as she could to head back to the Pod's caves.

It wouldn't take long to get back, but Ousran was already feeling the strain of a longer swim than she normally took. Even so, she ignored her aching muscles and continued to go as fast as she could manage.

When she got back to the pod's caves, she didn't bother going around the side. She swam right back in through the main entrance, where Queen Felati was floating with her guards, obviously questioning them telepathically.

::Your Highness! I'm so sorry, it's all my fault! Please punish me if you must, but find her, please!:: Ousran sent desperately to the beautiful white and gold Queen of the pod.

Queen Felati turned, her long golden hair swirling about her as she regarded Ousran.

::Ousran, why are you wearing a breather and what are you talking about?:: the Queen asked. ::And where is Kayla?::

::That's the problem, your highness,:: Ousran replied, desperately hoping that Kayla was still alive and all right. ::Kayla was taken by…what looked like a storm cloud…under water! She said it was magic!::

:;Calm down…tell me everything that's happened, Ousran. It's important, all of it, do you understand?::

::Yes, your highness. It started when I found Kayla lounging in the sun pool….::

Ousran told Queen Felati everything she knew telepathically as they began to swim back into the Pod's Caves. Queen Felati looked grim, but not as angry as she could have been.

"I will speak to your mother regarding your punishment later, Ousran. Right now, it's more important for us to find Kayla. And for that, we need help. I'm going to the Dragon's Keep," Felati announced as they emerged in the Council Pool with other Mermaids and Mermen arriving to sit and listen as the Queen announced her course of action. "While I'm gone, Counselor Enold is in charge as usual. Kayla is not the first taken, but I swear she shall be the last," Felati said in a quiet voice, her anger flashing in her blue eyes and her magic tingling and sparking at her fingertips. "Guards, come!" Felati cried before she took the breather from Ousran and put it on. The guards went to fetch their own as the Queen dove down to swim back to the Main Entrance to the caves…and to head for the Dragon's Keep.

"Young Lady, we are going to have a very long talk," Ousran's Mother, the Queen's handmaiden, said as she grasped Ousran's wrist and began to lead her back to their own home in the Servants section of the Caves. Ousran groaned but followed her, knowing that she was in deep, deep trouble.

Of course, she wondered what kind of trouble she had gotten Kayla into and that made her heart sink like a stone worse than any punishment she could get from her mother…or the Queen.

Ezra curled up in her bed, frustrated at how everyone was turning into a nursemaid over her. Granted, the contractions had been very intense this time, but they had finally subsided for the moment.

She was sipping on water and little else. Wine was forbidden while she was pregnant and she didn't want tea at the moment. Not that it mattered. Her stomach couldn't handle too much on days like this and it just added to her frustration. Ezra looked up into the beautiful decorations that seemed to dance at times in her vision, surging with the power that had been imbued in this Castle. She still was amazed at how Bael had managed to bring this vision of his to life because this was exactly what he had intended to do to their chamber back at the manor while he was alive.

Now, of course, he was part of Baelios, the Spirit of the Council. Her heart ached sometimes in these moments for Bael still, but he was beyond her reach.

Luckily, Derik had come into her life and while he was mortal, he was still a good man. The way he'd come back into her life just these past eight or so months ago perhaps was not the best, but he was here now. And she did love him dearly.

Lita is still insisting on a ceremony, one I do not have time for. I'm hoping that Derik and I can …manage to just exchange vows before the Gods one day. No fanfare, no frilly dresses. Just me and him. As it should be, as it was back in the days of the Temple of the

Warrior Goddess, Ezra thought, feeling a sting of tears coming to her eyes at the thought of the priestesses who had raised her and the other children she had grown up with. All gone. At the age of eleven, she had once again become an orphan and had had to start over. *If it wasn't for the Mercenary Company that found me and took me in, I wouldn't have made it to my twelfth birthday.*

Ezra's thoughts turned towards that company, who had found that she could fight very well for a young girl. The Captain, a big scarred Ogre named Dieb, had seen her potential and had made her part of the company at a very tender age. He'd given her a tent with other women in the company, both of whom had taken her under their wings. While the rest went out to fight, Ezra had stayed behind to help guard their camp.

A smile tugged at her lips as she remembered how those same women had taught her about her blooming womanhood and how to deal with men. Even though they themselves were lovers, which just seemed natural to Ezra at that time. She had heard and seen them in the darkness making love more than once by the time she was twelve. She had remembered how some of the priestesses in the temple she'd been raised in had looked at each other. Why anyone might have an issue with it, she couldn't understand.

Love is love, no matter what form it takes, Ezra thought as she ran her hand over her large belly, laying now on her left side and feeling the baby kicking and squirming. She chuckled and just reveled in the sensation, both strange and wonderful. *Why am I thinking so much about the past today? I have a future to be attending to…and duties to see to. Ah, Ezra, you're getting far too sentimental.*

::Ah, but my dear Ezra, this is part of what makes you uniquely you,:; Baelios replied in her thoughts as he appeared next to her to place a gentle hand on her belly. ::This child is going to be very special one day, I think. And you didn't have a mother or a father…but those priestesses and those mercenaries…. not only raised you as their own, Ezra. They helped to shape you into the woman you are now. They taught you the value of life, and love…and all of the beautiful things in this world and how it is all worth fighting for.::

::;How long have you been listening to my thoughts this time, hm?:: Ezra asked, chuckling softly as she saw his expression turn a bit wistful.

::Not long, I've just been monitoring you since your contractions began this time. I stayed close by, in case you needed someone to get Eve for you or food or drink. I don't want you straining yourself, Ezra,:: Baelios replied, a worried look coming over his ghostly features. Ezra reached up to touch the Spirit's ghostly cheek gently, feeling it grow solid under her fingertips.

::Thank you, Baelios. I don't know how I would've gotten through this pregnancy without you and Derik, honestly. I don't know why I'm thinking so much about the past when I need to be concentrating on what's happening now--::

Baelios shook his head.

::There's nothing wrong with thinking about the past, Ezra. Just so long as you remember the lessons they taught you and the importance of love, family and fighting for the right cause. As I said, they shaped who you are. You are an amazing woman, Ezra, one who has learned so much in a very short amount of time,:: Baelios told her, giving her a gentle pat on her belly and a look of pride.

::I don't feel amazing. I feel like I'm floundering lately,:: Ezra admitted.

::You're doing better than you think, Ezra. Now, why don't you take a nap and just be for a little bit? Derik and I can handle anyone who needs something for now, and Lita is off still trying to think of a way to make you accept a big ceremony.::

::;I don't want a big ceremony, Baelios. I'm not a ruler, I'm just….me,:: Ezra replied, feeling a surge of frustration surge up again which made her belly clench in response. She took a breath and closed her eyes, forcing herself to breathe…and relax again.

::I know, Ezra. We'll convince her somehow. For now, just rest…please?:: Baelios asked, looking into her eyes with concern written in his glowing orange orbs.

::Very well…I'll rest, Baelios. Thank you…for everything.::

::The pleasure is all mine, Ezra.:; Baelios replied as he disappeared again and Ezra closed her eyes, letting sleep take her for now away from the stress, the strain…and the worry.

For now.

Felati was impatient, pushing herself to swim as fast as she possibly could through the cool waters of the ocean her people called home. Her guards were even having trouble keeping up with her as she used magic to boost her speed but even that only drained her energy a bit, making her slow down again.

They paused as they spotted a ring of sharks, who were having a feeding frenzy in a school of fish. Sharks rarely attacked them, but they would attack while in a frenzy. Felati spotted a small passageway, a cave that would let out on the other side of the school and the sharks…but they would have to be careful!

;:Be on your guard, and be careful,:: she warned her guards telepathically as she adjusted her breather on her face…and dove, going for the cave that would keep them out of the sharks' view.

She willed herself to slow down while in the cave, carefully watching with her guards as the sharks circled still, striking randomly at the large school of fish. Felati counted them twice…there were at least ten sharks, and the school was unusually large. At least a hundred fish were darting and swimming, trying to evade the sharks.

First rule of survival: There's always a bigger fish, Felati thought, waiting to see if the sharks would disperse before they could swim for it. The Dragon's Keep was still another hour swim away from where they were now!

And between here and there was very little cover. If they weren't careful, the sharks would come after them if they were still hungry.

Felati cursed quietly into her breather, willing herself to calm down. She wouldn't help Kayla if she got herself seriously injured, which is all the sharks COULD do to her. She was immortal…but she really didn't want to see if immortality could survive being digested!

::Your Highness, some of us could draw them off--:: Her lead guard, Mavet, offered grimly.

::No, Mavet. You're all mortal. We've already lost too many of our people to whomever is snatching them, and we have no idea if they still live! I'm not going to lose all of you too. We'll wait a bit…those sharks have to be getting full soon,:; she replied, using her telepathy out of habit as all mer-people did when they were under the water. They couldn't breathe water, as they were mammals like dolphins and whales. They did have magic and psychic abilities that allowed them all to shift shapes into humanoid or elfin forms when they were dry and to talk via telepathy.

Finally, the sharks swam off, their bellies sated and the school of fish, what was left of it, had scattered only to rejoin into their formation on the other side of the tunnel. The school of sharks went one way, the fish another…and Felati breathed a sigh of relief as the sharks went away from the path they were taking towards the Dragon's Keep. She and her guards swam on, intent to reach it as soon as possible.

She had people to save and a daughter that she yearned to hug again.

I just pray that they're all right, Felati thought as she used her magic to boost her speed along with her guards as much as she could. Time was against them.

Chapter Three

Surala had had a rough night. Every time she'd dozed off, she'd had horrible nightmares. Dark clouds closing in over the sea and then the screams of all of the Ocean's creatures crying out as they died within those Dark clouds. The half-Dragon mage sat up, feeling the water of her sleeping pool running down her Draconic face and scaled hide as she cried out. Half Elf, Half Dragon, she had two forms and could easily transform from one to the other. When she slept, she preferred her Draconic form. When she was awake, she preferred her smaller Elfin form.

Shifting from the Draconic instantly into her Elfin, she rose naked from her pool and picked up the light thin robe that lay near it. Wrapping it about her, she made her way through the halls of her peculiar palace to her library.

In the center of the library was another clear, beautifully still pool that Surala used for scrying. She paused before it and pulled up her own magical power, weak as it was becoming with her age of fifteen hundred and sixty years, and began to look for the cause of her nightmares.

And was interrupted when Queen Felati of the Western Pod of merpeople suddenly swam up through the center of that pool.

"Your highness, what brings you here at this late hour?" Surala asked, bowing as low as she could and trying to hide her surprise.

"More of my people are missing. My youngest daughter, Kayla, was taken by a storm just beyond the reef in the boat graveyard. An older merman was taken at the same time by a storm on the surface. He was swimming to an island when he was taken. This makes ten people that have just vanished into cyclones that came out of nowhere or by sudden maelstroms on the surface. Surala, we need help," the white-tailed Mermaid Queen explained, her long blonde hair floating about her shoulders like a golden cloud.

Surala ran her long fingers through her own long pink hair and gave a nod. "I agree. I've seen more and more animals going missing too. And I've had nightmares of Dark clouds and hearing the screams of everyone in the ocean as they died in them. The nightmares have been consistent for a month and they're getting worse, not better. I've researched everything and searched with my pool and magic. I'm out of my depth and my magic is fading," Surala admitted, dismayed at having failed her charges and friends.

"Any sign of a successor?" Felati asked, concern written all over her face in the set of her jaw, the way her brows furrowed in worry.

"None. I have maybe another twenty or thirty years. Fifty if I'm lucky, and I'm going to need every bit of it to train my replacement. Which means either my successor hasn't been born yet or...."

"Or there's no one else who can take your place," Queen Felati finished for her. "How long have you been searching for them?"

"Seventy years, give or take a decade. And I've served here for nearly fifteen hundred years now. A drop in the bucket for most Dragons, but for a half-Dragon—" Surala began, holding her hands up in frustration.

"That's nearly your entire lifetime. Most merpeople live about that long," Queen Felati acknowledged.

"Yes. It's why my magic is growing weaker these days and it's all I can do to do my normal duties. This is beyond me. I'm not sure where to look for help."

"I'll help you search," Felati offered as she had many times before over the course of their friendship. "I'll boost your powers with mine."

"Your highness, you should save that power for your people—"

"I am serving my people by helping to find those who have vanished. Too many families are frantic over their loved one's disappearances. I can't protect my people if I don't know who, or what, is taking them. And my own daughter is one of the missing," Felati replied logically, as she was apt to do. Surala bowed her head, defeated by such sound reasoning, and nodded.

"Very well. Tomorrow night is a full moon. It'll be better to use that energy and combine it with ours—" Surala began, looking up towards the small break in the ceiling where the thin pane of glass separated them from what moonlight could shine down and within her Keep. There was a lever within the library that would lift and open it with the mechanical system designed to allow it to open and shut. Tomorrow, she would have to remember to open it.

"And give us greater strength and further reach. I'll see you tomorrow night, my friend. Try to rest well tonight. Tomorrow, we'll find someone to help us," Felati said gently before she disappeared down the tunnel that led from this pool to the ocean.

Surala sighed and rubbed her weary eyes.

"I could use a good night's sleep, but I doubt I'll find much rest," she murmured before she took herself back to her chambers.

Ezra wasn't finding much rest, despite how tired she was. Every time she closed her eyes, another nightmare would begin. Frustrated, she turned over yet again, attempting to try to rest.

Within her womb, she could feel the baby squirming and stretching. Running a gentle hand over her baby bump, she tried to soothe herself and the child within.

Suddenly, a Vision hit. A dragon, pink and purple let out a loud cry as she erupted out of a pool of water! Then it changed to that same dragon charging through a crowd of warriors, flinging them, stomping on them at times while she and several others clung to the creature's back.

It ended just as suddenly as it had begun, leaving Ezra puzzled and shaken.

That's not the same Dragon that I keep seeing with Angelica whenever I get a glimpse at her future. So, the question is…is it friend or foe? And who the hell are they? Ezra had sat up, shaking a bit as the Vision faded…and she found herself unable to go back to sleep at first. More and more questions were left than answers whenever she had a Vision like this…and she had no idea what to think of it all.

It took a couple of hours, but Ezra finally did doze off and finally slept peacefully for the rest of the night.

Surala dressed in her usual attire, a long flowing dress of pink and white with hints of gold and purple embroidery throughout the garment, and tried to breathe and relax as she waited for Queen Felati.

This is a big spell. Far bigger than any that I've done in the past decade. And we can't afford to fail to find someone to help us, Surala thought as she paced through her library. Normally she wasn't nervous, but with this particularly daunting task…she was. Surala took a breath and again tried to calm herself—

Then spun as she felt a tug. A tug from a previous cast spell that got her attention.

That…could it be that the one is…calling to me? She wondered.

Resting had helped, but Ezra was still concerned. It was late afternoon, slowly t urning into early evening and the contractions had begun again and this time, they weren't letting up! Ezra continued to breathe, trying to calm herself, to find that place inside that would allow her to relax. All of her techniques to calm herself, thus far, had done nothing!   The Vision also still had her puzzled, which didn't help as she kept mulling over its details today

:;Ezra, the Dragon egg! It's *moving!*:: Baelios suddenly called telepathically.

::It's moving…*right* now?:: she sent back, trying to hide the amount of pain she was feeling.

:;Yes…Ezra, what's wrong? I can sense something's wrong.::

:;Nothing's wrong. I just need a few minutes, Baelios--::

:;Ezra, I can send Eve--::

:;We can't bother her every time I feel a twinge, Baelios--:: She started when a fresh contraction brought her down to her knees!

::This is more than a twinge, Ezra!::

::;Stay with the egg! I'll be there in a moment,:: Ezra snapped back as she took another breath. It was just her bad luck that Derik walked into their chambers at that moment.

"What's wrong?" Derik asked as he ran to her side and knelt beside her.

"Contractions…but it's too early and I have to get downstairs," Ezra admitted, wishing for the pain to go away.

"To your chambers and I'll get Eve—"

"No…I have to go to my work room…I can make it from there," she replied as she started to stand. The pain was easing, but she sensed another contraction threatening to begin and sank back to the floor.

"All right, but I should still get Eve—"

"No…not until we know for certain that I *really* need her. I can't call her every time I feel a contraction, Derik. She said this would happen," Ezra explained yet again, feeling irritated by the fact that no one seemed to want to listen to her.

"I still think we should get her."

"Let me check on what I need to in my work room…then I'll go see her after, I promise."

Derik studied her for a few moments, then gave a resigned nod as he began to help her back to her feet.

Surala felt a stronger tug, and closed her eyes, letting her vison seek out where that tug was going to—

And found a barrier protecting it. Frustrated, she growled softly but didn't intrude. The barrier was thick, but was spun of nothing but good energy that glowed like a beacon in Surala's mind's eye. A mage of the light had definitely spun these protections and the tug was coming from behind it in the west. With a sigh, Surala opened her eyes.

"So close and yet so far."

"Is there news, Surala?" Queen Felati's voice rang out behind her. Turning to the central pool, Surala gave a slow nod.

"Yes, big news. I sense my sucessor. She's young, very young…but she's under some sort of protection. Even so—"

"That is good news, to hear that you sense her at last, if in the distance. Do you want to hold off on our spell working for today?"

"No, of course not! I still have a job to *do*, and I intend to do it. I can work on calling her here later, but as I said…she's very young," Surala replied, frustrated at being oh so close and yet unable to even see the one that she would have to teach to take her place. Surala paused to flip the lever that would open the sunroof and allow the moonlight to flow into the library, and looked up, making sure that she could see a hint of the moon up above.

"How young?" Felati asked, genuinely interested.

"I think she's a hatchling or still in the egg. She feels…like fresh dew on the grass, she's that young."

"That is young, Surala. Well, if you're ready, I'm ready."

"I'm ready. Let's begin," Surala closed her eyes and began to cast the spell, feeling Queen Felati's magic beginning to build and boost her own. Above them, the full moon emerged from the clouds and the soft silver light washed down over both of them.

Surala began to chant, going into a trance as they worked.

The contractions eased while Ezra moved with Derik to the work room. Once inside, she turned to him with a tinge of regret.

"I'll be out shortly, Derik. Don't worry, I'll be sitting," she promised as she closed and locked the door behind her. Turning and leaning against the wall, Ezra made her way to the secret entrance at the back of the room and touched a particular brick…then grasped the rail and made her way down the stairs.

I don't dare try to teleport while I'm like this! I could end up anywhere! Ezra thought, wincing as she felt another contraction beginning to hit. She forced herself to keep moving, taking the steps slowly until she reached the bottom and entered the chamber where the Dragon's Egg was hidden.

Baelios stood there, watching the egg as it wobbled and moved…and glowed!

"When did it…start doing that?" Ezra asked as she watched in amazement as she approached the egg.

"When you began to feel those contractions. I was down here last time when you began to have them, and it was moving *then*. This time, it's glowing…" Baelios said as he turned to her, and his face lightened in amazement. "And so are you."

"What?" Ezra asked in surprise.

"Your stomach is glowing, Ezra. Do you think it's…related?"

"I have no idea…you're more of an expert than I am, remember?" Ezra asked as she looked dumbly down at her stomach to see that he was right! There was a faint light coming from the round apex of her stomach! Ezra gently ran a hand over her baby bump, feeling the baby move within, feeling more wonder than she'd ever thought to feel while still pregnant with her child.

"Not with children," Baelios replied, his voice betraying his worry.

"I have no experience with children, as you know. Especially dragon hatchlings or…babies!" Ezra said, trying not to panic as the glow as growing brighter and stronger.

"I'm sorry, Ezra…this is out of my depth...perhaps we should—"

"Fine…fetch Eve and Derik. So much for keeping the egg a secret," Ezra snapped, having not wanted to reveal the egg's presence until she had found a proper guardian, a Dragon, for the little one inside of it.

"True, but at least those two can keep a secret. I'll be right back. Here, sit!" Baelios said as he conjured a chair for her. Ezra sank into it with a sigh of relief and Baelios vanished.

"Missing people, glowing eggs and stomachs…what in the blazing hells is going on?" Ezra wondered out loud as she watched the Dragon's egg. The glow intensified again—

Then Ezra felt something...sensed something! Something that was looking for them! Ezra closed her eyes, using her telepathic and magical senses to see who, or what, was seeing them.

"I see her!" Surala cried triumphantly and projected the image into the pool before Queen Felati so they could both see the person that Surala saw.

A young, pregnant woman was sitting in a warm chamber. Her belly glowed bright silver even as the Dragon's egg in a nest before her glowed a bright gold. The woman was clad in white and silver and was sitting in a chair—

::Who seeks me!:: Surala and Felati heard as clearly as if the woman was suddenly standing next to them and both Felati and Surala jumped in surprise!

"She's telepathic—" Felati said in wonder, her pink and blue eyes widening a bit in surprise.

"And a mage. And this means her baby and the Dragon hatchling are both my successors…I feel them both! She's their protector—" Surala said, amazed that the mage could contact them from that far away! It shouldn't have been possible.

"Then this is the best person to help us," Felati said with a sigh.

::Who seeks me!:: They heard again.

"Better answer her before she begins casting a spell to find us," Felati urged, a hint of amusement now dancing in her eyes. Surala shook her head and opened her mind even as Felati did the same, joining her in the link.

:;I am Surala..and this is Queen Felati. We seek your help, Lady—
::

::Sorceress. I'm the Sorceress of Ammora. You are trespassing—
:: the woman interrupted.

::We mean you no harm, Sorceress. We need your *help*,:: Felati
replied gently, sincerely.

::With what?:: came the reply, showing that the mage they were
talking to was growing short of patience, but hadn't quite run out of it
yet.

::Some of my people have been taken in a magical whirlwind
storm. We need help to locate them. We can't find them and we can't
seem to unravel the mystery of who took them,:: Felati replied grimly.

:;Other people have come to me with the same story. The storms
are magical in nature. I am looking into it,:: The Sorceress replied.

::We'd like to help. Please, if we all work together, we stand a
better chance at finding those who are missing,:; Surala offered
quickly.

:;I can't travel at the moment…::

:;I can come to you--:: Surala began.

:;We will come to you, Sorceress. Do you have accommodations
for a mermaid?:: Felati cut in, not wanting to be left out of the
investigation at hand.

:;No…I will see what I can do. Where are you located?:: the Mage
asked.

::The Dragon's Keep at the Eastern Seashore.:: Surala couldn't
believe their luck. It seemed the woman really wished to help them!

::I'm in Ammora Castle. I'll…be in touch soon,:: the reply came, the mental voice saying it now sounded weary and there was a hint of pain in it now. Surala's heart went out to the poor woman, wondering if she was already in labor.

:;Thank you, Sorceress. Our apologies for the intrusion,:; Surala said as she began to drop out of the link and began to disperse the magical energy holding the spell. She looked to Felati, who sat with a rather nice smile on her lips.

"Now that was some very fine magic, my friend," Felati said to her with a nod of satisfaction.

"At least we have a hope…and a chance," Surala conceded.

Ezra sighed as she released her hold on the telepathic contact she'd enacted at the feeling of intrusion. Another flash from the Vision had formed as she was speaking with Surala and Felati, and it was Surala's voice that had again invoked the image of the strange Dragon. *Perhaps she is the dragon, but it's too early to make assumptions,* Ezra thought as she again took a breath.

::Baelios, we have a problem. That intrusion—::

:;Should not have happened. Odd, very odd. I'm bringing Derik and Eve down now. Are you all right?:: Baelios asked as Ezra relaxed, puzzled at this new mystery that was before her.

As if I need another mystery right now, Ezra thought in frustration.

::I'm fine. But, when that happened…the egg and my belly both…glowed! It's so odd, Baelios, and I don't need Eve to tell me that that was *not* normal. Do you have any idea of what it could be?:; she sent to Baelios, having never heard of anything like this ever happening before.

::I've never heard of anything like this happening…Eve and Derik are nearly here, Ezra,:: Baelios cut her off as he rose to go unlock her work room door and to meet the pair as they came down the stairs. A moment later, she heard them just before they appeared, both at a run.

"Sorceress, are you alright?" Derik blurted out as he ran to her side and knelt by her chair.

"Derik, I'm fine, really. The contractions are slowing down but…the egg and my stomach were both…glowing."

"Glowing?" Eve and Derik asked in unison.

"Yes, glowing! Something is going on and I….*We* need to find out what it is. More people have been taken….*this* time from the Oceans. Lady Reanalia—"

"She arrived right after you went downstairs. She's waiting upstairs, in the throne room," Derik replied with a look of relief in his eyes.

"Good. Help me up and let's go. I need her to help me unravel this mystery," Ezra insisted as she began to rise.

"Now wait a minute! You've been having contractions again according to the Spirit and you're going to go right back to work? No. You can brief Lady Reanalia from your bed, and then you are on bed rest until we know that you're not going into labor. No work. No stress! You aren't taking this seriously enough, Sorceress, and if she's here to help you, then she can help by investigating. Got it?" Eve asked sternly, a light in her eyes that showed that she wasn't going to take any argument. Ezra sighed, then nodded.

"Very well. Until we know I'm not going into labor. But only until then! People have been taken, Eve. The Gods only know what's been happening to them," Ezra replied as Derik and Baelios helped her to stand. Derik surprised her as he swept her up into his arms and began to go back upstairs.

"You can't help them if you go into labor, Sorceress. You'd only put yourself and the baby in danger," Derik said softly into the cusp of her ear as he walked up the stairs. "So, for now, let's let Reanalia help out as much as she can. We have two sets of Elven visitors who might go for each other's throats any minute now. Their entourages also arrived today. The Dark Elf Ambassador is insisting that her servants dance for us all tonight to "entertain" us and I've been trying to put her off for your sake. The Forest Elf Ambassador is insisting on creating entertainment for us as well. If Reanalia can find out what's going on for us, maybe we can keep an all-out war from breaking out here, hm?" Derik gave a nod to Baelios, who was now holding open the door for them to go back into Ezra's workroom.

"I can't be putting off duties because of a minor inconvenience—" Ezra began, feeling weary at having to explain herself yet again!

"This is the baby and the baby's health we're talking about here. That's not a minor inconvenience. You're going to be a mother and there's going to be times when that's going to have to take priority," Derik insisted gently as he carried her through the workroom only to have Baelios open the next door.

"He's right, Sorceress. Being a mother is going to change everything," Eve said almost sadly to her as they walked. Eve came out to proceed them both down the hallway as Derik continued to carry Ezra in his arms.

Ezra sighed only to wince as she felt another contraction coming on.

"That may be, but I have my duty—"

"You'll have to find a new balance, Sorceress. That's true of any parent," Baelios offered out loud to her which made Ezra give him a rather scathing look.

"That may be…but not every parent has my circumstances. And we both know there's no one to take up the burden that I lay down, Spirit." Ezra said as she tried to just relax and breathe, wishing for the contraction to just stop and go away!

"True, but as we learned to work as a team, we will learn to balance our lives so that the baby won't feel neglected," Baelios offered as he opened the door to her chambers. Eve raced ahead of them now to arrange the pillows and cushions to make Ezra as comfortable as possible. Derik lay her down in the bed and Eve began her examination of her.

"Send for Lady Reanalia. If she's going to help, I need to brief her," Ezra told Baelios as she tried to relax and not feel so irritated at their attempt to comfort and educate her.

Chapter Four

"So, let me get this straight. Dark Elves, Forest Elves, Mermaids, sea creatures, humans…and various other people were taken in all these weird random storms? I know about the villages and cities near me saying that people disappeared after some clouds but…how could that happen under water?" Reanalia asked as she perched on the edge of the Sorceress' bed and looked at her with real interest.

"Magic, but not any sort of magic I've ever heard of before, to be honest. I need you to investigate for me, please. Eve isn't letting me leave my bed for the next week at least, if not for the rest of my pregnancy. Derik hardly gives me a moment alone unless he's dealing with our guests. I've been told not to use any magic or anything like it for the next week at least by the Spirit and Eve—"

"I'm surprised you haven't turned anyone into a toad yet." Reanalia sat back and crossed her arms, her face lit up with an expression that was clearly amusement.

"That would be a grave misuse of power…but the thought has crossed my mind," the Sorceress admitted to Reanalia as she shifted herself on the bed and those eerie ice-blue eyes flared briefly with anger and a hint of power.

"So where am I going?" Reanalia asked, excitement in her voice and in her eyes.

"To the sea, but to see a particular mage and the Queen of the Merfolk. Queen Felati and the Mage's name is Surala. I felt them trying to see into the Castle and confronted them telepathically. I'll go into the astral later to confirm their location, or at least Surala's location. It seems they work together often, the way they were finishing each other's sentences. Find Surala and Felati. I'll have a destination for you to go to before you leave tomorrow. I just have to make sure the Spirit isn't watching…or Derik or Eve."

"I can help you with that," Reanalia offered with a grin. "If I'm here, they're not going to come in because we're having a briefing. And I can always say you're asleep if they do." Reanalia gave her a slow wink. "Don't worry, I'll watch your back magically speaking, too."

"Thank you. Give me about a half an hour…I should have them fairly quickly," the Sorceress of Ammora replied with a bit of relief in her green eyes as she lay back against the pillows and closed her eyes.

Reanalia watched as the Sorceress closed her eyes to begin her journey into the Astral Plane. Naturally, right as she could see the Sorceress' astral form slipping into the Astral Plane, there was a knock at the door. She shook her head and rose, going to the door and cracking it open.

"She just fell asleep," Reanalia told Derik, keeping her voice soft enough that it wouldn't disturb the Sorceress as she moved through the wall and out of the Castle.

"Oh, sorry. I brought her something to eat. I thought it might help her to settle down for a rest maybe," Derik said as he glanced over Reanalia's shoulder. Luckily, with the Sorceress laying down, it appeared as though the woman was just deep in slumber.

"I'll let you know when she wakes, Derik. Don't worry. If you want, I'll take the tray for now and I'll use magic to keep it warm until she wakes," Reanalia said, trying to reassure him. "I'd let you in, but she was really irritated earlier. Seems you all have been treating her as though she's a child or something when she's a grown woman and older than all of you." Reanalia took the tray from him with gentle hands, watching Derik's expression.

"I guess we have. We're just worried. She's been through so much—" Derik started to explain.

"And she survived it. You can't protect her from everything, Derik. You'll make her miserable if you try," Reanalia pointed out, watching his expression still as she leaned against the door frame with the tray in her hands.

"I understand that, and I know I can't. She's protected me more than I have her. But I wish she'd let me in more. I love her and I don't expect to know every secret, but it would be nice if she would at least talk to me about things like this before it comes to a head." Derik ran his fingers through his hair, clearly worried about the Mage that he had entwined his life with.

"She will, she's just used to being independent is all. This is an adjustment for her just as much as it is for you. Once you two are officially married, I'm sure she'll relax and communicate better. Are you two doing a ceremony soon?" Reanalia asked, wanting to check. Plans sometimes changed at the drop of a pin, particularly in a place like this. She didn't want to assume anything, and she was glad she hadn't when she heard his reply.

"She doesn't want a big ceremony, but everyone is trying to push her into it. Like she's a big ruler," Derik admitted, looking sheepish.

"Well, she is a ruler," Reanalia replied with a soft chuckle. "Of a sort. She may not see it that way, but she is. Even if she has a council ruling the city, she still rules this place. And if she doesn't want a big ceremony, then she needs to tell them and you two should probably make your relationship formal before she does that. That way, if everyone is upset, you can both claim it's done and over with," Reanalia smiled at Derik and reached to pat his cheek in a sisterly fashion.

"I'll talk with her about it, and we'll see what we can do. I'd rather be done with this sooner instead of later," Derik replied. "I'll come check on her in an hour or two," he said as he straightened up and turned to go out for now.

Reanalia chuckled as she closed the door behind him and went to wait for the Sorceress to return to her body.

Going into the astral was easy, exhausting but easy. Ezra flew into it as easily as if she were a fish returning to water. Hurrying, she reached out with her magic, seeking the magical signatures she knew were in the distance…then flew at the tug as her magic encountered something familiar in the far distance of the East.

Ezra paused at the top of a hill that looked down at the Seashore. She sensed Surala nearby and gasped as she saw the fortress that looked as if it was made out of hard packed sand and seashells of every color of the rainbow.

Beautiful, Ezra thought as she looked it over in wonder. Ezra sighed and approached it, sending a tendril of thought.

::Surala?::

:;Sorceress?::

::Yes…so this is your fortress?::

:;Yes, Welcome to the Dragon's Keep,:: Surala replied into Ezra's mind.

::I'm sending a friend to you tomorrow. Her name is Lady Reanalia. She is going to help you to investigate the missing sea people. I'm unable to leave Ammora right now with so many guests here and with a baby on the way--::

::I understand. Any help you can send is welcomed, Sorceress.::

:;Thank you for understanding. If Reanalia sees something that needs my attention, she'll send a message to me immediately and I'll come then.   Whether or not the local healer likes it. But, in the meantime, she is very good at looking into this sort of thing and she's brought news of other peoples that have also gone missing around the same time as the Elves, Dark Elves and of course the sea people. I believe it's the same mage that is orchestrating all of this, but we *have* to be sure. It could be more than one…and that is why I'm sending Lady Reanalia to you. She'll be able to help you look for energy signatures, clues.::

::It'll be hard to look in the ocean if she's--::

:;She's immortal, Surala. And she's a powerful mage in her own right. I wouldn't send her if I wasn't absolutely sure she was capable of helping you out with this.::

::As I said, I'll take whatever help you send, Sorceress. We'll manage, I'm sure,:: Surala replied, a hint of resignation in her voice. Ezra felt for her, sensing her worry over her missing charges.

::She'll be there first thing tomorrow morning. She'll be arriving by portal. I'll be in contact shortly after she arrives, okay?::

::Yes, thank you, Sorceress. We'll talk to you tomorrow,:: Surala replied before she broke off contact. Ezra turned and raced back to her body, feeling weak by the time she settled back into herself.

Ezra opened her eyes and gave a nod to Reanalia.

"Any problems?" she asked softly.

"Nope. Derik brought you something to eat, and we had a bit of a talk while you were gone. Other than that, nothing," Reanalia replied as she rose to bring a tray over to the bed. Ezra struggled to sit upright, feeling her belly getting in the way as she pushed herself up on her side, then carefully turned so she didn't pull a muscle in her belly. Reanalia laid the tray over Ezra's lap and lifted a warming spell from it. "I didn't sense anything trying to come in from the Astral while you were gone."

"Oh good. I'm glad. The place you are going is beautiful. She calls it the Dragon's Keep," Ezra told Reanalia with a chuckle as she lifted the cover from the plate and smiled, seeing one of her favorite meals on the plate. "Oh, Derik certainly pays attention," she said as she picked up a fork to take a bite of the warm savory cheese, egg and a vegetable dish on her plate.

"He does. He said you don't want a big ceremony," Reanalia shared as she settled on a chair next to the bed and looked at her with wise-looking eyes.

"He's right. I don't. I've had a big wedding ceremony, I'd rather not be put on display again," Ezra shared after she swallowed that bite of food, feeling comforted and loved. *We should do something soon—* She thought.

"You just need to do something formal and those who are pushing for more will drop it. You are in charge of Ammora, you are its Ruler, whether you want to admit it or not, Sorceress. And Derik is quite a catch. Don't let him go," Reanalia said with a smile. "Now, I am looking forward to meeting this new Mage. "Dragon's Keep" is quite a title for a place! I can't wait to see it."

"You'll like Surala, too. She's quite a woman from what I've sensed and seen so far," Ezra shared as she picked up the teacup that had peppermint tea within it and took a sip. It was lightly sweetened with honey, perfect for her stomach that sometimes still felt somewhat sour.

"Oh good, that's wonderful! So, is there an Adventure to be had here?" Reanalia asked as she shifted a bit in excitement.

"Possibly, though investigations tend to be more waiting and trying to make sense of missing puzzle pieces than anything else," Ezra replied with a knowing grin to her friend.

"Oh good! I could use another Adventure and a good fight…but I'll help anyway even if it's boring," Reanalia teased with a smirk and a wink as she folded her hands over her own flat belly and put her feet up on Ezra's bed.

"Well, you'll still likely find both, especially once we know where all of these people are being held," Ezra told her, wishing that she could go herself, but knowing that this would be a better solution than wearing herself completely out.

"It's a good thing I came then because if I do…I know who to call in case I'm in too deep," Reanalia teased.

"Oh good…Eve will be thrilled."

They laughed together then and proceeded to talk about the months that had passed since they had defeated Juktis. Ezra shared about her own quiet but frustrating search and the preparations for the baby. Reanalia began to share how bored she had been, back in her tower.

"I really do need to just stay here awhile. I think you're gonna need me again, even after this is over," Reanalia said with a twinkle in her eye.

"Probably, especially if it is Juktis' partner behind it. But until we know for sure—" Ezra started.

"We can't count on anything," Reanalia finished for her, knowing all too well that it was true.

Alyra looked down through her scrying glass at her latest targets. Two humans, a Dark Elf warrior, a small but quite powerful mage in a dwarf body. She sighed and rubbed her hands together, trying to gather her energies.

My Army is slowly growing, but I need more. The more powerful and magical, the better, she thought as she studied their floating images in the mirror. She chuckled and looked back at her latest victims, two new merfolk sleeping still in their small, tiny tanks. She had left the water shallow so they could breathe more easily at the surface, knowing they did not have gills as she had discovered upon taking the first one.

Sadly, the first one had not survived her experiments, but she had high hopes for the next one.

She turned and walked towards her latest victim. A man in a long tunic, breeches and the remains of what had been a breast plate. She chuckled as she removed it from him and used her magic to remove his chains and to pull him to the altar in the center of the room.

It was time to play.

Derik looked up as the door finally opened again at his knock. It was dinner time, and he had brought a tray with Ezra's favorite meal. Reanalia smiled and held the door open for him so he could make his way into the room. Turning, he put it down over Ezra's lap, giving her a deep look of concern as he noted the circles under her eyes, the way she kept rubbing her belly.

"I'll go head over to my old quarters, Sorceress. I'll see you in the morning," Reanalia said as she rose and walked out the door gracefully before Ezra could say another word. Ezra sighed and rubbed her eyes, looking so frail and tired that it nearly broke Derik's heart seeing it.

"Want me to get Eve?" he asked.

"No. I don't need Eve right now, Derik. I just want you. I'm tired, oh so tired. I can't imagine getting through two more days much less two more months sometimes," Ezra admitted to him as she reached for him.

"You're nearly at the end, right?" he asked as he moved to hold her, wanting to soothe her, to reassure her that everything would be all right.

"Yes, and that end can't come soon enough. I keep having visions of her, I keep having dreams of her. And I have everyone treating me like...like…a walking womb instead of like a person," Ezra said, the frustration plain in the way she spoke along with the weariness.

"I didn't think about that. Eve's more focused on keeping you and the baby healthy, though," he said as he shifted on the bed and smoothed down the coverlet. He moved again carefully so he wasn't sitting on her leg and didn't knock her tray as she reached to take a bite of her soup.

"Eve forgets that I'm not a mortal woman. I'll survive having this baby, this baby will survive being born. That's not what she needs to be concerned with. She needs to give me some space to breathe, or I'm going to go crazy in a handbasket," she said, irritated still and tense…but she was eating. Derik reached for her hand and gave it a gentle squeeze then, trying to think of how they should be going about this. It wasn't fair to her, he realized, to treat her like she was a child. She was just having a baby!

But Eve was a force unto herself, and he had a feeling that she wasn't going to just back down on wanting Ezra to rest. Particularly during this crisis.

"And Lita keeps pressuring you to do a big ceremony," he sighed, knowing that that particular bit of stress wasn't helping anyone. Especially the love of his life.

"I don't' want a big ceremony, Derik. I'm sorry, I know you might—"

"No, no! Ezra, no…I really don't want a big ceremony. Something small and simple would be good enough for me," Derik admitted as he stroked through her hair.

"Really?" she asked, hope dawning in her face as she looked up at him with such a sad and unhappy expression in her eyes.

"Really. If you don't want one, I don't want one either. I don't need a fancy dinner or a big altar or tons of flowers. I'd rather just have you," he replied, tenderly stroking her cheek and giving it a gentle kiss and was rewarded as he felt her tense muscles relaxing.

"I love you, Derik" she murmured as she turned, clinging to him as he saw the tray lift up of its own accord and move. He chuckled as the Spirit of Ammora appeared a moment later, putting it down where it was safe and wouldn't tip over.

"I love you too, Ezra. Don't worry. Whatever is going to come, we'll face it, together," he promised her sincerely.

Ezra leaned up and kissed him then, a deep, passionate kiss that made his toes curl and his body ache for her. He crawled into the bed with her to soothe her, to remind her that she was beautiful and loved.

When they were done, they were both exhausted and sweaty and had no inclination to move anywhere. He held her close to his chest, feeling the swell of her belly pressing against his side and silently vowed that he would not be the one to bring her to tears like this again.

And Gods help anyone who did.

Surala paced the floor of her library. She couldn't seem to settle down, all of her thoughts were on her new successors.

Why are there two of them?   Why this particular pairing? Granted, there aren't many full-dragons left in the world, and the few there are have all withdrawn mostly from where the other creatures could readily find them.   But, why this particular baby?   Why this particular set of unborn babies?   It'll be years before they can take over— Surala thought as she just…couldn't help but think on the facts of this pairing.

"Having trouble sleeping?" Felati's voice rang out behind her from the pool. Surala turned, surprised and shocked at hearing another voice this late at night. "I couldn't rest either," the mermaid Queen admitted as she stretched out, her long white tail seeming to glow almost irredescently in the moonlight pouring down from the skylight above them.

"Yeah, me too," Surala admitted as she ran her long fingers through her long pink and purple hair.

"Excited or nervous?" Felati asked as Surala shape-shifted into her Draconic form and lay down by the edge of the pool, stretching her cramped wings out and just resting her head on her front claws.

"Both. And I can't stop thinking about my new successors. They're babies," Surala said, having been a little disappointed that they weren't older and puzzled at how babies would be old enough to replace her by the time she needed them.

"Mmhmm. Important babies at that," Felati said with a sage nod. "They'll be powerful when they're grown."

"Yes, but do I have the time to train them? I don't know how much longer I'll have left. I was hoping for an adult—"

"We don't always get what we wish for in this, Surala. Your successors are your successors because they're the only ones who'll be able to take over for you. And you're blessed in that one of the pair is immortal..and the other is a full-dragon. When they bond—"

"The immortality will be shared," Surala finished and nodded with a sigh. "They won't have the worry of ever having to find a successor…it seems the Gods have decided that my replacement will never need to worry about their own deaths." It was a solution that had never been seen before and one that made Surala wonder if the Gods were suddenly paying attention to the events on their world.

"Mmhmm. So, why are you so worried about it? Maybe the Gods will grant you a reprieve as well. Your powers are fading but you're not done yet. You're not weak and you're certainly not as foggy as your teacher was. Your mind is as sharp as mine is. And I have a very long memory just as you do," Felati pointed out, as she, too, was immortal.

"True…but I was hoping that maybe, just maybe, in this…I wouldn't have to wait for long for them to take over."

"At least you found them at all, Surala. And the gods work in mysterious and strange ways. Trust them."

"I do trust them, Felati. I just—" Surala started, but Felati cut her off with a wave of her index finger.

"Ah ah. Just trust them for once, Surala. Stop worrying about the why and how. You have a lot to look forward to in the future with this pair I think."

"True. And at least I did find them at all. At least they won't die after a few hundred years," Surala said in resignation, flicking her long, scaled tail in irritation and frustration.

"See, lots to think of in the more positive vein. So, any other reasons that you can't sleep?" Felatia asked as she gave a long, graceful and languid stretch with her arms and tail, making Surala a bit jealous at just how graceful and beautiful she was on the cushion of the large oyster that served as her perching spot in the pool.

"How is it that you look that graceful stretching like that? I have no idea why else I can't sleep…other than people are missing, being taken and I …I can't track down the source," Surala grumbled, feeling a bit put-out over the whole situation.

"I can't help it. Part sea creature, part Elf…not my fault that the Gods have a wicked sense of humor, Surala," she replied with a sardonic grin.

"Hm…well they could've passed some of that grace on to someone like me—" Surala grumbled.

"They did…you just don't see it, Love." Felati shifted a bit on her perch, giving her friend a sincere but amused look.

Surala grumbled and gave her friend a dark look…then chuckled darkly.

"Well, when we find who did this…I'm going to enjoy stepping on them."

"Oh, can I watch?" Felati asked, genuinely having stated in the past that she longed to see a Dragon step on someone.

Surala couldn't help it…she laughed long and hard! The halls rang with it and she felt a bit of joy for the first time in so long.

And hope.

Chapter Five

The next morning, Ezra rose early and ate a decent breakfast. She dressed in a new maternity outfit, which was a dress that was made of soft linen and was not what she liked to wear really at all. But it fit her better than her usual clothing did now...and she needed to feel somewhat more comfortable…even if it made her feel ridiculous. Her headdress went on as did her choker. Bracelets had been fashioned to match in place of her vambraces. She went down the corridors to the Entrance Hall and waited patiently for Reanalia to join her.

"Sorceress, you really shouldn't be out of bed," Eve said as she materialized seemingly out of nowhere.

"I have to be up for this, Eve. I'm sending Lady Reanalia to investigate these disappearances at the coast of the Eastern Sea. Since I can't go myself, I have to send her…and sending her by portal is the only way to get her there fast enough."

"Can't she do it then?"

"No, she doesn't know where she's going, and her reach isn't quite what mine is. Afterwards, I'll return to bed for today. But only for today. We have to get to the bottom of what's going on."

"You're going to put yourself into labor," Eve scolded her.

"No, I'm not. Eve, this is my duty! This is why I'm here. I *cannot* give it to anyone else. These people came to us for help. Just because I'm pregnant doesn't change that," Ezra told her gently, knowing the woman couldn't possibly understand. Of course, once upon a time, Ezra hadn't wanted to understand it either.

Being a warrior was so much easier. I would have willingly perished with the Council, but Bael did not want me to die. He wanted me to live, Ezra thought with a weary heart.

Her thoughts were interrupted by Reanalia, who arrived with a rather exuberant jump at the end of a long run down the hall.

"I overslept! Sorry, Sorceress. I'm ready to go," Reanalia said with a smile.

"This isn't a good idea. Can't she send herself?" Eve interrupted again.

"No, Eve. She doesn't have the reach to go quite that far, otherwise she would've teleported herself here! Or made her own portal. Besides, I know where she's going, and I've got the reach to get her there. Now, as I said, this is my duty—"

"And what happens if the baby comes early because of your duty?"

"Eve, the baby is immortal. No matter what, the baby will live."

"As your healer—"

"Would you allow a pregnancy to prevent you from doing your duty?" Ezra asked, growing tired of the argument. Eve hesitated, her expression showing a bit of defiance as Eve thought on it. Ezra gave her a sigh and a nod. "I thought not. Now, I promise I will go back to bed. But only after Reanalia is through the portal and begins her part in this. Reanalia, here's the charm I gave to Mara when she was playing spy for me. If you need to contact me—"

"Pfft! I'll just use a mirror spell," Reanalia said with a sage nod.

"Please don't. We don't know who will be listening. With the charm, you can send me a message directly through telepathy. You won't have to worry about being overheard and frankly, we still don't know who we can trust. I believe that Surala and Felati don't mean us any harm, but until we know for sure…I'd rather err on the side of caution," Ezra explained.

Reanalia took it and put it on her finger with a sigh.

"Okay, we'll play it safe. Let's get this show on the road."

Ezra gave a chuckle at Reanalia's exuberance and wished that she had that sort of energy today. As it was, she was going to have to draw on Ammora's power just to open the portal that would send her out so far.

Ezra closed her eyes, held her hands up before the empty space before her…and concentrated on finding that place again. Slowly she fed power into the spell, felt it spinning out, searching and finally it caught, and she felt the portal open. Lights and a bit of wind swirled around her as she opened her eyes and gave a nod.

"It's ready. Go! I'll talk to you later, Reanalia. Be careful!" Ezra urged her. Reanalia spun around with a laugh.

"I'm always careful! Talk to you soon, Sorceress!" Reanalia called as she ran and jumped into the portal. Ezra waited until she knew that Reanalia was safe on the other side and closed it down, feeling power pour back into her and she breathed a sigh of relief.

Only to feel her stomach tighten up and clench again. Ezra nearly doubled over as Eve tsked at her and began to scold her again.

"Back to your bed and no more magic today! In fact, I'm tempted to tell you that there'll be no more magic for a solid week!" Eve exclaimed as she gave Ezra a stern look.

Ezra sighed as they walked back to her quarters, taking it slowly and hoping that this pregnancy would be over before anything else happened.

Reanalia emerged from the portal to a beautiful sight. The castle before her looked like it was made from hard packed sand… and seashells of every color of the rainbow and every size she hadn't even dreamed was possible. She gasped and just stood in awe.

Who could have built this place? She wondered. And why use just sand and shells? Magic must protect it, or else it would've all been washed away long ago, Reanalia mused as she reached out with her own magic to touch it and see what held it all together.

And found a small amount of Earth magic holding it all together. Under the surface of sand also was a good layer of rock, which is what kept it all structurally sound while appearances were to the contrary. *A clever disguise,* Reanalia thought to herself as she just stood there, admiring it for a few moments more. Then, satisfied, Reanalia approached it, taking it slowly as she approached the doors.

Before she ever reached it, the door swung open and there stood, in all of her glory, a half-dragon! Pink and purple scaled, long pink and purple hair clad in a long flowing gown that was held together at the shoulders with pins and wearing an expression that was all business, the half-dragon mage approached Reanalia.

"Who goes there?" the half-dragon asked, a hint of mist leaving her lips as she spoke.

"Lady Reanalia. I've been sent here by the Sorceress of Ammora. Now, she's told me about what you told her so shall we go sit down, have a cup of tea and you can tell me everything that has happened here in detail. I promise, I will do everything in my power to help uncover what is going on."

*　*　*

Surala hated to admit it, but she liked this immortal mage! As they sat and she and Queen Felati filled the mage in, Reanalia had listened to every detail with the attention and patience of a priestess. She didn't ask unintelligent questions but waited for them to finish their tales.

"Okay, so we have two storms, one above water and the other below it. Which gives us two problems. I can't look at both simultaneously, but I can look at the one above water. The one below…well I am immortal, but I'm not really equipped for going underwater. I do have a transformation spell but that would be a big transformation and might take some time to master. Alone, I might not be able to pull that particular spell off, but it'll depend on how complex a creature I'm willing to transform into. I'm powerful but…I do have my limits, unlike the Sorceress of Ammora. So, for now, let's put that place aside. The one above the water I would like to see. How far away is it?"

"About a three-hour flight," Surala replied with a sardonic smile. "I can get you there fairly quickly, though magic might be faster. For a human…it would be a month by boat."

"We don't have a month, so I'll take your flight if you don't mind carrying me. We'll start there and see if there's any traces left that I can find. Most of the other sites didn't have much of any sort of signature according to the mages that the Sorceress has spoken to in those areas. The one under the water might be different since it probably took an astronomical amount of power to be able to create a storm like that under the water. Sooner or later, I or the Sorceress are going to have to see it," Reanalia admitted, looking very thoughtful. "And if there's witnesses, I'd like to speak to them."

"Of course there's witnesses. Kayla had a friend with her, Ousran. I'll send for her and have them here to talk with you when you return from the island where Libor was taken," Queen Felati said with a regal tip of her head. "Will you be back tonight?"

"Try for tomorrow. The sort of things I'm looking for might take hours just to find," Reanalia replied with a sigh. "Are you up to that flight now, Lady Surala? Or would you prefer to start off in the morning?"

"Let's go now. The sooner we get to the bottom of this mess, the better I'll feel," Surala replied as she rose.

Kayla woke with a soft groan. She was wet, at least. Kayla preferred being in the water. Although mermaids could transform into a human or elven form, though being directly under the sunlight was sometimes a bit too hot. Kayla preferred to be in her mermaid form at all times. Eyes slowly opened as she looked around herself. Hand brushed against something cold and smooth, and she turned to find nothing but glass on one side. She looked down underneath herself and found more glass, forming the bottom. To her other side, she found another glass pane. Panic forced her to turn over again and swim the short distance to the surface…

Of a tank. A rather large one, but for a mermaid it felt small, and cramped. Luckily it was just her within it. It was scarcely large enough for her to turn around and swim in very well and her head broke the surface to find nothing but bars above her, keeping her from escaping it. But at least it allowed her to breathe, which explained why she hadn't drowned—she'd been floating face up at least.

She looked around, hearing groans from other creatures nearby and the rattle of chains. There was a soft drip of water somewhere nearby. A few lone lanterns burned on stone walls that she had never seen before in her life.

In the center of the room, stood a single woman with long black hair, black tattoos interlacing all over her skin and wearing nothing except a long black halter dress made of a material that Kayla had never seen before.

On their knees before her was a dark elf woman. Blood ran down her arms and under the shackles on her dark wrists. Her long white hair was spattered with bits of blood and other gore. Her eyes had been removed, leaving nothing but empty sockets behind.

The woman was screaming as a knife ran over her flesh, slowly skinning her skin away from the flesh on her back.

Kayla looked around in panic and heard a soft "psst!" somewhere near her.

She turned and saw the glowing eyes of another dark woman, clad in blood-stained armor, who motioned with one chained hand to go back down into the water. The next motion was for her to feign sleep.

Kayla looked back to the horror before her tank and allowed herself to lay back in the water and lay limply, feigning sleep. She closed her eyes again and just tried not to hear those horrible sounds coming from across the room.

Goddess, please help me! Please send help for us! She thought desperately as she tried to block out those horrible screams.

Ezra woke with a scream! The nightmare lingered as she sat up, reaching out of habit for a sword she no longer wore. She looked around in the darkness, her heart racing until she realized where she was.

Safe at home. Not in a dark dungeon…

The dream was still lingering, refusing to let her go. The creatures she had seen, the horrible noises she'd heard—

Magic tingled at her fingertips, waiting to be used as she took a breath and concentrated. Sometimes she knew her dreams weren't dreams, but visions that had interrupted the dream she might have had.

As she concentrated, she felt the vision beginning to form anew. She saw the mermaid she had been watching through in the dream.

Then she saw the woman. Dark hair, pale skin, tattooed head to toe and wearing a very skimpy black gown and holding a bloody knife.

A dark, sickly green glow of magic was beginning to emanate from her victim's empty eye sockets, making Ezra's skin crawl with revulsion.

A dark elf woman was kneeling before her, her screams having turned to whimpers and the thoughts of the panicked mermaid touched Ezra's senses, pulling her attention back to her.

Goddess, please help me! Please send help for us! The thought was desperate, making Ezra's heart go out to her.

::Calm yourself, Little One. Help will come as soon as we can find you. I'm the Sorceress of Ammora and I have been looking for those who have been taken. How long have you been there? What's your name?:: Ezra reached out instinctively, trying to soothe the mermaid, sensing her panic.

I don't know how long I've been here. I don't even know where here is!

::It's okay. What's your name?:: Ezra asked as she tried to discover where this dungeon was—

And was suddenly shut out by a large wall! The mermaid's presence faded from her mind as Ezra realized that the woman with the pale skin and tattoos had blocked her out! The vision shattered, leaving Ezra sitting again in her bed, far away from the dungeon she had managed to catch a quick glimpse of.

No! So close! Ezra thought desperately as she continued to try to trace the mermaid's location, working desperately to break through that wall—

And found no relief. Ezra swore loudly.

"What's the matter?" Derik asked beside her as he stirred, his arm curling around her waist and pulling her down to him.

"I had a vision, Derik! I saw the captives! They're in a dungeon somewhere. I could sense a mermaid's thoughts and I was trying to soothe her and then suddenly, there was this wall! That woman must've sensed my presence somehow."

"Maybe she's telepathic like you are?" Derik asked groggily as Ezra cuddled down into his arms.

"Maybe," she replied quietly, frustrated to no end. "The Elves and Dark Elves are both nearly at each other's throats and this is so frustrating, I can't make heads or tails of it anymore!"

"I'll plan a tournament for the Elves' entertainment with Captain Lita if you'd like. It might give everyone a chance to relieve some of that pent up energy," Derik offered with a yawn.

Ezra looked back up to him.

"You'd do that for me?"

"Of course!"

"Thank you, Derik. That would help tremendously," Ezra sighed in relief at feeling one more pressure being removed from her shoulders.

"You're welcome. Now let's try to get some sleep and we'll talk more…in…the morning," Derik yawned again then began to snore softly.

Ezra shook her head and settled next to him but was very slow in finding her own rest until nearly dawn.

Alyra chuckled as she sensed that presence. Someone was watching somehow. She continued her work, allowing the watcher to watch for a few brief moments…

Then she put up the shield, blocking it out from the watcher. She had felt that tinge of light within it, the revulsion of what the woman had sensed her doing.

Reason enough to shut the meddler out. Wonder who they were watching through and how they managed to penetrate my defenses all the way down here in the first place, Alyria thought as she completed the spell…and motioned for her new puppet to be taken to the keeping place with the others. The Dark Elf would obey her mindlessly now as there was no longer a mind, or a soul, left within her. *A perfect new servant for the Darkness that I shall unleash upon this horrid world,* Alrya thought as she turned to look at her other victims and nodded to the servants to feed them.

These servants had been hand-picked by herself. They were greedy, foul little humans who wished to have the best of all life had to offer. Sex, money, and they enjoyed unleashing pain onto others. They hungered for the magic that she could potentially give them.

And why would I do that, when they are such perfect little puppets to do my bidding without it? Last thing I need is a contender, competition, for my little army. But, for now, they shall do. And I intend to make sure they only get enough to be sated with their lot…until I'm done with them. Then…then I'll take it all back and they shall be left as nothing more than a new set of mindless slaves. Alyra chuckled as she turned to go back to Jarod's chamber. The fool needed another dose of her company, lest he begin to grow suspicious of her.

The charm she had cast upon him was still holding, but she was starting to sense that he was beginning to fight it a little. She would have to strengthen it again with a glass of wine tonight and a good night of sex afterwards. Alyra smiled as she entered the bed chamber to find him pacing there and went to pour his nightly constitutional. She brought it to him with a smile and leaned up to kiss his lips after taking a sip of it herself…and poured the charmed wine into his mouth with the long, deep kiss.

Jarod turned to her and wrapped his arms around her, a troubled look in his eyes until the kiss broke and the charm began to take effect.

"Where have you been? I've been waiting for you," Jarod said with a smile as he began to relax, seeing everything he wanted in her now as the charm took over his senses. Alyra just smiled.

"Oh, just been puttering about, my Love. Come, let me make you feel good to make up for my absence," Alyra crooned, tugging lightly on his arm.

Jarod took one step as she tugged on his arm, then another. Soon, they were falling into his bed and ripping each other's clothes from the other's body.

Followed by carnal screams of pleasure that echoed throughout the halls.

Aeryn was patrolling along the upper parapets of Ammora Castle. He patted his laser pistol in its holster while slinging his new mace over his other shoulder as he looked down in the darkness towards the moat and small landing for the bridge across the way from the Castle.

The drawbridge was up, thank the Goddess, so he was relaxed as he watched.

Then he tensed, seeing shadows moving on the other side. He looked out into the darkness, trying to get a sense of who might be over there. Demonic shaped shadows moved, moving oddly in the very dim light as the moon was down to a bare sliver in the sky above Ammora.

He slipped out a communicator from his pocket.

"Mara, you awake?" he asked, knowing that she rarely slept when he wasn't at her side.

"I'm awake, Aeryn. Everything okay?"

"We've got some odd movement across the way. Might need some back-up over here," he reported, as he continued to watch those odd forms shuffling and moving in the darkness.

"You got it. Sending out three big burly guys your way, Aeryn, and my hot sexy ass. Lita's up, she'll man the communicator for a bit. Need anything special for a warm reception?"

"Grab a laser rifle or two, love. We might be here awhile," he replied, relieved that she was always ready to come up and keep him company during what might be a long watch.

"On the way," Mara replied before the communication dropped. He put the communicator away for now and nodded as three of his fellow mercenaries walked up.

Ash was tall, broad-chested and held his sword handle with one hand while stroking his own laser rifle with the other as he held it against his shoulder. He had blonde hair that was shaved on both sides of his head, but the top was long and held back in a long braid that hung down his back. The ladies were always flirting with him as he had an infectious smile, no filter to speak of and a rather light sense of humor for a man who had spent most of his life in battle.

Bear was large like Ash, but heftier. He outweighed Ash by at least 30 pounds, if Aeryn was any judge. And he was all muscle, sinew, and bone. He did like his beer, but he worked longer and harder at training daily than most men would over several days. He had a grim sense of humor, but he made up for it in honesty and the odd random bit of kindness he tended to do when he thought no one was looking. Red brown hair spilled down Bear's shoulders and was kept loose, but there were streaks of gray beginning to appear at his temples. *Age catches up with us all in the end*, Aeryn thought as he shifted his weight, noting that Bear had a pistol like he did, but a large bow was slung across his back along with a quiver full of deadly arrows.

The last was Wahya. Wahya wasn't a mercenary per se, but he and Tala had remained at Ammora and now had their own house in the city. They were friends with the Sorceress and Derik and had become friends with every mercenary that had settled here. Their own tribe was camped nearby, ready to come at a moment's notice. A rare gift for the tribe to stay somewhere for any length of time as they tended to move more often than not. Wahya's blonde hair was loose with several braids twined in it. He looked young, no more than maybe 30 years or so…but his eyes showed his age. Aeryn had gotten drunk with Wahya and Tala once and had gleaned that they had been cursed with immortality for past offenses in their true youth.

Gotta be a living hell, knowing you'll never die but have to live with what you've done. Poor bastards, but at least they turned it around and try to keep others from making the same mistakes, Aeryn thought as they all looked down.

"What are they?" Bear asked as they watched the flickering movements of shadow shuffling around the outer edges of the moat.

"I've never seen anything like it. Have you, Wahya?" Aeryn asked as they watched one nearly topple over the edge before it caught itself and climbed back up the small shelf backwards in a weird crab-like move.

"Not in all of my years have I seen anything like that. I've seen a lot. Vampires, wraiths. Mages of all sorts. Dragons. Never anything like that, Bra."

"Brought you all some hot tea and a couple of rifles," Mara said as she emerged from the door behind them. She passed out the cups of tea, all made of a hard wood that wouldn't easily shatter if it was dropped. It was sweetened with honey, Aeryn discovered to his relief, as he hated unsweetened tea.

"Thanks, love," he said as he put an arm around Mara and took one of those rifles from her once the lads had all taken their cups. They stood there for the next hour or two, just watching, waiting…

Then, just as suddenly as they had appeared…the shadows vanished, and the night grew still again.

"Did you feel that energy surge?" Wahya asked as Aeryn kept watching, expecting the shadows to reappear.

"No, what energy surge?"

"Magic, Bra. They were probably dropped here by a mage…and now they've been taken back again. I don't like it. The Sorceress is gonna have a cat when she finds out that a mage is dropping something like that this close. Especially since Eve is giving her a hard time with her pregnancy and making her rest," Wahya explained, his face grim.

"We should keep watch like this every night. Somethin's comin', Bra. I feel it." Wahya stretched his neck and made a face, showing his distaste for what had just happened.

"Lita'll probably agree with you. I don't like it, either. It's been too quiet, except for all of the kidnappings all over Axrealia…but none have happened here," Aeryn mused.

"We're too well protected. The Sorceress has a magical shield over us. It's small but it's there. Keeps unwanted mages from poking around doing as they want," Wahya said.

"How do you know that?"

"Bra, I was cursed with immortality by a mage. I'm sensitive to this shit, Bra," Wahya said with a near-savage grin. Aeryn chuckled and grasped his forearm then.

"We'll keep watch until dawn, lads. Wahya, you and I will report in the morning to the Sorceress. She needs to know."

"I can't wait until the baby is born. She'll feel so much better once the little one's here," Mara said with a nod.

"We all will. She'll be able to do magic freely again. That'll be a happy day and more than just about the birth of the little one," Wahya agreed as they all turned their attention back across the way, expecting to see more shadows.

But there were none for the rest of the night.

Chapter Six

"Shadows? Shadows of what, Counselor?" Ezra asked the next morning as she sat on her throne, gazing down at Lita, head of the ruling Council of Ammora City. Ezra had her place on the Council, but she insisted on only being an Advisor as she didn't need to add being a Ruler of a city to her list of duties. *Besides, I'm not a Ruler. I'm the guardian of this place, and the last thing I need is to be worrying about is everyone's little squabbles when I have real work to do,* Ezra thought yet again as she tried to fathom what it was that Lita's men had seen last night.

"They were unnatural, Sorceress. One minute, there was nothing…then these shadows were moving around all around the moat. If there'd been more moonlight, we might have seen them for what they really were, Ma'am," Aeryn spoke up behind Lita. Ash and Bear stood behind them as did Wahya.

"After the rest of us arrived, we watched 'em for another good hour or two, Sorceress. Then there was this energy surge, and they were gone," Wahya added grimly, a troubled look on his immortal features.

That took Ezra aback. She knew how old Wahya was, one of the few who truly knew. She also knew that he had seen just about everything that anyone could see in Axrealia over the centuries. Very few things troubled him like this.

"Have you ever seen anything like this before, Wahya?" she asked.

"No, Sista. I haven't. Not in all of my long years treading this world. And whatever it was, it wasn't friendly. I'm going to join the watch every night until we figure out who, or what, they are," Wahya said with a grim nod.

"Tala as well?" Ezra asked.

"Oh yeah. She said she won't miss this party for the world," Wahya said with a grim look. Ezra breathed a bit easier, knowing they would help to watch each other's backs, along with those who were mortal.

"I'll make sure that there's plenty of hot things for you all to have tonight while you stand watch to help against the chill of the night. Send Tala or Mara to wake me if they appear again. I need to see this for myself," Ezra decided on a whim, knowing Eve would probably have a cat, but she was beyond caring.

Some days, I swear, she's more concerned about the baby than she is about my well-being. But I'll make this work...somehow. Ezra sighed and turned to the next order of business.

"Lita, there is something else I need you to begin arranging. In light of this, I may ask the Dark Elves and the Forest Elves to have one of their retinues come up to watch with the others in case this happens again. They may have seen this before. But they are nearly at each other's throats. Every day they find a reason for an argument. I'd like to give them a chance to bond a little. You can take your time doing this of course, but I'd like you to arrange a tournament. Nothing where anyone will get seriously hurt. But a chance for everyone to take out their spleen on something more than a set of pells. Including our warriors. Can you take care of this for me, please?"

Lita's jaw dropped and Ezra resisted the urge to laugh a bit at the look on her face.

"That's not something we can arrange at the drop of a hat, Sorceress! It can take months! Prizes would need to be arranged, food as well. Plus, we'd need to set something up for it and we don't have that quite built yet," Lita protested.

"There is the training field, and it can be altered slightly for an audience, Lita. Plus, if we get enough hands in the kitchen here, the Castle will provide the feast for it. Snacks and drinks can be brought down to the field to hand out to the crowd as well as to the participants. As for Prizes well…I believe you have some fine artisans who have been creating things but haven't had many customers yet. So perhaps they will be willing to donate some special items in the hope of getting a bit more attention from the citizens of the town afterwards," Ezra replied, hoping to take the main bulk of the worry from Lita's mind so she could concentrate on the main task.

Arranging for Dark Elves and Forest Elves to fight each other in a way that would escalate the tensions between them but might build camaraderie between them.

"It doesn't seem so important in light of certain events that have been going on, Sorceress," Lita protested, huffing a bit.

"Lita, I need to investigate the disappearances as well as these other strange events that have been happening. I can't do that with our guests bickering every day and trying to take up my time or attention over petty nonsense. We need them to at least put their differences aside…and to help us. Whomever is taking these people, we have no idea what they're doing to them. So, let's give everyone a bit of fun and a chance to put their pasts aside. In the meantime, I will speak to them about helping to stand watch here and there, at least one of their guards from each retinue. That'll give a couple extra pairs of eyes to watch and who knows? They may see something we might have missed," Ezra added with a grim nod.

Lita hesitated for another minute or two, then bowed her head.

"As you wish, Sorceress. I'll make the arrangements, but it's going to take time."

"Take the time you need to do it right, Counselor. Thank you all for your diligence and for watching each night. Oh, and Lita? I'll send Derik to come and help you with the arrangements for the tournament," Ezra added, feeling grateful to them all. Without this small bit of news, she wouldn't have had any idea that anything had happened last night.

But then, I was quite exhausted!

Lita, Wahya and the others moved out and Ezra was left alone for a few moments to ponder her next move.

;;Baelios?;; she sent tentatively, wondering if the Spirit had seen anything that had happened last night.

::Yes, Ezra?:: Baelios asked as he suddenly popped into existence beside her chair, one solid hand coming down to touch her shoulder. She reached up and touched his hand and studied his face.

::Did you sense anything last night that was unusual?::

::;The shadows were glowing with magical energy, Ezra. I was going to bring this up to you later when we had a few moments alone. Lita and her men beat me to the punch.::

::What were they? Could you tell?:: She asked.

::;I've never seen anything like them or read about anything like them. Whatever, whomever, they were…it's nothing like anyone has ever seen before. But they glowed and the power they glowed with; I've never seen it's like. Dark, twisted and foul. And whoever sent them left very little signature in their magic,:: Baelios' mental voice sounded a little irritated and frustrated in her mind.

::Little…but not none?:: Ezra felt a gleam of hope.

:;Little, but not none. Which means--:: he started.

:;I can identify who cast the spell if I see it for myself,:: Ezra breathed a sigh of relief as she leaned her head back against the throne. :;I'll go and rest this afternoon in case they come again tonight.::

::They might. The moon is going to be nearly gone tonight, so it'll be very dark. And if they prefer the cover of darkness--::

::They'll love that the moon is gone. My thoughts exactly,Baelios!:: Ezra sent telepathically back, feeling hope for the first time in a long time.

::Let's hope that it's our quarry,:: Baelios agreed in her mind.

::Oh let's hope that indeed! I'm growing tired of chasing phantoms.::

::As am I,:: Baelios sent, giving her shoulder a gentle squeeze.

::Send for the Dark Elves and the Forest Elves, please. I'd like to arrange for them to join the watch and to tell them about our upcoming tournament. It'll give them all something to train for…and look forward to.::

:;It might spur them into keeping busy in the training fields for it too. Not a bad idea to tell them now.:; Baelios chuckled before he disappeared.

Ezra sat back then and relaxed in this moment of quiet and chuckled as the baby chose to kick and stretch.

"Soon enough you'll be here, little one. Soon enough," she murmured as she got a flash of a Vision. A dark-haired woman, strong and proud, dressed as a Warrior yet she glowed with power. A smile on her face as she rode on the back of a mighty dragon through the sky. It wasn't much, just a flash, but enough to look forward to.

Her daughter. Ezra had been having visions of her for months, but it was something that she cherished with each small peek into the future.

Then the delegation arrived and brought Ezra thoughts of what may be spiraling back to focus on the present.

"Shadows? What do you mean Shadows?" Reanalia asked as she and Surala spoke with Felati over breakfast. Surala, for someone who lived alone, was a very good cook! And Felati's people had brought plenty of fish though somehow the Half-Dragon Mage had managed to get eggs and sausages along with fruits for this morning's meal.

"That's just it. Shadows. Odd ones that moved weirdly in the night. I sensed something nearby and I went up to the window..and I saw shadows moving. Unnaturally so. They looked a little like various sorts of people but...I couldn't get a clear view of them. They kept in the darkness as much as they could, I could barely see them," Surala admitted as she poured Reanalia a cup of tea and held it out to her.

Reanalia took the tea and looked at her, puzzled.

"Anything else?"

"They glowed with power. Evil energy. There was a signature, but it was barely there," Surala admitted as she ran her fingers through her long blue and pink hair. "If I could get a little longer to watch them, I might be able to identify which mage sent them. Maybe."

"Or maybe not? We've been dealing with a very odd Mage as it is already, Surala. One who doesn't want to be found. I doubt they'll leave a signature any living mage could identify," Felati pointed out as she toyed with a bit of fruit. "We might get lucky, but we can't count on it. It'd be nice if we could catch one of these shadows, whatever it's connected to and see for ourselves just what it is."

"That isn't a bad idea. Why don't we set a trap for one, in case they come back?" Reanalia said as she touched the charm on her finger, the one that could connect her to the Sorceress of Ammora to send a report.

"I'm game. We have plenty of supplies to set up a trap with…and lots of nets," Surala said with a near-savage grin.

"Then that's what we'll do this morning. Too bad we didn't' find much of anything on the island where the merman was taken, Queen Felati. The underwater one should help more, if I can manage to go down there. Going underwater and feeling like I'm drowning won't be fun unless I can manage that transformation spell," Reanalia admitted, wishing that she had the reserves that the Sorceress of Ammora had.

Of course, the price for that, being soul-bound to a spirit and a living castle…not worth it for me to take that on, Reanalia admitted to herself as she had seen the cost with her own two eyes.

And it was not one that she would have ever been willing to pay.

"As soon as we're done with breakfast then, we'll get to work. Felati, if you have any extra bits of driftwood floating out there, could you have it sent up to the cliffs? The pulley system still works very well if memory serves," Surala asked her friend with an excited grin.

"Oh yes, I'd be delighted to. Soon as we're done eating, I'll go have some of my people go find what's floating around," Felati chuckled as she bit into the fruit she held and groaned with pleasure at the taste. "I love this fruit. What's it called again?"

"It's an apple. Juicy, crisp and quite delicious in the summertime," Reanalia replied, tilting her head a little as she watched the Mermaid Queen's reaction. "You've never had one?"

"We don't get a lot of fruit in the ocean. Plenty of salty things, but very little sweet. Though sea grapes are nice, as is kelp and shrimp. Crab is my favorite, but as I said we don't get anything like this in the ocean. It's a nice treat," Felatia replied with a grin before she took another big, juicy bite.

Oh, I wonder if I could fix that for her…at least make it easier for her and her people to get a treat now and then. That would be a good thing for Ammora, or someone nearby to trade with Surala for, Reanalia thought with pleasure as they finished their meal.

The rest of the morning was spent setting up the traps around the Dragon's Keep. Surala found herself impressed as Reanalia wasn't a large woman, nor as strong as a man. Yet Reanalia had used her own magic to help set up the traps and they had several now set and ready to go in the places where Surala had seen the shadows prowling around the night before.

Though why they are prowling around out here is beyond me, Surala thought grimly as she stretched out into her full Draconic form and lay upon a rock to sun herself for a little bit. *It's not as if my Keep has a lot of magic or anything really rare inside. We just help the creatures of the ocean and the shore.*

It troubled her, though she couldn't put a claw on exactly why. Why would a mage be watching this place? It didn't make much sense.

Then again, not much about this past month or so has made sense, Surala thought as she relaxed on her large basking rock, glorying in the feel of the sun upon her scaled back.

She shifted again, letting her tail flop down around her front claws, feeling it twitch as her agitation grew.

Surala felt the muscles on the back of her neck itch…and sensed a small surge of energy.

Someone's watching me, Surala realized and tried, too late, to trace it!

But the sensation vanished as if it never was…

Leaving her with more questions than answers.

Ezra was relaxing in her chambers. The reports she had been given alarmed her. Shadows prowling about on the other side of the moat.

But why? What purpose could they possibly have? She wondered as she rubbed her large, rounded belly while the baby kicked and squirmed inside of her. Ezra mulled that question over, wondering what the Shadows even were.

Mages often used to send various sorts of creatures to spy for them on other mages. That seemed to fit the puzzle before her.

What didn't fit was that they hadn't attacked or revealed what they were at all.

Most mages enjoy showing off to each other, so why not this time? Again, she mulled it over, feeling it bugging her.

Then it hit her like a ton of bricks raining about her.

If they're using these shadow-creatures to spy for them, they want information. They're investigating…as we've been investigating.

That also fit...and fit far too well into the mental puzzle she was assembling.

Ezra took a breath as she felt a twinge in her belly and all thoughts turned from the mental puzzle to the baby—

And she was hit with a Vision! She found herself outside in the dark, looking down at the moat—

And across the moat were shadowy shapes, swirling and moving about! Ezra looked to her left and right, then looked down at the center…

A woman with dark tattoos on her pale skin stood there, dressed in a black dress and crowned with a black onyx headdress.

She looked like a dark mirror of herself to Ezra…and Ezra heard shouts behind her.

"Sorceress, we have to get you to safety! We'll be overrun!" Lita screamed down the hallway.

"No, get everyone out! Get Angelica and Derik to safety! Hurry, there isn't much time!" Ezra called back.

"Mommy!"

The vision melted, leaving an echo of her unborn daughter's cries ringing in her ears!

Ezra looked around herself, frantic, trying to get herself back under control!

Seeing no one around her, she took another breath and rubbed her hand over her belly.

"Shh, little one. It's all right. Won't be for years yet, I promise."

But it left her with a chill running down her spine.

Not every Vision comes to pass. This one, I'm forewarned. I won't let it happen.

Alyra watched her prey from the shadowy realm. She slipped into it from time to time to watch, to listen.

She couldn't go inside Ammora—those shadows were magically protected, keeping her shut out!

But she could use the shadows to watch others. Her soldiers were already out, watching from across the moat again in the Dark.

And the Destruction God ruled the Dark and had given her dominion over it as well.

From the shadows, she watched her soldiers prowling about, watched the reactions from across the way as those who protected Ammora responded.

She watched as hands pointed, watched the bodies as they surged and moved…

And a single white figure stepped forth.

The Sorceress of Ammora looked back and Alyra smiled in her shroud of Darkness.

She can't see me, can't touch me. And one day, my Darkness will eclipse her light at last…and then…I'll take all of Axrealia into my Darkness and use it to spread my Darkness to other worlds.

Ezra jerked awake after having only slept for a few hours…Derik looked down at her with concern in his eyes.

"The Shadows are back," he told her.

"Show me," she told him as she got up, having not bothered to dress for bed tonight as she got up to follow him.

Together, they walked up to the parapets where Wayha, Tala, Mara, Aeryn, Lita, Bear, and Ash were all standing watch again. They parted before Ezra and let her get a good look at the opposite side of the moat below.

The shadows surged, glowing with a foul energy that Ezra had only sensed once before. It was barely a signature, but it was enough!

"The Mage that sent them was Juktis' partner," she breathed as she watched them, sensing the hot hatred that seemed to emanate off of the shadowy figures. Ezra used her mage senses, trying to read them further, sensing something of the one who had created these creatures, feeling the raw hatred….

But why? What had she ever done to this woman? She didn't even know her name! Much less had ever seen her!

::For some, that does not matter, Ezra. They hate us for what we represent. We have the magic they desire, the power they crave to have for themselves. They will do anything to obtain it.::

:;But why?:: Ezra asked, knowing that if she'd had the choice, she wouldn't have taken the power she possessed for the world.

::Sometimes there is no why. They just are evil, Ezra.::

::There must be a reason, Baelios,:: she replied telepathically, continuing to study the shadows.

And just as quickly as the shadows were there, they were suddenly gone. A surge of portal energy nearly blinded Ezra for a moment…

Leaving nothing behind in its place but the empty landscape around the Castle.

:;Next time, I am grabbing one of those creatures, Baelios.::

::I'll help, Ezra. I'll--:: Baelios' thought was cut short as the Castle suddenly began to shake under them.

And just as suddenly as it started, it stopped.

::;Ezra, the Castle just created…a dungeon,:: Baelios reported.

::Good…because we're going to need it to contain one of those things when we catch it.::

It was a small comfort when the sun rose that morning…showing nothing but random footprints in the dust on the other side of the drawbridge.

Chapter Seven

Reanalia paced the length of the library at the Dragon's Keep. She had been trying, without success, to change herself into a mermaid.

Mermaids were not part fish...they were *all* mammals.   Their tails were not scaled, but they were iridescent. Their lungs could hold more air that could allow them to dive deep into the waters and, according to Felati, they were able to get a breath of air in the deep caves and in large oysters that held large caches of fresh air…

"Where do you sleep when you need to sleep?" Reanalia asked the Mermaid queen as she again considered what her transformation spell would need to work.

"In caves…or on the shore. When our tails get dry, we transform into humans, elves, that sort of thing," Felati replied with a smile.

"Oh…and that's how you've hidden your presence for so long."

"Exactly," Felati replied with a mischievous smile. "No one knows if they're looking at a mermaid or a merman unless we get wet. So, we avoid going to certain places on rainy days. We don't feel the urge to go into villages or cities usually anyway. We prefer the sea. It's where we belong."

Reanalia rubbed her aching temples and tried to think of how her transformation spell would work.

"The transformation spell I have might work…might. Since it's not a full transformation…but I can't guarantee I'll be able to hold my breath as long as you could."

"Of course not. Who could have expected that? Magic has limitations, of course," Felati replied with a dry chuckle. "So, we'll make extra stops or…maybe we can give a bit of extra help," she said as she pulled up a harness with a large seashell on the back that had a long hollow tube running from it and ended in a face mask. "This is how we make long journeys in the areas where we know there isn't a lot of air. It should help," the Mermaid Queen said. "We came up with this a long, long time ago."

Reanalia was stunned speechless as she wondered how in the world—

But then, we have laser guns, sky chariots and all sorts of new technology is coming into the world each day, Reanalia thought.

"Okay, let's give it a try then."

Reanalia took a moment, took a breath, and began to use her own magic, pulling more from the world around her as she worked.

*   *   *

Three hours later, Reanalia finally managed the transformation! Dripping with sweat, she felt her legs give out beneath her…and felt an odd, painful sensation as they fused together.

Next, she felt webbing growing between her fingers…her feet elongated, flattened…and her bones inside changed! A scream left her lips, but she kept her mind on what she was doing, refusing to give up!

And felt the magic drain away as she lay there on the floor, her new tail flopping helplessly against the stones as she felt the pain pass at last…leaving her in a new, transformed state!

"Well done, Reanalia!" Surala called as Reanalia felt the half-dragon mage's magic lifting her up and carrying her towards the pool. The cool water felt good on her newly transformed fins and Reanalia lay back against the side of the pool, feeling exhausted in the aftermath of the spell.

"Thank you…so tired. That took more out of me… than I thought it would," she admitted.

"Rest here then. It's a special bed for Merpeople. Just rest and in the morning, we'll go to see the underwater site," Surala soothed Reanalia by stroking her long fingers through Reanalia's sweat-soaked locks. Reanalia couldn't argue with her. It would be there in the morning.

But now I'm helpless in this form, at least until I learn how to swim, Reanalia thought. And yet that thought cheered her immensely. *I'll be able to swim like a mermaid. How many others would give their right arm for that?*

A smile curled the corners of her lips as she drifted down into a very deep sleep.

"When your Castle builds a dungeon…it certainly does it right," Lita said as she walked around Ammora's new dungeon. Shackles hung from the walls, each cell had only a single barred door. Levers were the only way to open those doors and were out of reach of anyone who might end up being a prisoner in the place. It was as well-secured as any that Lita had ever seen.

Derik was even impressed with it. He looked to Ezra as they walked around, exploring the space. There were no instruments of torture, but the brick work was sound. The doors were sturdy. The chains and shackles were new and had no weak links that Derik or Aeryn could find.

In short, it was perfect for one of those creatures.

"I've never seen one this well-made either, Lita. I've seen quite a few over the years, but this one will do. Those creatures won't be able to escape us if we catch some. Even one might be strong enough to break out of most dungeons. But this…just shows that Ammora knows what it's doing…and what we're up against," Ezra said with a tilt of her head and a troubled look on her face. Ice blue orbs sought and caught Derik's gaze as he turned to look to her.

"So, when do we want to try and trap one?" Derik asked as he motioned to Lita to open one of the cell doors. It swung open easily with no creeks or squeaks and Derik moved inside to check the bench bed that hung from the side of the wall in it.

"As soon as we can manage it, Derik. The sooner we catch one, the sooner we'll either have answers…or more questions," Ezra replied with a hint of humor in her voice though her gaze was serious. She was trying to make light of the situation, Derik realized. But he could see the worry in her eyes, in the set of her jaw.

If Ezra's worried, that's bad, Derik thought as he moved back out of the cell and Lita closed the door again with the lever on the far wall.

"Hopefully we'll get more answers than questions," Lita added, a worried gaze of her own as she glanced about one more time. "Let's head back upstairs and start putting together a plan."

Derik nodded and held his arm out to Ezra, and they left the new dungeon of Ammora together. Derik took a deep breath once they were back on the ground floor, feeling better once he saw the light shining in through the windows in the hallway.

"I've never liked Dungeons. Always made me feel like I would be stuck in one forever," Derik admitted as they walked.

"I've never been a fan either. I was glad when I saw that Ammora didn't have one when I first began to learn magic. I hoped we would never need one but unfortunately, that time has passed," Ezra said with a sigh.

"Hopefully we'll never need it after this. Between people disappearing, these creatures and Juktis' partner still at large, this has been a stressful couple of months, Sorceress," he said, pausing to bury his hands into Ezra's long silver hair and leaned down to kiss her soft lips. Ezra's arms wrapped about him as she leaned into him, kissing him back with an eagerness that surprised them both.

"Very stressful and we still have to make a plan with Lita for tonight. After that, I want an afternoon off…with you, Derik," Ezra whispered as she buried her face into his chest after the kiss had broken. Derik paused to lean his chin on her head for a moment, letting her feel protected for once rather than being the protector.

"I know. I'd love that too and I vote that we take it. We don't have much time together these days. I want to spend a few hours just with you," Derik said with a grin as his fingers continued to stroke her long, soft locks. "So, let's do it. Let's take the afternoon off together."

"Sounds like a plan, my love," Ezra replied before she lifted her head and kissed him gently once more. He wrapped his arm around her shoulders as they turned to walk down the hallway where Lita was impatiently waiting in the Council Chamber.

Vincent shoved the latest gift to his Benefactor through the gate. The girl was gagged, bound and young. She was no more than perhaps twenty years of age, and yet here he was, presenting her for the slaughter.

The night before he had found her in an inn at one of the neighboring towns at the base of the mountain. He had spent his time charming her, flattering her and that night, he bedded her.

Come morning, she woke to find herself tied up, gagged, blindfolded and her face and hair hidden with a clever hood. He had put her into a heavy burlap sack and carried her down and put her in his wagon, being sure to put her in the secret compartment hidden in the floor. No one could hear her screams as he snuck her out of the town and back up to the Fortress.

"Here, M'Lady. Another volunteer for your experiments," he said proudly as he presented the red-haired, blue-eyed beauty to Lady Alyra in her dungeon.

Alyra circled the girl, taking pleasure as he did while the pretty thing trembled in fear. He removed the hood and the blindfold so the girl could see her new fate, though he didn't remove the gag.

"She'll do. Here's some more silver for your trouble, Vincent," Alyra said as she tossed him a small bag that jingled with the coin hidden inside. "Now go so this pretty one and I can get acquainted."

"Thank you, M'Lady," Vincent said as he turned and walked back out.

After all, it wasn't as if the girl was worth anything anymore to Him. He had what he wanted.

Tomorrow, he would seek out another town and another girl.

Surala watched from her hiding spot, on top of the Dragon's Keep as the last of the sun's rays faded from the horizon. She was curled up on top of the Keep, determined to keep an eye on her traps below.

Her tail and claws twitched with impatience as she waited for the minutes, and hours, to tick by.

They have to be coming. It's not as if they haven't come often since we first spotted them, Surala thought, feeling even her wing tips twitching in anticipation and hoping beyond hope that their traps would work.

The hours dragged out and Surala fought exhaustion as she watched, feeling her other senses, both physical and magical, growing as the darkness grew. The Moon was small tonight, barely a sliver on the horizon....

And then it winked out as if someone had blown out the candle flame.

Darkness fell and silence grew to a deafening clamor as Surala waited, scarcely daring to breathe as she waited for what she hoped would come.

A crash through some foliage near the traps sent Surala's senses into high alert and she turned, using her Dragonic eyes to see through the dark where others could not have seen. Not even an Elf could see as well as a Half-Dragon like Surala and she used those senses now, desperate to understand what it was they were dealing with.

All she could see were shadows gathering around another shadow that was caught in their trap.

"Yes," she whispered softly, seeing that one of the creatures WAS indeed caught! Another crash fell and she winced a bit, hoping that the trap had held! There were so many creatures around it now, she could barely tell if it was still caught in it or not!

Just as suddenly as it began, the creatures suddenly just disappeared from her sight…

Even the one in the trap was gone, and the trap was but a ruined broken thing that was likely beyond repair!

Surala growled in frustration as she flew down to double check the trap just as the sun began to break over the horizon. The creature, whatever it was, was gone and there was nothing that she could do about it.

The half-dragon mage sighed and began to gather new materials to try to catch one again and hoped that they would be able to deal with it…whatever it was.

Ezra was standing with the others on top of Ammora Castle. Waiting as the night stretched on and feeling her baby kick and squirm in time to the racing of her own heart.

"Easy, little one. Easy…We'll have our answers soon, I'm sure of it," Ezra said gently as she rested her hand on her swollen belly and prayed that the baby would come another night and not now.

Contractions were becoming a regular part of her day and night. Eve had reassured Ezra that they were harmless, just the muscles warming up for the big event that was, she assured, months down the road.

But Ezra had counted the days and nights and knew that she had already been carrying this child now for nearly Eight and a half months. The child was immortal, and Ezra was out of her depth as to how long an immortal had to carry a child.

All she knew was her belly felt ready to tear itself into two!

Be patient, Ezra, she chided herself silently. *The baby is going to be here before we know it and it's not going to be easy dealing with Duty and a newborn.*

::No, Ezra, it won't, but it won't be impossible, either. You have plenty of people willing to help you with the baby and to defend Ammora and Axrealia. In short, you're in the best position you've been in since you became the Sorceress one thousand years ago,:: Baelios chimed into her thoughts. She normally would have been annoyed, but he was right. And, as usual, she knew it.

::One day, I'm going to figure out how to take you by surprise--:: she started.

::That won't be easy, considering that I'm a Spirit and can be anywhere within the Castle, Ezra,:: Baelios replied playfully before he settled down. ::But with all due seriousness, Ezra, just be careful out there tonight.::

:: I will be, Baelios. I will be,:: she replied as she settled in with Derik and the others for a long wait.

*   *   *

"Sorceress, I'm seeing movement," Wahya whispered in the darkness somewhere off to Ezra's right. Ezra rose from where she'd been sitting and resting…and used her mage senses to peer across the moat.

Just as before, she could see nothing but shadows…but as she used her mage senses, there was an eerie, almost sickly green glow of power about them.

"Someone has changed them," she murmured very softly, waiting for the creatures to find the pit the men had dug and disguised so very carefully early in the morning. They had toiled for hours and when they were done, even Ezra couldn't tell where they had worked.

A loud crash answered Ezra's silent prayers and she silently cheered, relieved that it had worked! They had at least one creature, possibly more and that meant that soon they would have some answers.

Hopefully the answers would not give them more questions.

"What now?" Derik whispered softly.

"We wait for morning…or for when the rest disappear," Ezra replied in a hot whisper. "We'll be able to get it safely then."

Across the moat, the creatures were pouring around the trap, trying to figure out how to get their fellow creature out…the shadows moved, sinister and creeping around the edge of the pit. Ezra could hear the creatures making frustrated sounds that sounded like hisses and growls echoing across the deep moat that separated Ammora Castle from the other side.

About time we find out what you are and who sent you, Ezra thought quietly as she waited for the creatures to disappear.

After another half an hour of the creatures swarming and stirring, Ezra sensed the magical energy as it began to gather… and activated the spell that would keep whatever was in the pit trapped where it was.

A moment later, the rest of the shadows disappeared.

All but the one that was moving about in the trap.

Ezra waited, counting the moments, sensing something trying to snatch it away too…it was too low to get a signature, too far away to sense exactly where it came from.

But it felt all too familiar.

"Wait a few more moments, then go and get that thing and bring it to the dungeon," Ezra said. "If it's too dangerous, I'll teleport it directly into the dungeon and I'll use magic to chain it up."

"Not to worry, Sorceress, we'll get it done,"Wahya said as they watched for a few moments more before the men turned to walk down to go and get the shadowy creature.

Ezra watched from the parapets with Tala, praying no one would get hurt.

Derik approached the pit with a torch in his hand, looking down into it, trying to see what the creature was.

The creature shrieked in the light as he came close, the stench of an unwashed body hitting his nostrils like an assault. The flesh was discolored, mottled with bruises but it was quite pale for a Dark Elf.

The eyes were gone, leaving nothing but a sickly green glow from inside the eye sockets, showing that magic was all that was keeping this creature alive!

"Have you ever seen anything like this before?" Derik asked Wayha as they studied it.

"Never in all my years on this world have I ever seen anything like this, Bra. I've never ever heard of anything like it either," Wahya admitted as he took out his ropes. "Whatever it is, we're dragging it to the dungeon for the Sorceress to get a look at. Maybe she can figure out how to heal it or…put it out of its misery."

"Get the ropes…and the chains ready," Derik said grimly. The men around him all had ropes, some had chains and shackles. They all nodded to him, ready to go in and get this creature to where it belonged. "On the count of three. One….two….three!"

The men converged on the creature in the pit! There was tussling, fighting, the cries of men as they narrowly avoided being bitten by the thing!

Finally, they managed to wrestle it to the ground and bound it up and chained it so tightly it couldn't move. Derik, Wahya and Aaron managed to wrestle it out of the pit and into a wagon. They began to make their way home, across the drawbridge and back into Ammora.

Derik smiled as Ezra and Eve as well as other healers met them at the Entrance Hall.

"Is anyone hurt?" Ezra asked, her eyes filled with shock as she finally saw the creature.

"No, we managed to not be bitten or clawed, luckily. Thank the Gods…who knows what might happen if we were," Derik said with a smile as he leaned his forehead against hers, glad that they were both well and whole.

"Good, now to get some answers from this thing," Ezra told him grimly as she leaned into him.

"Not until that thing is secure *and* I've checked everyone over," Eve said, her voice showing that she would brook no argument in this.

"First things first then. To the dungeon!" Derik agreed as the men picked up the creature, which they had strapped to a board, and began to carry it through the maze of hallways to the lower level of the Castle and into its new dungeon.

*   *   *

"I've never seen or even read or heard of anything like this," Ezra said as she studied the creature, looking at how it was secured to the wall. The men had shackled it, ensuring the chain lengths were short enough that the creature couldn't come from the wall very far. Mere inches perhaps, but certainly not within killing range.

She was shocked at the change made to the creature before her. It had been a Dark Elf, so far as she could tell…but now it had no eyes, the flesh was damaged and yet it was still alive, but without a soul.

"It's not necromancy nor is it a vampire. It's…not a corpse and yet it's as if there was never a soul within it," Ezra said, trying to read the magical signature and finding nothing.

What magic there was, made her skin crawl.

"Can you cure it?" the Dark Elf Ambassador, Lady Talice, whom Ezra had had summoned to the dungeon, asked, concern in her voice.

"Perhaps, maybe. I'd have to find out what was done to her first, then there might be a chance. We need to find who did it but…if this is what's happening to the people who are being taken, then we need to find who is behind it and soon."

"Why?" Derik asked, a worried look in his eyes.

"Because this took time and they've taken so many. Who knows how many more have been changed," Ezra replied gravely, yearning to find, and kill, whoever was behind this horror.

So much for the tournament, Ezra thought as she turned to Counselor Lita. "I think you were right, Lita. Cancel the tournament. Ambassador Talice, I'd like you and Ambassador Suidan to help us with patrolling each night along with your entourages. If these creatures break into Ammora, it could be disastrous for us all."

"You're right, Sorceress. My people and I are willing to patrol with your people and with the Forest Elves. This common enemy is too dangerous. We need to apprehend them," Talice replied gravely.

That took Ezra by surprise. The Forest Elves and the Dark Elves had been at each other's throats since they'd arrived.

Thank the Gods for small favors, Ezra thought.

"Let's go speak to Ambassador Suidan together then and begin to set up a rotating schedule for everyone taking patrols. That way it's not on any one group to do it all," Ezra said as she turned to walk with them to the Forest Elves' quarters.

Chapter Eight

Reanalia surged through the water. Each day, she grew a little stronger, could hold her breath a little longer. Several days now she had been at this, working on learning how to swim with her new tail.

She was loving it. The water felt like silk against her skin, though her lungs burned towards the end when she needed to take a breath.

The new breathing apparatus that she was trying today was making a significant difference. Surala had managed to catch a creature in the trap they had set up, but unfortunately their prey had broken free, leaving them with more questions than answers.

The trap they had used was made with the strongest materials they had, and Surala was at a loss to explain how it was possible that it had been broken so quickly or easily. So, they regrouped, and discussed amongst Surala, Reanalia and Felati how to go about this puzzle.

The answer was to simply investigate the sites where the merpeople had been taken by magic and to find a clue, any clue, as to where they had gone.

When they arrived, Reanalia used her magical senses, looking for signs.

As usual, there was nothing that could be used to trace the source. However, there was the incident itself…using the residual magic, Reanalia used her own magic to recreate the incident, to show them all what had happened at the time that the mermaid here had disappeared.

They watched as she and another mermaid played and swam through the shipwrecks, through the water around the ship graveyard.

::They shouldn't have been here, Kayla knows it's dangerous,:: Felati shared telepathically with Surala and Reanalia.

::The problem is they were here. So how did the mage know that there would be anyone here if it's forbidden to be here in the first place?:: Reanalia asked.

::A good question, my friends. One that I can't even fathom an answer to. How would they have known?:: Surala asked, her mental voice tinged with worry.

::They might have scryed and watched her. Meaning the people they took, they took for a reason…but why a mermaid so young?:; Reanalia looked to Felati, hoping she might be able to shed some light.

::Kayla is my daughter. My youngest. A future queen of her own pod. She's immortal, like me," Felatia told her.

::Are all mermaid queens immortal?::

:;Yes, and very few are born immortal. Even from an immortal queen, our children tend to be mortal. It's a fluke that happens only once or twice in each generation. When Kayla was born, I saw she was like me—blue in color now. When she matures, her tail will turn white and gold…and she'll stop aging. Her magic will become stronger. And when the pod is big enough, she'll take half of it with her to go off and find her new pod's place to swim and live,:: Felati looked more worried now. ::Whoever did this, knows who and what I am, what she is.::

:;That puts her in danger. And makes me wonder if any of the other targets have similar fates where they're about to all come into a great amount of power,::; Reanalia replied grimly. ::I need to report all of this to the Sorceress.:;

::Grab on, both of you. I can swim faster than you can. Let's go,:: Surala replied, not one to waste any time. Felati grasped and settled herself onto Surala's back and Reanalia did the same. They both lay down as flat as they could against the Water dragon as she began to swim back to the Dragon's Keep.

Time was working against them.

"One of the mermaids is a *what?*" Ezra repeated, feeling her belly clench a little in dread.

"She's a future Queen, Sorceress. Felati told me that all Mermaid Queens are immortal. They're born with a blue tail, but when they hit a certain age, their tail turns white and gold, and their hair turns blonde. They cease to age, and their magic grows significantly. She was targeted for a reason so whomever this is, they know the secrets of the merpeople, who excels at keeping secrets, Sorceress," Reanalia replied gravely in the mirror. Ezra shifted a bit in her chair as she thought on the significance of this news…

And felt oh so cold at the thought that followed.

"We need to know more about the other people taken. Some are probably just..people..but others—They took the Forest Elf King and his consort and the Dark Elf Queen and her consort. And now a mermaid princess…how many others that are royalty, or near royalty, have they taken I wonder," Ezra said, feeling chilled.

"They're probably hostages, Sorceress. We need to find this person *now*," Reanalia replied. Ezra rose, feeling the need to pace even though her belly muscles clenched. Ezra sighed as she felt the baby kicking hard in response to the sudden movement.

"I'll send messengers out to all of the villages and cities that have sent complaints regarding their missing citizens. We need to get a list of people who may have been targeted to be hostages...versus those who were taken to be changed," Ezra replied. "The royal heads are obviously hostages, but we need a count of how many of them we're expecting to rescue."

"We'll go over the other kidnappings, but so far as we know, only Kayla and Felati are people of any importance to Felati's pod," Reanalia sighed.

"Keep me posted. Good work, Reanalia," Ezra replied before Reanalia broke off contact with her charm and Ezra was again alone in her chamber.

:;Baelios…were you listening?::

:;Always, Ezra. It's a bit hard not to listen, particularly when it's news of importance. Hard to believe that a mage could have targeted specific people like this, but someone who had the energy and the time--::

:;Like Juktis' unknown partner. My Dark counterpart...the pawn of the Destruction God,:: Ezra replied as she ran a hand over her belly where the baby was still frantically squirming and kicking. She took a breath to calm herself and felt the baby respond to it as she let go of the stress.

:;Exactly. She would have the energy, the time…the ability and capability to find those who are vulnerable--::

::;And would know when and where to strike if she is watching them ahead of time. Baelios, this is bad, very, very bad. Those creatures…I've never seen anything so foul or evil,:: Ezra said as she sighed.

::;It could be part of what's to come, Ezra,:; Baelios said, his voice tinged with sadness.

::This could be how she intends to bring the darkness or part of it at least. Those clouds could have had thousands of these creatures attacking in it and the Wizards Council just couldn't have seen it--:: Ezra started, feeling both anger and sorrow rising at the thought.

::;All too easily. All they saw was a cloud, they couldn't see what was within it. This may be what is coming, or at least….part of it,:: Baelios replied grimly.

::;We're running out of time, Baelios.::

::;I know, Ezra. I know. One thing at a time. Start with the Ambassadors and summoning the City Council and sending out messengers. We need more answers as quickly as we can get them,:; Baelios advised. Ezra gave a nod and pushed herself up awkwardly, feeling the weight on her shoulders as well as the weight of the unborn child within her.

::;Then let's get to work. Summon the council. I'll send someone to get the Ambassadors.:; Ezra turned to walk out, willing the twinge in her belly to stop as she took slow, deep breaths. She needed to stay calm and that was getting harder and harder to manage.

An hour later, the Council of the City assembled in the Council Chamber of Ammora Castle. Derik and Lita sat in their seats, whispering anxiously as the Council waited for the Sorceress' arrival.

"What's going on, Derik?" Lita asked, a hint of concern in her eyes.

"You know as much as I do, Lita. I don't know why we were summoned but the Sorceress, last I saw, was having a meeting with the Ambassadors from the Elves and Dark Elves," he replied.

"Think she found something out?"

"Maybe. We'll...ah here she is."

Lita rose as the Sorceress swept in and hit the round orb that was used to call the meetings to order upon its hard pedestal.

"The Council of Ammora City will come to order. The Chair recognizes the Sorceress of Ammora, who has called this meeting," Lita announced in a loud, clear voice.

"Thank you, Chairwoman. My lords and ladies, I have learned something about two of the abducted people. Kayla of the merpeople is a future Queen of a pod that will form when she is ready to rule. The Heir of the Head Priestess of the Dark Elves was also one of the victims taken. I believe that some of the kidnappings are random, and others are for hostages. We need to find out how many people are of importance, or future leaders of importance and we need to find out as quickly as possible. I'm asking for runners to be sent to each of the cities and villages that have sent messengers to tell us that people were missing...and to be sent today. I'm willing to provide food and provisions, even portals to send them closer to their destinations, as well as coin to pay for information, if necessary," the Sorceress said, a grave look in her eyes. Lita shifted a bit in her chair as she and the other councilors shared looks.

"Sorceress, you claim you're not a ruler—"

"I'm not, Chairwoman. I'm the Sorceress and guardian of Ammora. I'm not a ruler. But I can't leave Ammora with shadowy creatures showing up every night. I can't ignore the importance of this information. I'm asking you all for help. I prefer to do things my way, but in this instance it isn't wise. I need your help to get this done, please," the Sorceress pleaded as she turned, looking at each Council member in turn.

"That's twenty people that we would need to send, at least. How many can be spared from the city?" Aaron asked. "Would it be voluntary, Captain?"

"Of course, it would be voluntary! We don't force our own to do anything they don't wish to do. Let's put it to a vote. All in Favor?"

The resounding "Aye!" made Lita proud. Not a single member was opposed.

"Very well. Sorceress, we'll send the messengers to the Entrance Hall in the Castle within the next two hours," Lita informed her.

"My thanks, Chairwoman and Council. I'll go and get the provisions in order. Thank you…thank you all," the Sorceress said as she swept out. The resounding clicks of her heels echoed as Lita heard the steps go from a walk to a run.

"Send word to the city to assemble. Any who wants to go gets double the pay from me. Council dismissed!" Lita lifted and lowered the orb again with a loud clang and rose to go back to the city where her own house was to gather what she would need to pay the messengers.

It was good to be back in action.

Over the next few hours, various men and women came forward to act as messenger. Aaron, Mara, Wayha and Tala were amongst the first to volunteer. Derik watched his friends as they picked up a pack of provisions in the Entrance Hall and were each given an assigned city and a contact to speak to once they arrived.

I'd go, but Ezra needs me here. Any day now, the baby could come, she doesn't have much longer, Derik thought, torn between the need to go and help and the need to stay and help his beloved.

"Nineteen…we need one more," Ezra said beside him as the last messenger departed through the last portal she had created. Derik turned and saw that there was no one else. No one else had volunteered.

And Derik knew she'd rather send someone that she trusted and knew with something as important as this.

"I'll go, Sorceress," he said, sad that he had to go again and leave her. "I don't want to, but I'll do it if there's no one else."

"Derik, are you sure?" Ezra asked as she looked at him and reached to touch the side of his face, caressing his cheek with her soft fingertips.

"I'm sure."

Relief flooded Ezra's ice-blue eyes and she gave him a deep and passionate kiss. Derik wrapped his arms around her and just held her, one hand caressing the small of her back and the other stroking through her long silver hair.

"If you're going to be away, then we need to take care of something before you go," Ezra whispered as they broke the kiss and stood, forehead touching forehead for a few moments.

"What's that?"

"Come with me up to the parapets," she replied, slipping out of his arms with a mischievous look in her eyes as she tugged on his hand. Dumb founded, he found himself following her first at a walk, then at a light jog all the way up to the outside of the Castle and looking down at the beautiful green landscape that now surrounded Ammora.

Ezra held his hands with hers and looked up into his eyes.

"In this day and in this hour, we stand before the Sacred Power. Goddess, come and bless these marriage vows we make…no priest, no witnesses save that of the Gods," Ezra began. Derik smiled, seeing what she was up to. He had known she didn't want a large ceremony.

This was perfect. Private, small…and without pompous grandeur.

Derik took a breath and began his part.

"I, Derik, take you, Ezra, to be my beloved wife…before the gods. I swear to respect you, to love and cherish you all my days," he said, joy and happiness resounding in his deep voice.

"I, Ezra, take you, Derik, to be my beloved husband. Before the Gods, I swear to respect you, to love and cherish you all my days," she said in reply.

They sealed their vows with another deep, passionate kiss. Derik felt as though he could burst out of his skin with happiness as he held her, and it wasn't until Ezra looked around them and gasped that he realized there was anything else there but them.

Butterflies of every size and color had suddenly flown up and surrounded them. Butterflies sat on their clothing, on their heads and hair.   There were more butterflies about their feet and all over the parapets.

Ezra looked ready to cry and smiled happily up at Derik.

"It seems the Gods heard us…and have sent their blessing."

As if those words had broken the spell, the butterflies all flew up in a cloud about them and fluttered away. Derik and Ezra watched as the butterflies returned down into the green wonderland below.

"Then let's go for a little time together in our Chambers…and you can send me off this evening," Derik said as he scooped her up to carry her, feeling content as he began the journey down the stairs. If he was going to be away for a while, he wanted to leave her with something very pleasant to look forward to when he returned.

Vincent had his eye on a new target. This time, he was in a larger city and eyeing a pair of twins. They were short, red-haired, blue eyed and had volumptuous curves underneath their clothes accentuated by their corsets.

He picked up his tankard and approached them as they served in the local pub.

"Hello there, ladies. Could I entice you to join me for the night? I've never been to a large city before and I'm awfully lonely," he said putting on the charm as if it were a fine cologne.

They fell for it, hook, line, and sinker.

That night, after he bedded them both, making sure that he gave them the night they deserved. A Night of passion to prepare them for the pain ahead.

Before they were all to go to sleep, he gave them a final nightcap. The drug in the drink worked quickly and he was able to tie them both up with ease. Rolling them into the rugs he'd bought earlier, he carried them down to the wagon, one by one. The wagon rolled out into the darkness quietly, heading back towards the Fortress.

His patron was waiting for more victims.

Vincent was determined to ensure that he kept her quite occupied with them and to reap the rewards She had promised him.

*   *   *

Kayla was trying to act like she was asleep, but it was nearly impossible. The screams…she just tried to block them out, but they always cut through her head like a nail on a chalkboard. The one time she'd reached anyone telepathically, it had been cut off and she hadn't managed to reach anyone since.

Since then, she had despaired, watching as one prisoner after another was changed…their souls ripped out and stored in a magical container. Today was no different.

One of the merpeople was being changed today. Five had been taken thus far from the pod. Out of the five, only Kayla remained untouched. She heard the merman screaming as his eyes were removed, and she watched quietly in horror as his skin paled, his eyes began to glow…and he sagged, nearly lifeless at the woman's feet. His soul, pearly white, was drawn into a necklace at the woman's throat…a black gemstone with a poison red center that gleamed with an evil aura in the dim light of the dungeon.

Their captor turned to regard the rest as her guards took the merman away. Kayla closed her eyes again before the woman could regard her and she kept her breathing soft, floating at the top of the tank so she could easily breathe.

The woman in chains and the bloody armor next to the tank, the Dark Elf, shifted a bit, causing a soft clink of metal next to Kayla's small tank.

"Why are you doing this to us? Why haven't you just killed us all and gotten it over with?" the Dark Elf demanded as she jerked in her chains as if she yearned to fight the woman.

The black haired, heavily tattooed woman turned, a horrible smile on her red painted lips.

"I'm evil, Your Highness. I enjoy what I've been doing, and as for what my plans are for you. You are part of a much bigger plan, Queen of the Dark Caves. I'm interested to see what happens when She comes for you," the dark-haired woman replied, her tone cold and amused.

"Who?" the dark elf woman demanded, her face twisted into a snarl.

"You'll see," the woman replied with a cold, haughty laugh as she turned and swept out of the dungeon.

The door slammed and the torches went out all at once...

Leaving them all in nothing but oppressive darkness.

Chapter Nine

It was strange waking up without Derik next to her the next morning. Ezra reached for his empty spot, wistfully wishing that someone else had gone in his stead.

But no one else had volunteered and she trusted him as much as she trusted Baelios. Her heart ached with him being gone again, but they had been separated before. He would be back, and Ezra knew that it would be all the sweeter upon his return. She would survive just as she had before he had come to Ammora. Though she missed him dearly.

Ezra rose and took out a fresh tunic and leggings, started to pull them on and paused. She had been wearing her maternity dresses, but today, she just wanted something familiar.

They were far too tight! Ezra sighed and used a bit of magic to expand the clothes so they would fit her and looked at herself in the mirror. Her belly hadn't dropped yet which meant she wasn't about to go into labor yet. In the meantime, there were still duties to attend to and Ezra knew she needed to get to them.

She reached for her boots and couldn't quite bend down enough to pick them up.

"Oh, for crying out loud!" Ezra snapped, feeling frustrated and wishing this baby was at least on the way if not already here! She was tired of feeling tired, she was tired of not being able to move as she wished, and she was heartily tired of not being able to wear what she wished without needing help!

"Ezra, what's wrong?" Baelios asked as he appeared beside her.

"I can't get my boots, much less put them on!" Ezra snapped back.

"Sit down and I'll help you, Ezra," Baelios said good-naturedly as he picked up her boots with ease and knelt on one knee to help her. Ezra sat back down on the edge of the bed and held her foot up so he could ease the boot onto her leg.

"Why isn't this baby here yet? I'm so tired of feeling like I'm about to burst, not being able to eat much and not even being able to dress myself," Ezra said, feeling more irritated by the moment.

"It will be here soon, Ezra. It's not much longer, you're nearing the end," Baelios told her with a sympathetic look. "Once the baby comes, I'm sure you'll feel much better."

"Then I'll just be exhausted from caring for a newborn," she said as she held up her other foot so he could put on her other boot. "We should go down to the dungeon and see what sort of spell turned the Dark Elf into the creature it is now," she sighed as she rubbed her swollen belly.

"Take Wahya and Tala in with you at least. They can help and protect you if it gets loose," Baelios urged as he finished lacing up her boots.

"Of course, Baelios. I wouldn't ever go in alone. How's the dragon egg?" she asked as she hadn't been down there in several days.

"I checked it again this morning. It's doing well, no sign of hatching, yet."

"Good. Let's hope that it'll wait until we've found the hostages and the rest of those who were abducted," Ezra replied as Baelios rose and offered her his hand so she could rise. Grasping his hand with gratitude, she awkwardly rose up to her feet, stomach first, and shifted until she had her balance before releasing him.

"I hope so as well, Ezra, but as Eve says—"

"Babies come in their own time. I know. She's said it far too often lately," Ezra replied as she smoothed down her tunic and headed for the door.

::I'll send for Wahya and Tala to come and assist you,:: Baelios sent telepathically as she opened the door. Ezra gave a nod and gave the Spirit a smile before he vanished from sight.

She made her way slowly through the hallways. She felt heavy and awkward, a feeling she hated.

I'm hoping Derik won't want too many more children. I don't think I could handle being like this each year, Ezra thought trying to remind herself that this was not a planned pregnancy. But she still wanted the baby and since the baby had two immortal parents, it's not as if she could have ended the pregnancy even if she had wanted to.

The click of her own heels on the marble sounded ominous even to her ears. She walked down the hallways and to the door that had the stairs that would take her down to the dungeon. Wahya and Tala were already there, waiting for her.

"Hey, Sista! What're we doin' today?" Tala asked, her long curly blonde hair brushing against Ezra's face as Tala hugged her.

"Oh, we're going into dangerous territory. I'm going to see what sort of spell changed that creature in the dungeon."

"Damn right you should have someone with ya Sorceress. Not a good idea to be alone with that thing. Besides, it gives me the creeps," Wahya said with a grave look on his rugged face. "You can't expect it to behave and what if you can't change it back or figure out how it was made?"

"If I can't, then we need to see if it can be destroyed," Ezra replied, not liking this task at all. It wasn't something that she could look forward to.

"Okay well, let's get goin' then. Daylight's a burnin' and I don't wanna be with that thing in the dungeon when it gets dark," Tala said matter-of-factly as she opened the door. Wahya went down first, Ezra followed, and Tala brought up the rear.

Ezra's feeling of dread grew as they walked into the cell.

The creature looked up and lunged, hissing and spitting as Tala closed the cell door. Ezra stayed back out of its reach, using her magical senses and beginning a spell…one that might unravel this mystery.

Alyra was working, creating a new Dark-Born. She'd chosen that name for her creatures as they would be essential to the darkness that was to come. *And of course, they're born of Darkness, as I am,* she mused as she hummed while she worked.

The hair rose on the back of her neck suddenly and she turned, looking for someone that wasn't in the room. Granted, she had plenty of prisoners now, plenty of fodder for the war-machine that was to come. And of course, plenty of hostages that she could use to keep those who might oppose her at bay.

But she had been extra cautious since the day she'd sensed the breach and sensed that someone had managed to contact help.

This wasn't someone looking directly into her space, however, but someone who was exploring one of her carefully crafted spells…

Someone must have caught one of my creatures! Only one didn't return when I checked the head count the other night. Drat and damn, I can't let them figure out how it was created! Alyra thought desperately as she ceased her casting, letting the human female at her feet sag and cower in terror!

Alyra quickly began to cast a new spell, one that would destroy the creature that hadn't returned—

Ezra chanted, keeping her magical senses open as she continued to explore the spell. It was carefully created, made to be as seamless as possible.

It lacks a signature that's significant to the caster, but at the same time…that is a signature all its own. Looks like they took the Dark Elf and removed her eyes while casting the spell. Ezra continued to explore it, going over it with her magical senses as if it were a magical globe and her mental fingers continue to go over and over it trying to see if there was a specific order to the way it'd been cast…and perhaps a way to undo it. *Ironically, their soul is gone…how in the name of the Gods did they manage that?*

Then the Castle shook, nearly throwing Ezra off of her feet as a powerful spell struck Ammora's protections in a powerful hammer-blow!

Alyra found the source. Ammora Castle! She sent her spell hurtling at it, expecting the creature to suddenly snuff out of existence—

And found a backlash of energy that flung itself back at her that threw her off of her feet!

How in the world are her protections THAT powerful?!? Alyra thought frantically as she lay on the floor of her own dungeon, her head ringing in a way she hadn't felt since she'd been changed.

Ezra clung to Wahya and Tala, who had each moved to steady her as the Castle had rocked around them. She felt the spell backlash back its caster and used her magical senses instinctively to follow it!

And found it going into an all-too familiar direction. The Fortress…Jarrod's Fortress now.

But that wasn't Jarrod's signature! I'd know if it were! Ezra returned to her body quickly after looking over the Fortress again from the Astral.

It wasn't Jarrod's Signature. She had sensed him in the fortress, but there was something else. Something else that felt foul and evil.

Ezra straightened up as she sank into her body and looked back to the creature. It was still alive, still sitting there looking at her.

"What caused that?" Tala asked in wonder, looking at Ezra with alarm.

"Whoever cast this spell tried to destroy the creature. Ammora's protections protected us and it…barely," Ezra admitted, feeling a headache coming on. "I need to go lay down—"

Without further prompting, Wahya scooped her up and took her from the dungeon.

"This is some bad juju," Wahya muttered as Ezra closed her eyes, feeling the pounding in her temples getting worse by the moment.

Alyra crawled back up to the chambers that she shared with Jarrod and looked in for him. She was grateful, for once, that he was out and about working with the guards today.

Don't need a million questions as to what just happened from him, not today. As it is, I've got a big problem. The Sorceress is trying to trace my spell. She may have found me. That's bad news, especially for me! Alyra groaned as she stretched out on the bed that had become oh so familiar over the years and closed her eyes, trying to will the pounding in her temples to stop.

And instead felt it just getting worse by the moment.

Kayla had been watching as their captor was flung by something she'd done magically and almost cheered as she nearly heard bones crunch as the woman hit the hard dungeon floor.

She watched carefully from the surface of the water of her tiny tank as the woman rose, struggling to do so, to her hands and knees and crawl from the room.

Kayla felt a glimmer of hope as the door was left open!

Only to see that hope dashed a moment later when a guard closed the door with an ominous thud!

Kayla sank back down into the water, and looked at her fellow captives, seeing the despair in all of their eyes.

I can't give up! Kayla thought in desperation as she began to swim in the tight confines…determined to find a way out of this tank…

Or die trying in the process.

Sunshine washed into the large chamber as Ezra woke the next morning. She groaned and let her fingertips roll out, let her toes stretch and felt her large belly tense as she stretched…

Then she rolled over very awkwardly out of bed, feeling her belly and body protesting every movement. Her headache, thankfully, was gone but the rest of her wasn't going to let her forget just how much it despised what had happened the day before.

That spell hitting our defenses yesterday…I should have anticipated that! Amateur move, but now I know that whoever made these things, they want them back or they want them destroyed. That means there's a way to destroy them…but there may be a way to reverse the process, Ezra thought as she rose. It was a potential shot in the dark, possibly a disaster, but she had to try.

She knew deep down if she didn't, she'd never live with herself if she did not at least try to save these poor people.

Ezra dressed and bolted a quick breakfast, ignoring how her stomach wanted to repel it almost immediately. She made her way down to the dungeon, taking a couple of guards with her that she found as she made her way through the hallways.

"I just need a small sample to work with of their flesh, it won't take long to get," she reassured the guards as they opened the door. The creature was still there, hissing and making soft growls at them as Ezra made her way towards the creature with a small dish and a set of tongs.

The creature lunged and Ezra twisted herself to avoid it, nearly losing her balance as she did and grasped a bit of flesh from the creature's thumb before she moved back. Dropping the sample into her dish, she motioned for the guards to follow her and went back upstairs to the main rooms of the Castle.

Leaving the guards behind after leaving the dungeon, Ezra went straight to her work room. Using her magical senses, she explored the bit of flesh, the spell that had made it…

Then the experimentation began.

*   *   *

Three hours later, Ezra was still no closer to breaking the spell or reversing it. She was, simply put, astounded!

I've tried everything that I know...every reversal spell, every single way to break the spell that I can find...I'm not finding a weak spot anywhere...but there has to be one. Every spell has a weak spot...somewhere. Ezra looked it over again, using that bit she'd taken from the creature as a way to get as good a look at the spell as she could manage.

And yet, she still couldn't see a weak spot, or a way to reverse it. She'd even tried reanimation spells that left the original being's mind intact...

Nothing. Nada. ZIP! Ezra sat back in her chair, feeling her headache coming back as she tried to think of yet another way to tackle this problem—

::Ezra, not everything is solved in a day. Come back upstairs, you need to take a break from all of this,:: Baelios sent telepathically to her as she just took a breath.

::Baelios, I need to solve this riddle--::

::The riddle will be here tomorrow. Take a break. The messengers should be reporting tomorrow. Maybe we'll get lucky--::

::And maybe we won't!:: she snapped back, feeling her frustration growing rather than ebbing.

It was only when she felt the baby within her womb kicking frantically that she took a breath again and tried, truly tried, to calm down.

::Maybe you're right. Can you have someone bring me something in my chambers? I'm going to lay down after this if no one needs me for anything,:: Ezra said, feeling despair creeping within her as she caved like a house of cards.

:;Of course, Ezra. I'll have a tray for you delivered shortly,:; Baelios said, his tone tender and gentle and not just annoyingly cheerful.

Granted she was used to the cheerfulness in his tone by now, but the tenderness brought tears to her eyes.

Over a thousand years, and I still mourn Bael. Will the hurt ever go away? It was a glum thought that kept her steps slow instead of her round, swollen belly as she walked through the hallways back to her chambers.

The answer, of course, was no.

As much as she loved Derik, he wasn't Bael.

And Bael did live but within Baelios.

Beyond reach and while she had lived with this fact for a Millenia now, it never made it any easier.

Derik rubbed his eyes yet again as he went over the abductee list, those that were known anyway, with the Herald for the King of Kestos, a kingdom so far that only a portal could get him here in any decent amount of time.

Thank the Gods that Ezra can send anyone within a day's journey or less outside any city protected by Magic.

Which was the case with nearly any city these days in Axrealia, he remembered, and in these dark times was it any wonder? Strange disappearances, someone tampering with nature, warping people into strange creatures? Derik couldn't blame any ruler for wanting to keep their people safe as he felt the same way. He'd give anything just to keep Ezra and his friends safe!

"Are you sure that the King's Cousin, sister, no one related or important to him at all is missing?" Derik asked as the Herald had been droning on and on for quite some time.

"Quite sure, no one is missing from our Court, Sir. But we're a small kingdom. We're a peaceful kingdom and hardly anything ever happens here," the Herald said wistfully. "I wish I could help you, Sir, but all of the people that are missing are peasants, craftsmen. No one of any greater importance to the Kingdom, Sir. Although if you get information, I would still like you to notify us if you find where our people were taken."

"Well, I had to be sure. Can I have the list, please? At least a copy of it? This way, if we find them, we can ensure that they are returned home as quickly as possible," Derik explained.

"Of course, Sir and thank you. The Sorceress' help is greatly appreciated in this matter, Sir."

"Why is that?"

"Word has spread of her deeds to bring that foul mage, Juktis, to justice. He has been a blight on the land for years and thankfully we were far too far out for him to be bothered with us. Even so, our Mages have had a chance to finally rest. The King ordered them all to keep us hidden from Juktis, to ensure that he didn't try to plunder our Kingdom, Sir," the Herald replied in a grateful tone that took Derik by surprise.

"I see. He attacked her first, but she was determined to do what she could to put a stop to his plans. It took quite an army to free the

Fortress from his grip. And, well….it was worth the effort to ensure that no one else went through his…attentions," Derik said with a nod.

The Herald swiftly copied the list for Derik and handed it to him.

"Thank you again, Sir and we'll do all we can to help, should you need us. The King himself has pledged it," the Herald told him solemnly.

"Thank you. We may be taking you up on it. Now we just have to find where these people have been taken to," Derik sighed as he rose and offered his forearm to the Herald.

The Herald clasped Derik's forearm in a grip that was surprisingly strong for a man who was so slight! The Herald was very slender, some may say wirey. His body was all bone and sinew that was well hidden by his Palatial Uniform. Derik couldn't help but feel reassured by this Courtier and smiled.

"I'll send word when we have any, Sir—"

"Oh Tallus, Sir. It would be greatly appreciated, Sir," Tallus said with all the air of propeity.

Derik left the Herald's record chamber with a great deal of relief.

They had another ally; one they would probably need in the days to come.

Tallus watched Derik go and chuckled as he closed the door. He walked over to a secret door and slipped through it—

And back into his real chamber. That of the King.

"Any problems, Sir?" Tallus' true Herald, a man named Portus, asked.

"None at all, Portus. He had no idea that I wasn't who I said I was. Thank you for aiding in my little deception, but I wanted him to leave knowing that Ammora has our support should they need it," Tallus told Portus, feeling grave at the news that Derik had shared.

Whomever is behind this foul plot, they are toying with all of us. Stealing future rulers and current rulers to use as hostages? To ensure their own agenda is left alone, but for what purpose? Luckily, I don't have an Heir of any sort yet, but I'll need to declare a successor soon. But not until this mess is sorted out. I won't put anyone else in danger, Tallus thought, wondering how many other rulers were frantic over the thought of their successors or Heirs being held somewhere, possibly tormented or worse. Not to mention those who had been taken that were already rulers.

It was a thought that chilled him to the bone and would give him a restless night, most likely, as it all too easily could have been him that had been taken!

"Anything to help you, Sir. Is there anything else I may do to help in the deception?"

"Yes…you're standing in for me tonight and we're going to let him continue to think that You're the King…at least until he leaves. We need to know we can trust this emissary, but from what I've heard of the Sorceress he serves…she'll have sent only the most trustworthy."

"Of course, Sir," Portus said with a slight bow and a smile.

This was a ploy that Tallus had used for years. He and Portus looked much alike, and the King's name had never been well known here, a necessity for the times when they needed to switch places.

Not even the courtiers really knew which was really the King.

But that was why Tallus was glad that his father had had so many affairs. Thus, the resemblance.

But Portus had never once tried to betray Tallus, for which Tallus was deeply grateful and afforded Portus with so much trust.

And why a mere Herald was given a bit more responsibility and power than in other kingdoms. If anything ever happened to Tallus, Portus would be the one to wear the crown and Tallus' death kept a secret.

A necessity in these dark times, but one that Tallus accepted and hoped would never come to pass.

Chapter Ten

Reanalia stretched as she read through yet another book in Surala's library.

"So how did that creature manage to get loose?" Surala mused as she was looking at a magical recreation of her trap and watching the shadowy creatures that she had magically recreated into a hologram getting caught in it. "I can't see how they did it, other than destroying most of the trap…again. But I thought I had made it strong enough."

"Not sure either, it was a sturdy trap. Maybe whoever sent them took it magically back just as they did the others?" Reanalia suggested as she looked up from her book.

"I don't know either. Can we report this to the Sorceress? I don't know if this is related at all but, I'd feel more comfortable if she knew what was going on," Surala said. Reanalia straightened up on her watery perch and nodded.

"Sure, and we should report on what we've seen anyway," Surala said, knowing this wasn't going to help the Sorceress' stress levels. But it had to be done.

She began to activate the charm, using her own magic as she flipped her tail lazily in the water.

Ezra was musing over her own problem. Most of the scouts were starting to report back and out of all of those who had been taken, about ten were people who would be future leaders of their people though not all. Some of course were already rulers.

She looked up as she sensed Reanalia's charm awaken and opened her mind telepathically.

:;Yes, Reanalia?::

:;We've been seeing shadowy creatures at night when there isn't a lot of moonlight, Sorceress. We tried to catch one, but it got away,.; Reanalia reported as Ezra settled back in her chair in her work room.

::We've had the same thing happening here, but we managed to catch one. They're the people that were taken, some of them anyway, we believe. They're being changed into creatures that are, for lack of a better word…undead. I'm working on trying to undo what was done to the one we caught, but I'm not having a lot of luck over here, Reanalia,:: Ezra replied as she reached up, stroking over the bridge of her nose as she thought.

::Oh my. What about Kayla? She's a mermaid, an immortal one at that--:; Reanalia started.

::I don't believe she or others like her are being changed. I think whoever is doing this is holding them as hostages. This is a deep game, but I have no idea what their end goal is. We need more information, but I have no idea where to look for it,:: Ezra admitted as she laid a hand on her belly, wincing as the child within kicked very, very hard.

::Perhaps you could trace the spell that took Kayla. The rest of us can't, the magic keeps us from tracing it to the origin," Reanalia replied solemnly.

::;I can try. I'll be there in a little while,:: Ezra sent back as she rose.

"All I can do is try," Ezra murmured out loud as she rubbed her belly, hoping the child would calm.

::;Eve won't approve of you traveling just now, Ezra,:: Baelios sent telepathically as Ezra shut the communication down.

::;I don't have a choice, Baelios. This is my duty and this time…I can't send anyone else,:: Ezra replied, feeling tired and wishing that just this once, she could lay the burden down.

But she couldn't. There was no one else to carry out her duties.

::;I understand, Ezra, more than anyone. But is it wise?::

::Of course not, Baelios. I'm risking going into labor any day now. I'm risking everything but I have to find where these people were taken,:: Ezra sent back as she headed downstairs to go and visit the Orb of Eithal.

She would need the power boost.

*   *   *

An hour later, Ezra walked through the portal and out into, what could only be called…Paradise.

The Dragon's Keep she had seen in the astral, but this was different in person. The colors were brighter, more vivid than she had seen from the Astral realm. For a moment, Ezra felt overwhelmed as she looked at the Keep and how it was so cleverly constructed and kept together with sand, shells…and a bit of magic.

"Greetings, Sorceress," Surala greeted as she arrived at the door. Ezra found herself quickly ushered in and allowed to sit, which helped after such a long journey by portal.

Not to mention the protest from Ezra's ankles from both the walk across the sand and the weight that Ezra had gained during her pregnancy.

"Greetings, Surala, Reanalia and Your Highness," she said, giving a courteous nod to each as she relaxed back into the chair that Surala had summoned to her. They were seated in the middle of a large library and Ezra was amazed at how it had been adapated so that the Mermaid Queen and Reanalia, who looked stunning as a mermaid, could sit with them. "I'm surprised, Reanalia. I wasn't expecting to see you with a mermaid tail," she said with a teasing wink to her friend.

"I'll be changing back soon, Sorceress, but not quite yet. Not until we've exhausted every part of the investigation. Now the place where Princess Kayla was taken was fairly far away from the Pod's normal swimming grounds, so to speak. It's awash with magic, and I can't tell where it leads if anywhere. We've done all we can but…we need fresh eyes, Sorceress," Reanalia admitted, and Ezra could see the look in Reanalia's eyes. Of failure and defeat echoed in those beautiful eyes and it broke Ezra's heart to see it.

"Very well, I'll be glad to take a look. Which spell did you use to change yourself, Reanalia? I'll probably use the same—"

"Oh it's too risky while you're pregnant, Sorceress," Surala said immediately. "We couldn't ask you to do that—"

"This is why I'm here, Surala. To help and to do all I can and since this situation is growing more dire by the day, I'd rather do all I can and not worry about the risks. Now, please, which spell did you use?" Ezra insisted, not about to be deterred.

Reanalia sighed and gave a nod to Surala.

"She's right. We're running out of time, Surala. It's a simple transformation spell, Sorceress. It took me three hours to manage it for myself, but you should be able to manage it in no time. Mermaids and mermen are mammals, so you won't need to grow gills. They have a superb lung capacity so they can hold their breath for a while, but they utilize things in the ocean that keep air pockets to stop and take a breath. Long journeys, they have a special breathing device they wear," Reanalia explained as she took a pen, a small slab of marble and a piece of parchment and began to write the spell down.

Ezra took the parchment as it was handed to her by Surala, who acted as a quick go between the two mages and Ezra took her time, looking it over and gave a nod.

"I should be able to manage it. How quickly did it take effect?"

"Nearly instantly. I fell when it happened so I'd suggest you do it in the pool or sitting on the side of it so you don't fall as I did," Reanalia suggested, a look of concern in her eyes. "It would be horrible if something happened to the baby—"

"The baby is immortal, Reanalia. Just as I am. There's nothing to fear for the baby," Ezra explained.

"Oh good! Still, no point in taking pointless risks, Sorceress," Queen Felati said with a grave look in her eyes. "I'm still not happy that you're willing to do this but…we should get it over with. The sooner we rescue Kayla and bring her home, the happier I'll be," Queen Felati admitted, the frustration quite plain on her face.

It was a mother's worry for their child. Ezra could sense it as if the Mermaid Queen was screaming it in her ear.

"I'll do all I can, Your Highness. So, where can I put my clothes and where do I sit?"

Surala showed Ezra to where there was a private chamber and gave Ezra a simple chemise of soft white linen. Ezra took off her attire with Surala's help and put it all aside.

When she was ready, she sat at the side of the library pool and began.

Taking a breath, Ezra drew on her magical power deep within her. She could sense, far off, the Castle and the Orb as well as Baelios. They were not quite out of reach, but she didn't attempt to draw on their magic. They needed it to keep the Castle safe in her absence, so instead Ezra drew on the power deep within herself.

She pulled on it, forced it up until it came to life as she worked the spell, concentrating on the form that she wanted to have…and felt her legs suddenly glue themselves together before her bones melted and reformed into the proper shape that she would need for a powerful mermaid tail.

Ezra felt the chemise about her melt away and become something else as well, becoming a simple top that kept her breasts covered..and a wrap about her hips though the wrap she could have done without. She opened her eyes and looked down—

And found a beautiful white mermaid tail instead of legs and feet. Her fluke was beautiful, a startling white with a hint of blue and gold in each little line of fin tissue. Ezra looked to Reanalia and to Felati, who chuckled.

"Should've known that you would be another Queen now that I'm seeing how powerful you are," Felati said before she handed Ezra a special apparatus to wear. "This will help you to breathe under the water...we're going a long way," Felati explained before she put on her own and handed one to Reanalia as well.

"Hold onto me in the water, Sorceress. I'll pull you to where we're going…Reanalia's been swimming since she transformed but… it takes a bit of practice," Surala reassured Ezra as Ezra put on her breathing apparatus and sank under the water. The shell acted as a tank and the smaller shell sealed itself around Ezra's mouth. The tube that connected the pair brought fresh air to Ezra's lungs..and there was a small hole or two in the small shell that allowed the air she was breathing out to escape.

Oh, so clever these people, Ezra thought as she tried to emulate Reanalia and Felati as they all moved down and out of the way.

And just in time for Surala to splash down between all three of them…in full Draconic form!

This is beginning to be a regular thing, being stunned so much here! What other wonders will I see today? Ezra mused as the three of them all found positions on Surala's back to hold on to…and the journey to the ship graveyard began.

Baelios was a little perplexed! He had seen Ezra just this morning but now, he couldn't find her anywhere in the Castle!

She wasn't in her chambers or in the library. He couldn't sense her anywhere as he checked the Throne Room, the Work Room, the Dungeon, even the Nesting Room with the Dragon's egg and the Power Chamber.

She wasn't anywhere in the Castle and when Baelios reached—

He sensed her very, very far away.

It's not like Ezra to not tell me when she's leaving, Baelios mused, hearing the Wizards within arguing as to why she was suddenly just...gone! *She must have gone to see Reanalia in person, even though I warned her not to go. Oh well, Eve will have a cat when she finds out!*

Naturally, today was the day that some of the messengers were due to return, including Derik. As each charm activated with the message for home, Baelios was the one in the Entrance Hall opening the portals to bring them home. It meant he had to use the Castle's Magic himself, but this was one of those times that he knew it was necessary.

One by one, the Messengers arrived home to find only Baelios and Counselor Lita waiting for them. As Derik came through, he gave Baelios a puzzled look.

"Spirit, good to see you. Where's the Sorceress?" Derik asked and Baelios immediately drew him aside.

"I haven't seen her anywhere since this morning, Derik. When I reach to find her, she's not here...but very far away," Baelios whispered to him, keeping His own voice low so it wouldn't carry.

"Is she in trouble?" Derik murmured back, picking up on the hint immediately.

"Not that I can tell, but we shouldn't let Eve or anyone else find out that she's not here for the moment. Why don't you go to your chambers and get a quick bath and I'll bring you a meal and we can discuss a quick strategy to keep word from spreading?" Baelios whispered.

"Okay, but find out where she is please and make sure she's all right?" Derik asked. Baelios gave a nod.

"I know where she went and I'll have a meal brought to you," Baelios promised before he disappeared and teleported himself directly into the Power Chamber.

He reached for Ezra telepathically, using the Orb's power to boost his own and prayed that Ezra really was all right. The last thing they all needed was for her to be in trouble, too.

Ezra was surprised at how fast Surala could swim! She was having to work to stay on Surala's back and felt her belly brushing against the Dragon Mage's scales from time to time. Inside, the baby was quiet, kicking now and then but mostly just resting from what Ezra could tell.

Which was all to the good as Ezra wanted to concentrate on what she had to do here.

::Ezra….can you hear me?:: A faint message sent from Baelios made her realize that she hadn't told him where she was going.

::Yes, Baelios, barely. I'm with Surala and Reanalia. We're going to look at the site where the mermaid, Kayla, was taken. Sorry, I meant to tell you--:: she started to send.

:;It's all right, at least now I can tell Derik where you are and that you're safe! We're going to keep it quiet that you're gone for now. How long are you going to be?:: Baelios asked.

Ezra shifted a bit in her position, trying to find a more comfortable one that she could still keep her grip on Surala's back with.

:;I should be back tonight or tomorrow morning, Baelios. As soon as we're done here, I'm intending to return back home,:; She sent, not daring to let him see what she'd done to herself for now.

::Very well, Ezra, let me know if you're delayed. Be safe,:: Baelios sent before he cut off contact.

Ezra sighed and just tried to remain positive for the moment. They needed answers and there were some answers here.

She just needed to find them.

Surala finally pulled up and gave a draconic nod towards the depths ahead.

The water was very clear despite the amount of sand and rock that kept these boats from ever leaving the water. Each boat was badly damaged and had sunk long ago. Ezra rued with sadness that many lives had already been lost here.

Ezra shook it off and began to look at everything around her, using her magical senses to reach—

And frantically grabbed Felati and pulled her back along with Reanalia as she sensed something happening!

A gigantic whirlpool opened before them, pulling and trying to suck them all in!

Surala, seeing the danger, grabbed all of them and pulled them back and away from the whirlpool trap even as Ezra frantically used her magic to try to trace it!

She found a line of power and seized on it, leaping from her body into the astral and following it…following it, feeling it pulling her spirit up—

Swimming and flying along that line, Ezra didn't resist for the moment until she saw…

The Fortress. Jarod's Fortress nestled in its place in the mountains.

But this isn't Jarod's magic, Ezra thought as she looked at the line she had followed. *This is someone else's…something familiar. It feels a little like…Like the magic that really animated that Necromanced Dragon that Juktis was controlling.* Ezra gasped at the realization. *This is his partner's magic…maybe that's why it drew me here? That or…Or Jarod has been playing us all along?* Ezra thought but immediately pushed the thought away. She knew that Jarod had desired her, had wanted her to be with him. But he reminded her far too much of his twin brother, Juktis, for her to ever really be able to trust him with everything she had.

Not to mention the fact that his family's Fortress needed someone to look after it and the people there. Ezra frowned and tried to shake off the feeling of betrayal and failed…

I need to get home! I need to speak with him as soon as possible, was the frantic thought on her mind as she raced back now, fighting against the magic that tugged and pulled at her, trying to draw it further into its trap.

But it wasn't quite strong enough and she shook it off, following the line that led back to her body and rushed into it with a feeling of Relief!

Ezra opened her eyes to find Surala, Reanalia and Felati all looking down at her.

::It was a clever trap, but I used it to find out where the spell originated,:: she told them telepathically, her mental voice grave and worn.

:;Where, Sorceress?:: Felati asked and Ezra heaved a heavy sigh.

::The Fortress…Jarod's Fortress now…I don't think it's him. But there's one person it could be…::

:;Surely not Juktis?:: Reanalia asked.

::No….I think it's his partner though, the one that got away,:: Ezra replied. ::I need to get home to Ammora…I need to get a hold of Jarod and find out what the blazes is going on over there--::

::Shh, you're weary, Sorceress. I'll carry you back to the Dragon's Keep. Reanalia, Felati, hang on, my friends. I'm going to get us all back there as fast as I can,:: Surala said, giving Reanalia and Felati barely time to settle as she cradled Ezra in one massive set of claws and forearm..and took off!

Any creatures that saw their passing saw nothing but bubbles.

Chapter Eleven

Jarod was more than a little concerned. Alyra had been more and more reclusive, occupied more often and not with him as often as she had been in the beginning when he'd met her. Something was off, but he couldn't put his finger on it.

"Where is Lady Alyra this morning?" he asked one of the servant girls as she changed the sheets on his large opulent bed.

"I don't know, M'Lord. Perhaps she was called away," the servant girl, Ayteri, said as she bobbed a quick curtsy to him. She was petite, curvy and dark skinned with long black hair and beautiful melted chocolate brown eyes. He found himself normally smiling with her, but today he frowned. This wasn't a good thing that he couldn't find the woman, nor was it a good thing that the servants had no idea where she was either. These two servant girls he'd had assigned to his chambers were very nosey, kept on only by Alyra's insistence.

If it were up to me, I'd have sent them both packing or at least assigned them elsewhere. Those two are not trustworthy! Jarod thought as he looked wistfully around his chambers again.

And each day he noticed more of his mother's jewelry was gone. More of his cufflinks as well. It was at the point now where Jarod had narrowed it down to just the two servants who had access to his chambers.

Which was unfortunate because it meant Alyra vouching for them also put her in a bad light.

I don't know why I ever took up with her in the first place. Granted, I was jealous that the Sorceress and Derik were together, and that the Sorceress really didn't want anything to do with me. I had hoped she'd see past the resemblance to Juktis, but…he did hurt her very badly. I can see now why she might not want anything to do with me outside of being allies. Jarod ran his fingers through his hair, ashamed of the fact that he'd hidden Alyra from the Sorceress. But she didn't seem to be a bad person.

But she also didn't seem to be a very good person either. He was having trouble just tracking her down and the two servants who were supposed to know were either telling the truth or lying through their teeth.

Either way, it's still not good! Bad enough that Alyra doesn't help me with the day-to-day running of this place, but now not being able to find her? What is she up to? Jarod sighed, noting that yet another pair of his mother's earrings was gone from where he had put them out yesterday. Ayteri and the other chambermaid was nearly done and were beginning to take his laundry out and Jarod could swear he saw a flash of gold coming from the top of one of Ayteri's apron pockets.

He frowned and let it go for now as he strode out to see to what his people needed today. Thus far, there was a long, alarming list of things that needed to be done to see to their welfare.

I'll track her down this afternoon, Jarod resigned himself to the idea that what he wanted wasn't going to be what was going to happen right now.

It was what needed to be done that mattered.

In the Dragon's Keep, Ezra felt so very, very weary but she managed to transform himself back to her human form. Feeling the baby kicking within her with a vengeance, she sat back in the chair and accepted the cheese, bread and fruit that Surala gave her.

"Thank you. I need to get home as soon as I can. The Spirit of the Council is keeping it very quiet that I'm here, but…he'll only be able to do that for a short while I'm afraid. Eve will be furious if she finds out I traveled all this way without telling her," Ezra sighed as she tried to relax. "I traced the magic…all the way back to the Fortress..but it isn't linked to Jarod. That's what makes all of this so troubling," Ezra admitted as she picked up a bit of cheese, trying to decide if she had the energy to even eat it.

"Eat and rest, first, Sorceress. We can help you with the portal after that if you'd like," Reanalia said gently, worry in her eyes. Ezra shook it off with a wave of a hand.

"I'm fine, I can manage it—" Ezra started, not wanting them to make a fuss over her.

"You're pregnant...half of your energy is going into making a baby. And I know you don't recover very quickly when you're away from Ammora, Sorceress. It's not a bad thing to admit you need help—"

"I'm fine, Reanalia. Since the Orb of Eithal was added to Ammora's power source, I've had more energy than I've ever had before," Ezra countered before finally just takin ga bite of cheese. Better to eat and satisfy them for now, then perhaps they'd allow her to go home.

When did my life become a drama with everyone fussing over me? Ezra wondered.

When did my life become a drama with everyone fussing at me? Derik thought as Eve continued to rant and rave. Eve had discovered when she couldn't find the Sorceress that the Sorceress was not in the Castle.

"Where is she, Derik? I need to check her and the baby again," Eve snapped at him as if it was his fault.

"I don't know. The Spirit knows, otherwise he'd have sent out a search party by now. Calm down, the Sorceress isn't a child and she's immortal. I'm sure she and the baby are fine," Derik said for what felt like the fiftieth time just in the past five minutes. "She left while I was gone, I just got back myself, Eve!" He said insistently, hoping against hope that she might actually believe him!

Naturally, that wasn't in the cards!

"Derik, we need to find her, we really do. She's due any day now! Don't you want the baby to be born here?" Eve asked, her voice ringing with desperation.

"Of course I do, Eve! But I can't control what she does, and no one should try! This is her home! We are just guests in it, and you need to remember that! She has been here for far longer than most of us have been alive," he retorted, beginning to lose his own patience! He was tired, despite the rest and the bath and he was just not willing to listen to her ranting and raving any further.

::Nor should you, Derik. Ezra said she'll be back soon, probably by tonight. And Eve is getting on my nerves,:: the Spirit whispered telepathically into Derik's mind. And that was the only warning Derik got.

Suddenly, the room shook! Derik nearly lost his footing and Eve grasped onto the nearest chair to keep from falling over.

"ENOUGH! Eve, the Sorceress is fulfilling her duties and will be back as soon as possible. She will see you after she is back, but she is NOT at your beck and call. I'd suggest finding something to do that is more constructive than yelling at everyone in the meantime!" The Spirit's voice suddenly bellowed about them! It was so loud, even Derik had to grab his ears to try to muffle the sound.

Eve looked around, visibly pale and swallowed as it went quiet again.

"Sorry," she whispered before she turned and hurried back out of the room. Derik sighed and just sank into his chair.

::;Sorry, Derik…but it had to be done,:: The Spirit whispered apologetically into Derik's mind.

"Well done, Spirit…thank you," Derik murmured back as he just tried to sit back and relax for the moment. Which wasn't easy, considering that his heart was pounding in his chest like a rabbit, and he felt his adrenaline racing in his bloodstream from the shock of what had just happened. Derik took another breath, and closed his eyes, just using some mental exercises he'd learned in the Mercenary Guild to try to calm himself.

One never knew when the second shoe would drop.

Ezra was running down the hallways again. Behind her, she could hear an army of those creatures chasing her, stumbling blindly after her.

I've got to protect the Orb…I have to! Ezra thought frantically as she hurried on towards her destination. She had sent everyone from the Castle away, including Angelica and Derik, so the hallways were completely clear. *Just a little further,* she realized as she dashed into her work room.

"Come on, Alyra! You have to catch me!" she taunted over her shoulder as she ran down the steps towards the Power Chamber. She would make her last stand there—

But then she fell as a creature grabbed her legs and pulled them out from underneath her—

Ezra woke with a scream! She sat up, sweating and feeling the baby frantically kicking inside of her. She looked around herself, not knowing where she was for a moment—

"Sorceress, are you all right?" Reanalia asked her as she reached over to touch her hand. Ezra jumped from the sudden touch, then took a breath and nodded as she tried to calm down.

"I'm all right. It was just a nightmare," she said, brushing it off as lightly as she could. *That wasn't just a nightmare…it was another bloody vision and they're getting worse, darker not lighter. These creatures are connected to the Darkness…but how?* Ezra took another breath and just tried to appear calm even though inside, she was anything but.

"Do you want me to get Surala?" Reanalia asked, having transformed back into her human self. Her tail was gone, and she was dressed in a light lavender gown. Ezra shook her head as she took another breath.

"No…I need to get back to Ammora though, Reanalia. You know I won't recover as easily here. I need to get home," she said as she rose, giving it up and getting dressed in her usual clothing again. The tunic was getting too tight, and she used her magic to expand it again—

RIIIIP! The sound of ripping fabric was plain to even Ezra's ears and she sighed. The spell hadn't worked this time. Ezra looked down at the rip in her tunic and pants and just blinked back furious tears.

I guess even fabric has a limit as to how far it can be magically stretched, Ezra thought as she just brushed that off too. She picked up her boots and gave Reanalia a hug.

"Time for a new wardrobe, Sorceress," Reanalia teased gently, hugging her back. "I'll help you with the portal and let Surala and Felati know that you were called back."

"Thank you, my friend," Ezra murmured as she fought the desire to both throw something, laugh and cry all at once. *Damned hormones, I'll be glad when this pregnancy is over.*

"You're welcome. Come," Reanalia said as she walked with her out through the doors of the Dragon's Keep. Within moments, their energies had merged to create a portal back to Ammora Castle. "I'll send you word if we find out anything else, Sorceress," Reanalia promised.

"And I'll let you know when I've finished unraveling this mystery. I have a feeling I'm going to need all the help I can get this time…there's a storm on the horizon. I can feel it, can you?"

Reanalia closed her eyes for a moment, then nodded.

"Yes, the energies are getting darker and wilder. Something is coming…a big storm of some sort. I'm sure Surala and I will be able to help you all we can. Felati may be willing to as well," Reanalia said thoughtfully. "Just send for me when you're ready."

"I will. Stay safe my friends," Ezra said before she turned and walked through the portal—

And came out into the calm quiet of the Entrance Hall.

::Ezra, welcome home!:: Baelios sent as he appeared next to her while she closed down the portal. She turned and hugged him, having missed him while she was away! Baelios hugged her back. ::What's wrong?:: he asked, his voice changing into the stern Draconic voice of the half-Dragon wizard.

::I've had another vision, Baelios. It was horrible. Those creatures were loose inside the Castle. They're connected to the Darkness, I can feel it,:: she sent back, feeling fear boiling within her.

::Well they're not here yet. Calm down, we'll figure out a way to either change them back…or to destroy them if we must,:: Baelios said, his mental voice changing mid-sentence back into the calmer voice of Bael. ::Eve was a handful while you were gone, I had to give her a verbal slap and remind her that you have your duties just as she has hers,:: Bael then told her telepathically with a hint of humor in his voice now.

::All right, I will talk with her after I've had a hot bath and..I need some new clothes, Baelios,:; Ezra admitted as she turned and showed him the rip down the steams of her tunic and leggings.

::;I'll get right on it. Derik is home as are the rest of the messengers and they all have reports for you to go over though…most of it hasn't changed,:: Baelios said as he wrapped an arm around her shoulders and began to walk her back to her Chambers. She leaned her head against his shoulder, into his quiet strength as she walked and felt oddly comforted by the Spirit.

::Thank you. I'm glad he's home. I've missed him,:: she admitted to Baelios as they walked, her bare feet making an odd noise against the floor instead of the usual click click of her heels.

::I actually missed him. He's good for you and he's brought help and people back into both of our lives. I'm glad, Ezra. We were alone for far too long.;:

::I know…and we may be alone again if that Vision comes to pass,:: she sighed wearily, feeling the weight of the world again on her shoulders.

::Then let's hope it doesn't,:: Baelios soothed her gently as he opened the door to her Chambers, revealing Derik laying on their bed.

Ezra went to him and cuddled in, dropping her boots at the foot of the bed and not caring a fig about how she looked in that moment.

Baelios closed the door and locked it for her as Derik began to welcome Ezra home.

A pounding on the door a few hours later woke Derik out of a dead sleep. Ezra was still asleep next to him under the covers, her nude body warm against his and he didn't want to disturb her.

"Derik, I need to talk to you!" Eve snapped from the other side of the door. Derik rolled his eyes and growled a little, then carefully shifted Ezra from his shoulder back onto her pillow. Ezra groaned a little in her sleep as he did but didn't wake. Derik picked up his robe and eased himself from the bed and went to the door and cracked it open.

"The Sorceress just got back home, Eve. She's exhausted and still asleep. I'll tell her that you want to examine her as soon as she wakes up—" he started.

"We have a problem. That creature just mauled one of the guards in the dungeon, Derik," Eve said, cutting him off. "You need to see this—" she said, her eyes showing both anger and a deep concern.

"Okay, I'll wake her, then we'll come and see. Give us a couple of moments," Derik told Eve before he closed the door again and turned.

I hate to wake her but…this does sound important, he thought ruefully as he got himself dressed before walking to Ezra's side to gently wake her.

Ezra woke but she was very groggy. Derik felt a stab of guilt at having to wake her but from what Eve had just said, this was something that needed to be seen to immediately.

"Ezra, Eve said that the creature in the dungeon has mauled one of the guards. She wants us to come and see…must be important," he told her gently, stroking her hair. "If you want, I can go and see and then have Baelios come and fetch you if it really is important—"

"No….no…I'll come," Ezra said wearily as she rolled over to push herself up to sitting. "I don't have anything to wear except my robe," she said as she nodded to the pile of her clothing on the floor.

"I can't expand them any further, Derik," she said with regret. "Even my maternity dresses have been too tight lately."

"Then we'll just have to lend you some of my clothes if you want…or you can go in just a robe for now," he replied with a grin, kissing her lips and stroking her hair as he just breathed in her sweet scent. "Whichever you want."

"I'll just wear the robe for now, but thank you," Ezra replied with a chuckle, kissing him back before she held out her hands as she required help these days to get up out of their bed. He gladly took them and helped her up, then walked to go and get her robe from the closet along with her slippers.

As she slipped both on, Derik couldn't help but just appreciate her beauty, the grace with which she moved despite her large belly. A belly that he reached for and touched with tenderness.

How is it possible that she grows more and more beautiful each day? Derik thought as he moved to open the door and wrapped his arm around her protectively. *Gods, I love her.*

Ezra smiled as they walked and whispered into his ear. "I love you too." That was enough. They could face anything.

So long as they were together.

Chapter Twelve

"Oh my," the Sorceress breathed as they walked into the dungeon and the make-shift infirmary that Eve had set up.

"He isn't stable enough for us to move him yet," Eve stated as she and her partner worked frantically on the mauled guard.

He was a mess! Bite marks, rip marks from the creature's long nails riddled his body. And worse, the veins were turning strange colors near those marks.

"Wait, is this normal?" the Sorceress asked as she pointed towards the discoloration of the veins.

"Not even a little. Bruising would be normal, but this isn't bruising. From what I can tell…whatever made that creature what it is, it's infectious if the creature bites or claws you," Eve told the pair as she continued to work. "And I have no way of knowing if I can stop the spread—"

"Then, let's stop it now before it gets any further. Where healing fails, magic may be what's needed," the Sorceress stated as Derik helped her down to the floor. The Sorceress placed her hands just over the wounds and closed her eyes—

The light that flowed forth, the energy that went into the guard then was beautiful, magnificent and Eve added her energy immediately to the Sorceress' hoping against hope that it might help—

"It's working!" Derik exclaimed as Eve looked down to see the discoloration disappearing.

The Sorceress and Eve kept it up until the guard's wounds were completely healed and the discoloration was completely gone. The Sorceress sagged but gave a smile as the guard's eyes opened.

"It worked…but why? Why not on the original when I attempted the same thing?" the Sorceress wondered out loud as Derik carefully helped her up.

"Perhaps it's because the original is protected by a powerful protection spell, Sorceress," The Spirit of the Council said as he suddenly popped into view right next to Eve, making her jump and scream!

"A little warning next time!" Eve snapped at the Spirit.

"Perhaps it's more than that, Spirit. Maybe it's a combination of Magic and Healing that reverses it. After I rest, Eve, we'll try it on the creature in the basement. See if we can get some answers—" the Sorceress started.

"Not until after I've examined you…and we find a way to put that thing out so it doesn't change either of us before we can help it," Eve replied. "And I want to make sure the baby is doing all right," Eve said with a growl, frustrated that the Sorceress and Derik were not focusing on the blessed event about to arrive.

"Of course, Eve. But I am knackered, and I really need to rest for a bit longer," the Sorceress said gently, reaching to put a hand on her shoulder. "Thank you for your concern and for all you do for all of us. I don't know what we would do without you," the Sorceress admitted with a gentle shake to Eve's shoulder.

"Thank you. I wasn't feeling very appreciated lately," Eve admitted as her partner came up beside her and put an arm around her shoulders.

"Well, you are appreciated, and I'm sorry if I haven't said it enough lately. Why don't you go and take an afternoon off together and just enjoy being together?" the Sorceress suggested before she turned and walked with Derik, wearing nothing but a robe and slippers Eve realized, back up the stairs towards the main level.

"That's the best suggestion I've heard all day," a sensual whisper rang against Eve's ear, making her smile.

"Mmm…me too, love. Let's go and relax together for a bit. I could use it."

"Me too," Phyla said with a grin as she tugged Eve towards the door. "So, let's go make the most of it!"

Eve couldn't find a single solitary reason to argue with that as they began to race up the stairs together.

Jarod couldn't find Alyra again. He had finished early with his duties and had hoped to spend a little time with her this afternoon.

And she was nowhere to be found! He was walking down the hall when he heard voices from around the corner.

"Well, well, pretty girls…so how is M'lord today? And has he asked for Lady Alyra again?" a deep, sinister voice asked. Jarod froze and pressed up against the wall and listened.

"Oh, M'lord is well, but he hasn't asked for her yet, Lord Lytarph," a female voice replied…Ayteri's he realized as he listened. Using an orb, he scryed and watched them magically around the corner. It was Maron Lytarph, a minor lord here at the Fortress, Ayteri one of his maids and his other maid, a short blonde haired and green-eyed woman named Seri. Seri was a bit too thin for his taste, but he never bedded the servants anyway.

"Good...if he asks again, just say you haven't seen her. She's been very busy with her guests in the dungeon. Fairly soon, she should be ready to enact the plan," Lytarph said with a dark smirk on his face. Lytarph was tall, muscular and had a short well-kept goatee and dark hair that fell as far as his shoulders. He had a look in his brown eyes that made even Jarod want to snarl as he looked at the two maids.

I don't like the sound of this...but that explains why she's disappeared so much. Last I knew, there were no prisoners in the dungeon...so WHO the bloody hell is down there? He thought furiously as he shifted and dismissed the scrying spell with the touch of his index finger. *I need help on this one. I hope the Sorceress won't mind a surprise visit.*

Jarod turned and went back down the hallway, making a portal with the wave of one hand and closing it with the other once he walked through. He looked up at the Aliicorns that looked sternly down at him from the Drawbridge of Ammora Castle. He swallowed and reached over, ringing a bell that looked like it had been put there for visitors—

And nearly fell through! He grabbed the post as he felt the ground give way and looked down at a clever trap that had been neatly put there!

"Help!" Jarod cried in surprise.

And looked up at spears as familiar faces surrounded him...then the spears lowered, and Wahya reached over to offer him his forearm.

"How's it, Bra? Didn't know you were comin' for a visit! Sorry about the trap but...we've had a lot of strange things going on at night around here lately. Strange creatures coming and going that look like walking undead, Bra," Wahya explained as Jarod got his footing.

"I need the Sorceress' help, Wahya. I couldn't send warning, mostly because I can't trust my own servants it seems," Jarod explained as he looked down into the pit below which was quite deep and with nothing to gain purchase on. "What do you mean the "walking undead?" Do you mean Vampires?"

"Reset it for tonight, just in case, Bras. C'mon, Bra, I'll take you in the back way if you'd like," Wahya said with a grin as he began to lead Jarod over to another path that would take them to the city through a nearby tunnel that was cleverly disguised. "No, Bra. It's not Vampires. Vampires I know how to handle, Bra. No, something else. Something I've never seen before, and I can tell ya...I've seen a lot!"

"Aren't you worried that someone *would* sneak in through here, Wahya?" he asked.

"Nah, we have a lever that closes a door that seals it off—makes it look like a big boulder. We leave it closed most of the time, especially at night," Wahya told him as they walked through the tunnel and out into Ammora City.

It was wondrous what they had done in less than a year! Beautiful buildings, lots of cozy houses...plenty of space for growth! And everything made with a sense of beauty in mind.

Jarod was just *stunned* at the sight of it. Wahya chuckled and nudged him.

"Something to behold, huh, Bra? C'mon, let's go in through the back entrance and we'll get you to the Sorceress. What's been going on in the Fortress that you don't think you can trust your own servants?" Wahya asked as they walked towards a small bridge that led to the Castle's back.

"I…have a lady who arrived shortly after you all left. She's very nice but…she's up to something. She distracts me whenever I'm with her and I think she's using magic to do it.   She's beautiful, gorgeous…but lately, whenever I want to talk to her, she's nowhere to be found. And just now, I overheard my servants talking with one of the minor lords in my Fortress about her…and about me. They say she has guests in the Dungeon…but I haven't sentenced anyone to the dungeons. We haven't had any crime or any problems whatsoever," Jarod explained.

"When there's no obvious problems, Bra..that's a problem in and of itself," Wahya said as they walked at last through the back door of the Castle and began to make their way through the hallways. "Spirit, we got a visitor for the Sorceress…Lord Jarod. Where're we meetin' her at?" Wahya asked seemingly into the air—

And the Spirit of the Council appeared right next to them, making Jarod jump visibly and Wahya laughed a bit.

"It's all right, Bra! He startles us all when he does that," Wahya said with a wink to Jarod.

"The Sorceress is eating her lunch in the library at the moment, Wahya. Greetings, Lord Jarod. If you make your way there, I'll have refreshments brought up for both of you," The Spirit said before he disappeared again.

"I never can seem to get used to that," Jarod muttered.

"Ha! You do if you hang around long enough. This way, Bra. Hallways changed around again recently, shouldn't make too long a way," Wahya said as he took the lead, leading him through the maze of halls that could change on their own whenever the Castle took it into its head to change them around.

"Wonder why the hallways are changing so often. I thought it did that more when intruders are around."

"With this many people inside, I think it likes to keep us on our toes…and we've had a lot of Visitors so…could be it just wants to make sure that no one can easily find their way around unless they live here," Wahya explained as he turned again, then began to go up a winding staircase that led to the next floor up.

"Why so many visitors, Wahya?"

"A lot of people have been kidnapped from all over Axrealia. Some are being held as hostages we think. Others are being changed. Ah here we are. How's it, Sista! Lord Jarod's got a problem at his Fortress," Wahya said as they entered the library and he sat himself down in a chair, propped his feet up and grabbed a muffin from the table.

Jarod sat down in the other chair, taking a moment first to just appreciate the Sorceress' beauty.

Her belly was much bigger than he last remembered it being, but by now she *was* nearing the end of her pregnancy. Even so, she looked radiant and beautiful in a loose-fitting linen gown. She was sitting back in the best chair in the room and resting one hand against her swollen belly.

A belly that he could hear singing with a child of his family's lineage.

"Greetings, Jarod. What's your problem? And how have you been?" the Sorceress asked with concern in her features as she shifted in her chair.

"It's a bit of a long story, but Wahya says that a lot of people have been kidnapped. We haven't had any kidnappings at my Fortress, though a couple of towns near it have reported some young ladies that have gone missing," Jarod explained. The Sorceress gave a grave nod.

"Yes, and well I have a theory about that. Why don't you tell me your problem and then I'll tell you the whole story of what has been going on here?"

Jarod thought on it, then gave a solemn nod.

"All right...well it began shortly after you all left the Fortress..." he began.

*　*　*

Ezra was stunned! Absolutely stunned! She listened as Jarod described the very woman she had seen in her vision of Kayla! And of course, it explained why there were no kidnappings at the Fortress.

However, it doesn't mean that other kidnappings of a more common kind have been happening near it. She's been playing a long game here...I wonder just how long this has been going on? Perhaps since Juktis ruled there, who knows? Ezra thought as she took a breath as he came to the end of his tale.

Then she began to explain hers, beginning with the first reports of kidnappings from the Dark and Forest Elves....

*   *   *

Jarod didn't think he could be more stunned in his life. He sat there as the Sorceress finished with how she had tracked the magic back to His Fortress.

Oh Gods…I've been duped! He thought in horror.

"So you're sure that Alyra is the woman that you've tracked down to My Fortress?" Jarod asked, horrified at what might have been going on under his very nose.

"Not completely sure. But I am fairly sure that she was Juktis' partner. I'd like to get someone into that dungeon, better yet I'd like to see it for myself. Now these servant girls that she vouched for? Are they honest or are they…perhaps of the more troublesome sort of servant?" the Sorceress asked with a tilt of her head.

"More troublesome these days. More and more of my mother's jewelry and even my cufflinks have disappeared lately. They're getting bolder by the day, the little thieves. I've a mind to dismiss them—"

"Not yet, Jarod. Let's use this to our advantage. If they're thieves, then I'll make two charms, one for each of them to steal. Or you can gift it to them directly. Whichever you prefer. I'll use a very well disguised spell, so it won't alert Alyra to what we're doing. Then we can use those charms to watch everything they do from here in Ammora. When we have verified that it is who we are looking for, and that it is where they are taking those who have been taken…then

I will contact you and you'll return here so we can make our plan. We'll get her, these servants and whomever else is on whatever plan it is they are hatching. We will get justice, Jarod, I assure you. I have one of the creatures still in my dungeon and tomorrow…I am going to break the protection spell on it. Eve and I are going to see if we can save that person. If we're successful, we should get even more answers from them…hopefully," Ezra explained.

Jarod looked at her, astounded and grateful all at once.

"You're not angry with me?" he asked.

"For what? You were duped by a clever woman; you aren't the first man to fall for a woman's charms. I doubt you'll be the last. If it is the woman that was working with Juktis, then we need to make sure we get her this time. We can't afford to let her slip from our grasp," Ezra said as she shifted again in her seat.

"Agreed, but you're pregnant, Sorceress. You really shouldn't go into battle," Jarod said gently as he picked up a pastry and took a bite, not realizing how hungry he was until he took that single bite…and found himself polishing it off quickly. He reached for another, feeling his stomach growling for more.

"Pregnant or not, I don't have a choice. We're running out of time. It's working against us every step of the way. Whatever this plan that she has is, it can't be good for the rest of Axrealia," the Sorceress replied as she placed a hand on her belly and lifted her chin. "And as the Guardian of this place, I can't allow the Wizard's Council's Sacrifice to be in Vain. If she is who I think she is…she is why I am the Sorceress of Ammora and why this Castle is alive to begin with," she explained gravely.

"For what?" Jarod asked, puzzled.

"To be the Light in the Dark…to stand against the Darkness," the Sorceress replied. "It is why I am here and have been here for so long, Jarod. Now, I do have some questions for you. When you're with this woman, is there anything that she says or does every single time you're with her? How do you feel when you're with her?"

"We usually have a glass or two of wine—"

"How do you feel after that?" the Sorceress asked, looking at him with concern.

"I don't want to be apart from her after that. We usually end up in bed together and talking for hours," Jarod replied.

"I think you weren't just duped, Jarod. I think she's been using a potion to charm you—"

"That isn't possible—" he started.

"It is. Unfortunately, it is," the Sorceress replied. "Whatever she's using, we'll need to give you something so that if she gives it to you again, it won't work."

"I haven't heard of any potion that could charm or guard—"

"It's not just charming you. She was controlling you, making sure that you wouldn't go asking too many questions. You must be building a tolerance to it though, otherwise I doubt you would be here. This is one of the reasons why we can't afford to lose."

"What happens after you defeat her then?"

"Nothing…except continuing to be here to aid those in need. I'm immortal, Jarod. Nothing else…will change."

"That doesn't seem very fair," Jarod observed, looking to her with real concern.

"Life isn't fair, Bra. Tala and I were both cursed with immortality for our bad deeds long ago. We turned over new leaves, began to help others before they became as bad as we were. Nothing changed…the curse doesn't end. But we see it as a good thing now. If we can't die, we can continue to help others. Hell, I can't remember the last time I even aged," Wahya laughed and clapped Jarod on the shoulder.

"I was born immortal, but I've always wondered what it might be like to have been mortal once," Jarod said with a shrug of his own.

"I've almost forgotten what it was like to even be mortal. It's not much different except you get old, things ache…but there are good things about it too," the Sorceress said with a twinkle in her eye. "All right, I need something to charm. Wahya, can you go and bring me two lockets, please, from the treasury?"

"At your service," Wahya replied and headed out into the hall to get them.

"Lockets?"

"They won't know that there's a spell inside this way," the Sorceress explained with a chuckle. "If they ever figure it out, I'll eat my boots."

Jarod thought on that a moment and laughed.

He wasn't a betting man, but he was sure that she was right.

Chapter Thirteen

Derik looked across the table at Jarod with a bit of surprise written all over his face. Ezra couldn't help but smile a little, seeing him so taken aback by Jarod's sudden presence.

::;I take it you forgot to warn Derik that Jarod has come to call?:: she asked Baelios telepathically as she shifted in her seat at the table. The rest of the Castle servants and guards were beginning to eat, as were most of the rest of the residents of the city along with the Dark Elf and Forest Elf Ambassadors and their entourages.

::I did, Ezra, sorry. I was trying to keep everyone from breaking down your door as you were working,:: Baelios replied sounding a little meek and sheepish, his voice a bit higher and sounding a bit like one of the Hive Clansmen. Ezra smiled and resisted the urge to tease Baelios. After all, he had a lot going on upstairs, more than some people she'd met anyway.

A little side-effect of so many people merging into one being, I imagine, Ezra thought quietly as she looked up and down the table.

::Indeed,:: Baelios sent back with a mental chuckle.

She bit back a laugh.

"Jarod is having a problem at his Fortress, Derik. It's why he's here. He's come to ask us for help and well…I'm obligated to help him. I may need your help in this task though, Derik," she said as she picked up a roll and carefully took a bite.

"What? What's the problem and whose ass am I kicking?" Derik asked, leaning forward on his forearms a bit against the table.

"No one's yet. But…I'm thinking I may have you return with Jarod, but in disguise. I won't talk of it too much here. We're just going to discuss it together, the three of us, before we all retire tonight," Ezra replied softly.

"What's with the secrecy?" Derik whispered.

:;Derik, I think I know where those people went…but until I'm absolutely certain, I don't dare say it where EVERYONE can hear! Just drop it for now, please, we'll talk about it *later*,:: she sent telepathically to him. Derik sighed and nodded.

All right, but I want the full story before we go to bed tonight. Where's he sleeping? Derik sent back, albeit much softer than Baelios would. But then, he was just thinking carefully on his answer to her as he wasn't telepathic.

::Jarod will have his old chamber. It's empty anyway and he's just staying the night. He doesn't want to raise any suspicion from his servants or a guest of his that has made herself at home there,:; she sent back with a wink to Derik as she enjoyed her dinner roll.

Okay, I can live with that, Derik thought back at her, and she chuckled.

"So, I understand that things have been interesting here at night, Derik. Mind if I come out to keep watch with you all tonight?" Jarod asked, throwing a bit of a wrench into the plans Derik and Ezra had just silently made.

"Sure, not a problem, Jarod. The more the merrier—a lot of the men are getting overtired. They could use the night off to just rest," Derik replied with a nod. "I was thinking of taking a turn tonight myself for a few hours," he added.

"Thank you. I'd like to see what it is that you all are seeing at night," Jarod replied with a nod as he picked up an apple from the bowl in the center of the table and took a bite.

"You're in for a show then. Oh, and be careful where you step near the moat...we're having to put up warning signs for anyone walking in or taking a sky chariot in," Derik said, watching Jarod intently as if he expected him to attack Ezra at any moment.

"I already found one of your traps today when I arrived, Derik. I took a portal here…you might want to put a warning sign closer to your trap or make it so no one can arrive in that spot and....end up nearly falling into the pit like I did," Jarod said with a look of incredulation on his face.

Derik's jaw dropped and Ezra bit back another chuckle.

::Poor Derik, he really is getting quite a bit of surprises tonight,:: she sent to Baelios.

::Quite so, but well so will Jarod.::

::How so, Baelios?::

::Jarod has no idea that you two are married.::

Ezra nearly fell out of her chair in surprise and steadied herself with one hand quickly.

:;You haven't told him, Baelios?::

::No, Ezra, that isn't mine to tell--::

:;And Wahya has no idea so…oh my. How could I have forgotten to tell him that?::

::Ezra, you are one person who is busier than most mortals or immortals ever are in their entire lifetime,:: Baelios replied. ::Plus your pregnancy is nearing its end, it's just natural that you lost track of a thing or two,:: Baelios replied with a mental chuckle.

::Thank you, Baelios, but…I really don't have an excuse on this one. I should've told him when he arrived but well…it'll be quickly mended,:: Ezra replied as she felt her little one kicking and then stretching inside of her. She just closed her eyes, feeling weary all at once.

::You don't have to push yourself so hard, Ezra,:: Baelios said gently into her mind.

::I know. Well I'm pretty much done with my dinner, best to get this all over and done with,:: she replied as she began to rise up to her feet. Out loud she yawned then said "Okay, why don't you two come up to the library with me for a quick word before I retire for the night," Ezra suggested before she teleported herself directly there.

A moment later, Jarod teleported in next to her with Derik beside him.

"Are you all right, Sorceress?" Jarod asked, concerned as she sank wearily into her chair.

"I'm very tired. This pregnancy is taking a lot out of me these days, Jarod. That and…well…just to tell you for your own information…Derik and I are married," Ezra said as gently as she could.

Jarod took it better than she thought.

"Congratulations to you both," he said with unfeigned joy. "I'm glad you're together and happy. And well…hopefully I can still be a doting uncle on my niece or nephew?" Jarod asked with real emotion in his eyes.

"Of course, Jarod. I'd like that. She should know her family. Well not Juktis but…I have no objection to her having her real uncle to go to as she gets older," Ezra replied as Derik sat down next to her and took her hand in his.

"Agreed. Besides, I know next to nothing about how immortals age as children…could use an uncle dropping in now and then to spoil her and give us both a chance to relax," Derik added, all signs of wariness suddenly evaporating out of him.

Both reactions surprised Ezra, which gave her hope.

Maybe my plan really can work, and they can get to know each other much better, Ezra thought as she relaxed back. She took a breath...and just jumped in with her plan.

Once she had explained it all, she sat back and waited for their reactions.

It was nothing like she expected.

How did I get roped into this? I had just gotten home! Derik thought in exasperation as he toiled away, digging in the trench that would become the new irrigation system for the Fortress.

Jarod had made some good changes here. There were farms up here in the Fortress grounds, thus the need for a new irrigation system. He was trying to make his Fortress independent from the towns at the bottom of the mountain. The reason being that those people needed most of their food there in their own towns and not going up the mountain every season.

It was a good plan; one Derik hadn't expected from the man he had once thought as his rival. After all, they had both vied for Ezra's affections.

But only Derik had captured her heart. Even so, they were family now, of a sort, so that meant he had to suck it up and get along with the man for the sake of Ezra and the child.

The man toiling next to Derik paused as well and looked around.

::See anyone interesting?:; Jarod's voice rang into Derik's mind as they worked together, side by side, in magical disguises that were invisible to all but each other…and Ezra.

Not really, Derik thought back. *Though I intend to try to seduce one of your maids later tonight…see if that gets me any closer to our goal of infiltrating those who are helping this woman you let in.*

:;Good. Try Sira first. She seems to be the looser one of the two, though if she doesn't go for it…try Ayteri. I've noticed they both smell like they've had a roll in the sheets whenever they come in first thing in the morning,:: Jarod replied with a mental chuckle.

The man beside him looked nothing like Jarod. Jarod normally had dark hair and was tall, lean but definitely had seen more than one battle.

The man beside Derik was blonde, still tall, but broader and seemed stronger in general compared to Jarod's leaning physique. He also had a far thicker middle than Jarod did. Jarod's disguised name was Bert. And Derik's was Talun. Easy enough names and easily forgettable, just as they intended them to be.

They continued to work, watching the other men and women. Everyone here seemed honest, hard-working and genuinely interested in just making the Fortress a better place for everyone to live.

Most of the people here aren't the problem. It's just the few bad apples that need to be rooted out, Derik concluded as they trudged back into the Fortress at the end of their shift to get their meal.

For that was another thing that Jarod had done. Juktis had allowed everyone a small, pitiful meal except for his soldiers. Jarod, on the other hand, was generous, making sure everyone got their fill three times per day without ever paying a copper. His wages were fair, and everyone got to buy and own decent clothing, good weapons if they wanted it, and of course a chance to have a family and move away if they wished or to remain and raise their families here.

Everyone, from what Derik could see, was content with their lot.

Of course, the bad apples would put an end to all of that. Derik was certain of it.

As they sat down with the meals and began to eat, Derik saw the little servant, Sira, flirting with a guard at the other end of the room. He winked to Bert aka Jarod…and rose to make his move.

"Greetings…Name's Talun. Nice to meet a beautiful rose, such as yourself," he said in a drawl that he didn't think he could've made before this assignment. Of course, hours with Wahya and Tala had helped him to learn to disguise his accent. They had drilled him endlessly until he had it right.

Sira blushed and giggled as he held out the rose that Jarod had magically sent to him, and it appeared as if he'd pulled it out of thin air. She accepted it and went on a walk with him.

He saw immediately that she was wearing the charm that Ezra had made for her and the other girl to steal.

Perfect, and they're wearing them. That'll give The Sorceress a chance to see whatever it is that they see, he thought, hoping Jarod overheard his thoughts.

:;Good. Let's hope this all pans out and for the better. I'd hate to think that people are being changed into those creatures you showed me before we left. I hope the Sorceress can get a decent glimpse into what's going on in my dungeon,:; Jarod sent back directly into Derik's mind.

Fingers crossed, Derik thought back as he set about seducing the pretty little maid as much as he could without completely betraying Ezra in the bargain.

"What is it that we're watching for again?" Wahya mused as he sat in the library watching the mirror that was active now every hour of the day and night and needed people to watch it.

In the mirror, was a view from the lockets of the two maids as they went about their duties in Jarod's fortress.

"Two maids…and we're waiting to see if they'll go into Jarod's dungeon," Tala replied wearily beside him. They were cuddled up together with a plate of cheese, bread and fruits and were snacking away quietly as they watched the two going about their day.

Lately, it was the closest thing to rest they seemed to get.

"They'd better hurry up. I wanna go and kick a lot of asses over there," Wahya grumbled.

"Ah, c'mon, Big Daddy. You know we'll get that in soon enough. I sent for the kids today and for all of the tribes to come back. Just in case," Tala told him with a grin.

"I love you," he said, feeling his heart melt a bit. That meant that Tala thought that this would be coming to a head soon.

For Wayha, it couldn't come soon enough.

::Any progress?:: Jarod asked a few days later as they sat down for breakfast before going out for their shift.

She's promised to introduce me to a man named Lytarph today. Said she thinks I could be useful to them, Derik thought back as he took a sip of his beer that came with his meal and wished for a tea instead.

The next sip, instead of beer, he discovered it was suddenly changed to a nice black tea, cold not hot…but good enough and even lightly sweetened.

Thanks, Derik thought in genuine appreciation.

:;Can't have you falling asleep on the job nor wishing for the comforts of home. Besides, I'm hoping that we'll be wrapping this up in the next day or two, hopefully sooner. Two weeks of this has been enough but…the Sorceress should be due any day now. Don't want either of us to miss the birth,:; Jarod replied with a wink to Derik.

Derik had become used to hiding his surprise around Jarod lately. But he took a moment, missing Ezra and of course…Jarod was right. She was due literally any day, possibly any moment, now.

I hope she's doing okay, he thought.

::She's an amazing woman, Derik. I'm sure she's managing quite well,:: Jarod replied with a careful, discreet nod back.

I hope you're right. Okay, time to get to work, Derik concluded as he finished his meal and rose with the other workers to get to their shift duties.

The irrigation project was going to be completed today, and for Derik that meant the next stage was going to be even trickier.

"I can't see why you aren't in labor yet, Sorceress. Everything looks great, the baby seems fine… you literally could go into labor at any moment. You've even begun to drop," Eve told Ezra as Ezra sat up and began to pull the lace-up side-seam to her dress closed again.

"Is this normal for a first pregnancy?" Ezra asked as she rose from the table, being careful as she moved, feeling as big as a whale and ready to burst at any time. "Ohhh….I can't wait to get my own body back," she grumbled.

"Not really for a mortal…but immortals might be different. Some mortal women have their babies early, even late. We'll just have to keep an eye on things and see what happens in the days to come," Eve replied as she put an arm around Ezra's shoulders. "In the meantime, I'd like for you to rest and not spend so much time in the library."

"I'll rest when this is all over…if the baby lets me," Ezra replied with a hint of a weary smile. "I have to see this through."

"Just remember to lay down when you get too tired to carry on and to eat, drink and keep everything small. Everything is squished inside so…you're not going to be able to eat or drink as much at once…so I'd keep every meal small and have snacks handy for in between meals, okay?"

"Okay okay…. thank you, Eve. And yeah, I can tell everything is squished in there! I can't wait for this baby to get here," she said before she headed for the library to give Wahya and Tala a rest.

Once there, and alone, she sagged…and hoped to see a hint of Derik today. Even in disguise she could recognize him.

Goddess, I miss him, Ezra thought as she picked up an apple, polished it on a clean cloth…and took a bite.

Then sat up and paid attention as their patience was rewarded…at last.

Chapter Fourteen

Both maids had finally entered the dungeon of the Fortress. Ezra couldn't believe her luck!

::Baelios, call Wahya, Lita, Tala all in here, please! Eve too! I want them all to see this!:: she sent hurriedly as she got out parchment and set a spell for it to write the notes as her mind and eyes took it all in through the mirror.

People hung in shackles just as Ezra remembered them. Though they were fewer but not by many. Fresh prisoners hung where others had hung not long before. And a pale woman with black tattoos, long black hair and clad in a black lace sheath-dress was working in the center of the room.

There were several tanks in the room as well. Though Ezra noted two of those tanks were empty. Kayla was forlornly watching from one, floating at the top where she could breathe in fresh air and save her strength. With dismay, Ezra noted the first signs of sickness in her. She had been there for far too long. Spots of ick were all over Kayla's magnificent blue tail...and she had a defeated look in her eyes as if she never expected to be free again.

I have to get her and the others out of there...and soon! Ezra thought as the maids walked to their Mistress and Ezra finally got a good look at her face. *That's Perothia! She's changed since the last time I saw her...but that's definitely her!* Ezra thought back on their last battle...nearly seven hundred years ago, when Ezra was still learning but was quite capable of defending Ammora after three hundred years of training.

And there was no mistaking the traces of magic that Ezra had sensed…she felt it again, stronger from the charm's presence inside of the Dungeon of the Fortress…where it was thicker, like a taint that stained the very walls of the place with foul magic.

The whole dungeon oozed not of Juktis' magic…but of Perothia's!

The tattoos were familiar…and Ezra thought from where she had seen them before—

The Vision flashed again before her eyes…of herself running through the hallways of Ammora, taunting a woman named Alyra….

"It's her," she breathed in realization.

"Who's her?" Wahya asked as he and the others walked in.

"We've found out who has taken the creatures…and where they are, Wahya. We need to summon Jarod and Derik back…and we need to move quickly—" Ezra started to say when Alyra's voice rang from the mirror.

"Good girls! My pets are well cared for…and tomorrow I shall take another. I'm taking another mermaid…a very special one," Alyra said in a seductive, sensual tone that sent chills down Ezra's spine.

"Oh, what sort of mermaid? A mortal one that I can toy with this time, M'Lady?" A higher pitched squeak of a girl's voice asked from one of the viewpoints of the mirror.

"A queen. I need an immortal mermaid for my next spell…and the Queen of that one's pod…will be just the ingredient I need for my next spell…the spell that will bring Axrealia and even Ammora to their knees at MY feet," Alyra replied as if she were casually discussing the weather.

"Felati…. we need to warn her," Ezra murmured as she listened. "Surala, Reanalia too…it's why the creatures have been at the Dragon's Keep…." She realized and looked at the others.

"Why, Sorceress?" Eve asked, clearly alarmed and puzzled.

"To attack the Queen where they think she'll be at her most vulnerable…" Ezra replied, then she rose to her feet…

They were out of time…and she knew it. The time for disguises and for investigation was over.

Now was the time for action.

"Lita, Call the Council! If they ask why, tell them the Sorceress needs to brief EVERYONE on the plan and that we need to summon as much help as possible—" Ezra started as she began to walk out the door.

"Help's already here, Sista! I summoned the tribes, the hive clans, even the Ogres and both Dark Elves and Forest Elves through our contacts. They just arrived," Tala reported, making Ezra turn and stare at her.

"How did you know?"

"You sent Derik with Jarod. That meant that a battle's brewing. You'd never send him away unless you were *sure* that he could get you some intel…and well while he didn't, your back-up plan *did*. I'll get the leaders of each tribe, clan and well the rest into the Council Chamber, Sista! Hope that you've got a good plan up your sleeve," Tala said as she shook her long blonde hair out of her eyes and gave Ezra a knowing glance along with a smile that showed that Tala was going to welcome the chance to finally fight again.

Ezra couldn't help but hug her, relieved that someone else had realized that this whole mess might have been coming to a head.

"Thank you, Tala," she said. "I…I don't know how to thank you enough—"

"Just doin' what I always do, Sista. Makin' sure we all have what we need…when we need it. Part of my curse, remember? I can sense when things are about to get heated up. I'm just glad that part of it still works right," Tala replied, giving Ezra a gentle squeeze, then nudged her towards the stairs just as gently. "Go to the Council Chamber…we'll all be right behind you."

Ezra couldn't teleport herself fast enough, but then she had to wait for the others to arrive.

Derik and Jarod had just finished their shift and were about to bathe when they both felt a familiar tug in their minds…the warning that Ezra had warned them about in case she needed to pull them through a portal for a briefing. They quickly ducked into an alcove, out of anyone else's sight.

A moment later, they were tumbling, disguises discarded, into the Council Chamber inside of Ammora Castle.

Around them, representatives of most of the residents of Axrealia had gathered along with the Council and at the Center of it all…was Ezra.

Derik looked at her, in awe of her beauty and seeing that the baby had begun to drop. That meant that very soon, she *would* be in labor—

:;Things must be desperate for her to pull us out so suddenly,:: Jarod whispered into Derik's mind. Derik gave a nod and listened as the meeting was called to Order…and Ezra was called upon to speak.

"People of Axrealia…the hour is very dark, and I apologize for the short notice. Lots of people from all over our world have been kidnapped. Many have been changed into undead creatures who are protected by magic from being changed back…and others are hostages being held within Jarod's dungeon in his Fortress. This is *not,* I repeat *not* done with his consent or knowledge…but by a greater threat," Ezra paused to take a breath as she turned around, her eyes seeking each and every person's eyes there before she continued.

"I have been investigating this since the Dark Elves and Forest Elves sent their Ambassadors to Ammora Castle. Since then, I have discovered this problem is like a sickness, feeding upon the very people of our world. It must be destroyed, root and branch…we cannot afford to fail. We must once again go to the Fortress…and fight! Not the people within it, certainly *not* all…but a minor few. I ask you….will we all see this DONE?" Ezra asked the room, looking at them one by one again.

Derik felt so proud in that moment of the love of his life. She was beautiful, she was patient…and right now, she was also deadly. Even though she was heavy with child, he knew that she would do anything and everything to see this enemy brought down.

And he knew he would do anything and everything he could to protect her while she did it.

"AYE!" the room suddenly echoed in unison. Ezra looked around again at them all...and gave a nod.

"Then let's get to work. The Mermaid Queen is in danger…I must go to protect her and take her place. When they try to take her…they MUST think I am her…therefore…we need a place for her to stay here in Ammora for now…Ammora…do you hear me? We need a place for a Mermaid Queen to stay…" and Ezra paused….

And the Castle shook in response, it's living walls moving somewhere within…

Everyone grabbed for something to hold onto as things shifted and changed…and in that moment, Ezra and Ammora's very walls seemed to eerily glow as the lights flickered.

And Derik understood in that moment…

Ezra, and the Castle itself…were the light in the dark.

But would it be enough to drive back the darkness?

"You want to do what?" Queen Felati asked the mirror in Surala's library as she sat up in surprise on her comfortable mermaid-designed seat in Surala's pool.

"You and I need to switch places, your Highness...and we need to do it now. Surala, can you and Reanalia help me, please? You both need to come with her…I won't have either of you in danger," the Sorceress' image that glowed within it explained.

"Wait a moment, don't I have a choice in this matter?" Felati asked, grumbling as she felt anger rising up. First her daughter was taken, now this?

"No. You're in danger…the person who took Kayla wants to take you next. We were just very, very lucky that we found out before they tried to take you. Time is out…I need you to come to Ammora. We have a special room the Castle has designed just for you to stay in so you can transform from your humanoid form to your swimming form with ease. Please…we need all the help we can get, and this may be the only way to bring troops into the Dungeon with as few casualties as possible," the Sorceress patiently explained, looking both desperate…and quite worn out at once.

"All right on one condition. That Surala be there and in on the fight…and me as well. I know how to fight on land…and I'm quite good at it. My guard retinue will come as well to make sure that we get Kayla out safely along with the others," Felati grudgingly agreed.

That took the Sorceress aback and she looked to Reanalia and Surala, both of whom nodded.

"We want in on this, Sorceress. We need to help in any way that we can," Reanalia and Surala both said at once.

After a few moments, the Sorceress gave a nod.

"Very well…but you must help to help secure the other hostages as well, not just Kayla," she said.

"Of course, I wouldn't have it any other way," Reanalia added with a wry grin of her own.

"And I intend to fight these people on my own terms…in my true form. Most will flee if they see a dragon," Surala added with a deadly edge in her voice and a firey glint in her eye.

"Thank you, my friends. Pack your things…and prepare. I will be opening the portal in less than an hour…Surala, please lower your protection spell…we don't want anyone to see us swapping places," the Sorceress told them before her image disappeared from the mirror.

They all looked at each other…and began to get ready.

None of them had nor needed much…but they all had preparations to make.

The scent of blood and battle was practically tangible in the air and the fight hadn't even begun yet.

"Are you sure you don't want me to go with you, Ezra?" Derik asked Ezra when he finally had cornered her, briefly, alone in the hallway. Ezra looked at him in surprise, her eyes meeting him with worry and fear dancing briefly in them…

But there was also a stubborn resolve. One he recognized.

"I'm sure. I need you ready with the others to charge in. When she realizes it's me that she's caught and not Felati…our prey might try to take the baby…or worse," Ezra said in a voice that showed both resolve…with a hint of fear.

"I can protect you—"

"Without magic, you won't be able to bring yourself to me...and her spell or whatever she's planning *might* involve those creatures she's been making. Eve and I are going to try one more time to undo what she did to them…let's just pray I'm right and that it works," Ezra said as she leaned up to kiss him…then hugged and clung to him as if he were her only shelter.

Derik wrapped his arms around the woman he loved and just held her.

There were no words in that moment that needed to be said.

There were only the feelings they both felt and their love for each other.

Goddess be kind...and see us through safely tomorrow, Derik thought, wondering if they would succeed…

Or fail trying to put things right.

Eve was still not happy as she entered the dungeon with the Sorceress. Granted, they had a lot of guards, two of which moved and managed to muzzle and secure the creature so it could not move, no matter what it did.

Not that it doesn't still creep me out! Goddess's tits, that thing is foul! Eve thought as Ezra made to move closer to the thing. Eve caught her wrist, stopping her short.

"We shouldn't get too close," Eve said with concern.

"It's secured and gagged…and I will paralyze it with magic if I must. I try not to do things that way but…this time…" The Sorceress said as she held out a hand and as easily as if she were swatting a fly, then cast a spell on the creature to keep it from moving. "This time, it's a necessity," the Sorceress said, her eyes looking grave and every line of her showing her weariness.

She's pushing herself too hard again, Eve realized as she moved with her.

"You're exhausted! You can't do this—"

"Yes, I can. I'll rest briefly after before I go to the Dragon's Keep. I have to see this through, Eve."

"The risk to you…to the baby—" Eve started.

"Is nothing, compared to the danger that Axrealia now faces. We have our duty, Eve. I will see it through," the Sorceress replied, a sadness almost glimmering in her eyes for a moment before it was concealed. The Sorceress lifted her chin and began to chant, holding out both hands…and began her spell.

Eve sighed and brought her own healing energy to bear on the undead creature.

Chapter Fifteen

People were gathering throughout the city. To hide their numbers, a lot were hidden within Ammora itself, and everyone was preparing. Blacksmiths were at their forges day and night along with the other weaponsmiths. Metal, wood and various other supplies were being brought in. Everyone went out to gather foodstuffs from the farms when they could, but hunters went out to carefully hunt for meat to ensure that no one would go hungry.

Everyone pitched in, everyone was sharing. There was no arguing between the Dark Elves and the Forest Elves. Everyone was working together.

Felati was amazed. She walked in a long linen gown and a pair of the Sorceress' boots with Surala and Reanalia.

"I've never seen the people of our world working together towards a common goal like this before," she admitted to the two women beside her. "They always found a reason to fight and bicker…but everyone is getting along. Even making jokes and boasts to each other," Felati said, just absolutely amazed at the sight she was seeing throughout the Castle.

"We all have a common purpose now. To survive the Darkness our Enemy would send against us," a man said as he appeared right next to Felati, making both Felati and Surala jump. "Oh, sorry…I didn't mean to startle you."

"It's all right, Spirit. Spirit of the Council, this is Queen Felati and Surala, the mage who guards the Dragon's Keep. Ladies, this is the Spirit of the Council. He's part of the package of this place," Reanalia said with a knowing smile and gave the Spirit a wink.

"Oh, the Sorceress mentioned that you would be here to help. Thank you so much for everything, Spirit," Felati said, feeling ashamed at how she'd reacted.

"It's why we are here, Your Highness. To ensure that we all survive. I'm just glad that the Sorceress has finally allowed others to help. For the first thousand years, she wouldn't hear of it," the Spirit chuckled, his voice changing from the tenor voice he'd had a moment ago to a deeper, more humorous Draconic sort of voice.

Felati looked at him in surprise and the Spirit winked.

"That happens, depending on which Wizard from the old Wizard's Council is speaking, Your Highness," the Spirit explained.

"Oh…that's unique," Felati said as she relaxed a little bit, her gaze turning to look over the crowded room.

"Quite unique…that sounds like a Dragon," Surala said with her own fanged smile as she turned to look the Spirit over.

"Half-Dragon, actually," the Spirit admitted, his voice still sounding in that Draconic timber as he chuckled. "Many sorts of creatures made up the Wizard Council before it dissolved in favor of creating our best hope."

"What made you all do it?" Surala asked, and Felati could see the curiosity was eating her up inside. Of course, it was also eating at Felati as well.

"A Vision of the Darkness that is to come…one that would destroy us all," the Spirit explained.

"That bad?" Felati asked.

"Worse. For we didn't see what we now have. A Light to stand against the Darkness for Axrealia. To protect all of Her Creatures," the Spirit replied smoothly before he disappeared again.

Surala and Felati both looked to Reanalia who shrugged.

"You get used to it," she told them. They both gave a nod and continued on with their tour of the Castle.

Ezra had changed back into a mermaid. No one else was in the Dragon's Keep…and she had reestablished the protection spell here and at Ammora to keep magic from being able to just enter here.

Reanalia had given her the basics of how to swim like a mermaid in a brief crash course and of course Felati had left a couple of the devices she would need to breathe under the water for a time. She also had a map of the underwater tunnels that led out of the Dragon's Keep.

And she had disguised herself, to make sure that she looked exactly like Felati.

Using a mirror, she watched the maids again through their charms, waiting for when Perothia, also known as Alyra, would cast her spell.

Derik and Jarod were back at the Fortress. Derik had finally seduced his way into Sira's charms… and had talked her into bringing Bert, the disguised Jarod, along.

After all, they were just two normal men to all around them. Ezra and Jarod had done everything to hide that their disguises were magical.

That was the hope as they followed her downstairs to go to the Dungeon.

And to see with their own eyes the horror that was contained within it.

People were beginning to gather within the Entrance Hall. Felati, her guards, Surala and Reanalia stood with them. Wahya was walking around with Captain Lita, and both were giving instructions together to everyone.

"Be ready. Portals are gonna open. Healers and Mages *first!* After they're through, the portals are gonna close. They'll open a second time and that's when the rest of us go through," Wahya was saying.

"Make sure your weapons are at hand, Mages be ready with the spell that we gave you from the Sorceress. Healers, find a mage and stand with them. We only have one shot at this to save all of the people who were taken. Our target is to capture the Mage who is causing all of this pain and sorrow. She's a woman with black tattoos, dark hair and pale skin. We cannot, I repeat, *cannot* let her escape. Mages, make sure once that spell is cast with the Healer's help that you work to trap her. We must not let her get away," Lita was telling everyone after Wahya had said his bit.

A copy of the spell was handed to Felati as well as to Surala and Reanalia and understanding dawned as to why they would need a healer with them.

Luckily, with all the tribes and the various people that had come, a whole regiment of healers had managed to come with them.

Everyone waited in the Entrance Hall, a pregnant pause in the air as they waited for the first of the portals to open.

Derik and Jarod both nodded politely as they "met" Alyra. She gave a smile that sent a chill down Derik's spine.

"Welcome to the cause, Talun and Bert. Glad to see we have more hands to help with today's…sacrifice. In a moment, I'm going to pull a Mermaid Queen through a magical portal. We're going to use her to power the spell I intend to cast," Alyra said as she walked around them to a table that had been put within the center of the dungeon and lovingly caressed the stone.

It had grooves…and of course chains, one designed for a mermaid. It was also stained with blood.

How long has she been up to this under my very nose? Jarod wondered as he gave a nod and pretended to follow her directions.

"You both will secure her to this table so I can begin to draw on her magic to power the spell," Alyra explained, pointing to two places, which they went to. "It will go quickly and then…the Darkness will fall."

They now knew what her plan was. To unleash the Darkness upon Axrealia.

They also knew it would fail. Felati was not going to be the one taken.

Derik gave Jarod a look as Alyra began to cast her spell. It was a long one and she swayed and chanted, dancing almost in the dim candlelight while the other prisoners against the walls were forced to watch.

Thank goodness this Dungeon is as big as it is. We'll need the space, Jarod thought as he glanced about discreetly while they waited.

The wind began to pick up inside of the Dungeon, whipping hair and cloaks alike about. An eerie, sickly green glow began around Alyra as the candles blew out.

Ezra watched as the spell began. She could sense something reaching out. In her disguise, she knew in that dim light, she would easily be mistaken for Felati.

Now, she thought as she dove, down through the tunnels and came out just beyond her spell…and headed towards the cove where Kayla was taken from. She sensed the magic reaching out for her and put a burst of speed on that she hadn't thought was possible in her pregnant state as she hurried towards the graveyard. She dodged around a bit, sensing the magic reaching out, trying to catch her. *Gotta give her a really good chase,* Ezra thought as she dodged again, hoping to frustrate her prey just a little so that Alyra would feel just a taste of triumph…

That was the plan, at least.

"Clever little Mermaid…but you can't outrun me forever," Alyra muttered in the center of the room as Jarod and Derik both continued to watch.

Derik shifted, wishing he could just kill the bitch now before she could do anything else.

::Don't interfere, Derik. Besides, this woman…isn't mortal. I thought she might be at first, but what I'm sensing from her now…she isn't mortal. She's at least as old as the Sorceress is and nearly as powerful,:: Jarod whispered into Derik's mind.

Wonder what the Sorceress is doing if she's having a hard time catching her, Derik thought back as he saw that Alyra seemed to be getting frustrated. Sweat beaded her brow and she was starting to tremble with the effort of bringing her prey to her.

::;Probably giving her a very good chase…but that's what the real Queen would do as well. Can't exactly have her catch her too soon, or she'll know something isn't right,:; Jarod replied quietly.

I hope she wears her out a little then. We need all the help that we can get, Derik thought back as he watched Alyra struggling, trying to reign in her prey.

Ezra dodged the spell again, feeling it chasing her…almost toying with her as she dodged and swam, pushing herself to make sure that she wore the caster out just a little bit.

I've got to make sure that she's a little on the weak side. Tired. I can't afford for her to have any advantages, Ezra thought as she made it at last to the ship graveyard and hid quickly in one of the ships. Finding an air bubble, she swam up and removed the device for a moment, taking a breath of air as she waited, sensing the spell searching again for her…and pretending to be scared. Her heart was racing in her chest and within, she felt the baby stretching briefly before it settled.

After a few moments, she put the mask of the breathing device back on…and dove again, feeling that searching spell seeking her again.

Alyra smiled grimly suddenly.

"Got you, Little One," she said in triumph as the spell suddenly burst forth and became a maelstrom…

One that was reaching out and pulling something into the center of the room.

::Be ready,:: Jarod whispered into Derik's mind. Derik gave him a nod and prepared himself for the act of his life.

Ezra felt the maelstrom as it began to suck her in, water and everything around her was pulled down into a gaping maw of sickly greenish light! Ezra screamed, reaching in vain out of instinct to try and save herself—

And felt the wood give way under her fingertips as she was ripped into the whirlpool that had appeared so far under the water.

The world spun, pulling, stretching. Ezra felt the mask being ripped from her face by the water and struggled, unable to take a breath as the world tilted…

The water suddenly disappeared as she fell onto hard stone, landing on her back. Stunned, she lay there a moment, groaning as she looked up at a very dark room. Her eyes seemed to take forever to adjust as she heard people moving about and then the light flared from the candles spread about the massive dungeon, making her eyes burn and water in response.

"What is this? You aren't the Queen I intended to take!" She heard an all too familiar voice ring out above her.

Ezra looked up and smiled…and waved her hand, opening the portals while simultaneously changing herself back into her normal form. As Ezra struggled to rise, all hell broke loose!

Chapter Sixteen

It was Chaos as the first portals opened. Healers and Mages rushed for their assigned portals, including Felati, Surala and Reanalia along with Felati's guards. They all had a healer beside them, and the first priority was to do what they could to create as much chaos as possible and to help any creatures that might be in the room by returning them to their original forms.

Pouring out of the portal, Felati barely got a glimpse of the Sorceress as she changed and rose with real effort to her feet before the Sorceress was helping to create the shield. The portals closed and they all looked about.

::I don't see any creatures. Just hostages and the Sorceress and four others—:: Felati sent.

::They aren't in here, but I smell them nearby. Stay alert and ready, in case they suddenly come pouring in,:; Surala sent back to her and Reanalia.

They kept the shield up, guarding as the next portals opened...then released the shields.

Ezra was on her feet. That was the last that Derik got a chance to see before the portals opened and healers and mages poured out. The shield was set up, to protect the next set of portals that opened. How Ezra was coordinating everything, Derik had no idea.

Now the warriors were pouring out with weapons drawn and ready—

And Jarod broke the spell disguising himself and Derik. Derik ran to Ezra's side who just shook her head and called "We need to get her—now! I'll keep her busy, just watch my back," Ezra told him as she raised her hands.

It was just bad luck that a man carrying a woman over his shoulder happened to walk into the Dungeon right at that moment.

Vincent had returned to the Fortress to deliver another quarry. He headed downstairs; the woman hidden in a rug until he reached nearly the bottom. Then he unwrapped his gift, opened the door…

And walked into Chaos.

Ezra saw the man walking in with another young woman, completely tied up and drugged from the looks of things, over his shoulder. In that moment, everyone in the room turned…and everything, for just a moment was quiet. Everyone stared at the interloper, some in disbelief. Others in grim purpose.

"Put her DOWN!" Ezra commanded him immediately, using her magic to force him to put his captive down. He gently lay down the bundle just inside the door and two of the warriors took the woman, untied her and sent her back through the portal with the help of a healer.

Ezra looked at Alyra and her gaze narrowed. Ezra raised a hand, and with her magic, picked up the man who had been delivering his prey to this foul wench...and tossed him into the wall so hard the entire dungeon could hear the crack as all of his bones simultaneously shattered, leaving him a bloody mess as he dropped to the floor.

Alyra laughed.

"If you think that was my only servant, you are mistaken, woman," Alyra said as she raised her hands. Magic spells began to fly through the air between them. Fire, snow balls, lightning all flew between the pair.

To add to the chaos, another door opened somewhere…and then Ezra could hear them…smell them. The creatures had been unleashed!

Surala was still with her healer, darting as spells began to fly through the air between the Sorceress and the enemy, Alyra. Suddenly, a door flew open, and creatures poured in and all the candles blew out. In the Darkness, Surala heard panicked cries from those who couldn't see.

And the Sorceress suddenly began to Glow…

::She's making herself a target!:: Felati cried into Surala's mind.

::No…she's making herself a beacon! She's lighting up the room, look!:; Surala sent back as she transformed herself in that moment into her full Draconic form. "On my back, we're going in," Surala cried as she swept her own healer up onto her back with a single set of claws.

Felati and Reanalia and their healers followed suit and the six of them began to work together as Surala dove into the chaos, running, dodging, tossing a man that appeared with a sword in his hand---a man with a goatee and black hair—casually into the wall.

"Maron!" Alyra cried as the body flew past her before it hit the stone and fell never to rise again.

The two servant girls were the next to fall to Surala's claws.

"That's for stealing and betraying Axrealia!" Surala snapped as the two servant girls were pounced once with Surala's full weight, leaving them as nothing more than bloody lumps before she surged gracefully into the center of the creatures. "NOW!" Surala screamed as they all began to caste the spell together, healers and mages all united through contact.

The spell glowed…and then erupted out in burst of light from the six of them, bathing the whole room in nothing *but* light!

And as the light faded…Surala saw that the creatures that had burst in had been changed back into the people they had been!

"We did it!" Felati cried, seeing about 30 more people standing around them, weak but alive once more…and whole!

Derik hid his eyes as the flash of light erupted through the room! And confusion happened in that moment as the warriors surged forward to rescue the unsteady people on their feet while freeing prisoners along the walls and taking them all through the portal.

He also saw two Warriors fishing out the one lone mermaid in her tank and fleeing with her through one of the portals to where the healers were now retreating to begin taking care of casualties. Half would remain here; half would go back to Ammora.

That was the plan anyway.

But then the door opened again…and warriors poured through it, all with weapons drawn and Derik found himself busy defending himself and Ezra against those that flooded in.

"Got ya, Bra," Wahya said as he blocked a blow that would've taken Derik's head off if Wahya hadn't been there.

"Thanks!" Derik cried back as they continued to fight.

Jarod growled as he saw his own warriors, at least thirty of them, pour in with their weapons drawn. He growled and leapt in, fighting them with magic and his own sword, refusing to give any of them that fought for her any mercy.

"After this, I am not taking anyone else's *word* that someone is trustworthy!" He snapped as he fought beside Derik and Wahya. While magic soared through the air behind them between the Sorceress and Alyra. Spell after spell rang out, some came so close to hitting Jarod, he could feel his own skin nearly sizzle or grow cold in response.

The warriors were very good, which is something that Jarod was both proud and resentful of. They had trained daily, trained hard in fact, but here they were, fighting against the very people he had brought in to help Him regain some sense of control!

"ENOUGH!" Jarod yelled as he took the head of the commander and held it up. "Stand BLOODY DOWN or I will send all of you, ALL of you to the bloody hells!" Jarod screamed at his own men.

The men looked at him, looked at each other…shrugged, and the fight began anew.

"So be it then!" Jarod growled as he and the other warriors that had come to defend Axrealia fought tooth and nail, sword and dagger, and laser gun alike for their world.

Surala growled, seeing that the Lord of this Fortress wasn't getting the respect that he was due from his own men.

"Cowards," she muttered as she took a breath…

And rained down ice all over the enemy warriors in front of her, taking out at least 10 of them in one blow. A quick stomp of her foot and the ice shattered, along with the encased flesh. Surala continued to dart and weave amongst those in the dungeon, intent on keeping Felati and Reanalia safe while wreaking as much damage as possible on the enemy.

Derik was having a hard time staying right beside Ezra. Warriors were coming at him from all sides, but he wasn't giving it up. Jarod was to his right, Wahya and some of the hive people and the Dark Elves and Forest Elves were to his left! Each time an enemy fell, more seemed to pour in!

"Where are they all coming from?" Derik called.

"She must've corrupted most if not the entire regiment of Warriors that had remained here," Jarod called back. "That or they're under a spell—"

"Check for one!" Derik called back. Jarod looked at him in surprise then as more of Wahya's tribe members and some Ogres came up beside him on the right, Jarod took a step back, held out a hand and concentrated.

Jarod was surprised! Surprised that Derik would actually think that his warriors could be controlled! *That would explain why they keep coming even though no one has sounded an alarm,* Jarod thought as he reached out with his magic, gauging the warriors, looking for traces of magic.

And found it! Alyra's sickly green taint was over every single one of the warriors.

"She's controlling them with magic!" Jarod exclaimed as he examined the spell.

"Can you break it, Bra?" Wahya called as he and Derik tossed another one or two back.

"I can try! Get me some more mages, we'll give it a shot!" Jarod called back.

"Mages, OVER HERE!" Lita cried as she came up to join the fight to keep the Sorceress protected.

Ezra heard a cry for mages, but she couldn't break off her concentration. She was focused, completely focused, on Alyra.

She was vaguely aware that the people behind her were working on keeping her safe. She was also vaguely aware that they were discussing the possibility that Alyra was controlling the warriors that had poured in.

None of that mattered in this moment. All that mattered was that she was facing off against the Darkness.

I can't afford to lose, Ezra thought as she readied another spell.

Surala heard a call for mages, and she turned lightly on her feet and ran over to Jarod and Derik, taking up a quick position in front of them and growling. The warriors didn't seem perturbed in the least and she readied another blast of icy cold breath to unleash on them.

"Surala, we need your help," Felati called, making her pause.

"Surala, join the spell with us," Jarod called behind her and she threw them both lines of her own energy while continuing to intimidate the enemies before her.

Another spell blasted out this time, it radiated from them, going through everyone, coating everyone in blue light for a moment—

Then half of the enemy warriors seemed to wake up and look around.

The other half continued on as if nothing had happened.

"What happened?" Felatia called.

"Only half were being controlled! This lot threw in their loyalty to her!" Jarod called back with a growl.

"So, what do we do now?" Felati called again.

"Keep fighting!" Surala growled and unleashed her icy blast on a warrior that was seeking to take her head and threw him with a flick of her tail as she turned to trample another one with a sword in his hands, seeking to try to hamstring her. Surala chuckled. "It's been centuries since I've had a fight like this!"

Alyra looked around her. Vincent and Lytarph were both dead. Sira and Ayteri were nothing but broken lumps of dead flesh upon the floor.

Her creatures were healed and changed back into their original forms. All of her plans...and it was all for nothing!

Even her warriors that she had thought were under her firm control had been released from the spell that forced them to fight with their fellows that had pledged their loyalty to her.

All for nothing! At least I still have my cave. I'll begin anew, Alyra thought, realizing that now was the time for retreat.

She glared back at the Sorceress and raised her hands.

"Time for me to be going," she said with a smirk.

Ezra heard Alyra over the din.

"You're not going anywhere," she snapped, trying to set up the containment spell as quickly as she could—

And suddenly Alyra was gone as if she'd never been, having fallen through the floor—

And her own shadow.

"No!" Ezra screamed as she tried to stop her, tried to keep her from getting away—

But it was too late!

To cap it all, the baby decided that now was the time to be born! Her water broke, it poured down her legs in a gush of unexpected fluid.

"Derik! The baby!" she cried, grasping her stomach as a strong contraction hit, stealing her breath for a moment as she sank to the floor.

Derik turned as Surala stomped the last of the warriors behind him, picked her up and dashed for the portals.

"Eve, we need you!" he called over his shoulder before he carried Ezra through. Ezra could only breathe and hold herself as he took her home.

"We have a problem, Sorceress. The Dragon's Egg...is hatching!" Baelios reported as he popped into existence right next to them in the Entrance Hall.

Ezra looked up at Baelios in dismay and groaned.

"I can't do anything, Baelios…we need Surala," she said as Derik held her. "I want my chambers, Derik…please," she moaned softly in pain, hiding her face in his chest.

"I'll fetch Surala," one of the other healers said as Eve came to touch Ezra's stomach with surprisingly gentle hands.

"You're at the beginning of active labor, Sorceress. Derik, take her to your chambers, put her in the rocking chair and have her rock. It'll help her to relax and help to move things along. I'll be there as quickly as I can to check on her," Eve said before turning her hands back to heal the wounds of those who had been hurt in the battle.

Derik gave a nod and began to carry his wife, the Sorceress, back to their Chambers.

"Hang in there, Sorceress. I'm here," he murmured as he carried her as carefully as he could.

Surala and the others had finished the fight! Healers were everywhere, helping those who could be helped while Wahya and Tala walked from person to person, giving water to those who couldn't be saved and helping to encourage those who would survive to change their ways.

"Lady Surala…the Sorceress needs you back at the Castle," one of the healers called. Surala turned, puzzled and said "Me?"

"Yes, you. The Spirit will explain when you return," the healer said as she motioned to the middle portal that was still open.

"Thank you. Felati?"

"We're fine. I'm going to tend to Kayla now," she said as she left the clean up to her guard retinue for now and came to follow Surala back through the portal. Surala had shifted back into her Elven form and walked through so she wouldn't accidentally step on someone on the other side.

She had no idea why they needed her, but she would do whatever she needed to help her new-found friends.

Alyra fled through the shadows from the Fortress. The Realm of Shadows was her second home and it helped to shorten the journey for her.

Her cave was far from here, but she knew she would make it in a few days. She had to exit from a shadow at the base of the mountain that housed the Fortress, then she began to run on foot.

Her creatures had been saved and turned back into the people they had been. Her allies were gone, dead and flattened.

But she had been planning this for a very long time. She just had to get back home, back to where she would be able to regain her strength.

The Cave was the best place to go. As the sun was rising, the shadows became shorter, smaller. She would have to wait until the sun set and darkness of Night came in.

It would link the shadows and make the journey home much shorter…at least for a few hours. She was tired, so tired as she

found a nice dark cove at the base of the Mountain and disguised it
with her magic. Alyra curled up and let her eyes close, allowing
herself to fall into dreamless slumber.

Chapter Seventeen

Ezra was tired. Oh, so tired! She was feeling the after-effects of the battle now as she rocked wearily in the rocking chair in her chambers.

"Derik, I want to lie down," she said, feeling so drained that she doubted that she would have the energy to push.

"If Eve says you can, Ezra. Hang in there a little longer," he encouraged as he offered her some water and kissed her cheek.

"Then send for her, I want to lie down," Ezra said, wondering why in the world no one would let her do as she wanted. She felt shaky and weak and just wanted to sleep—

::Ezra, sleeping might not be the best thing yet though I'll ask Eve if you may,:: Baelios whispered into her mind. Ezra sent him a flash of wordless gratitude and just tried to keep her eyes open as she waited.

Baelios appeared a few moments later right next to Derik.

"Eve says she can lie down and rest if she needs it, that it sometimes takes a while before the baby comes anyway," Baelios told him as he began to help Ezra up to her feet. Derik got up as well and between the two men, she found herself cradled and taken to her bed before sinking gratefully into its soft mattress.

"Thank you, Baelios," Ezra murmured as she closed her eyes, letting herself fall asleep.

Derik looked down in concern as he saw Ezra drift off so fast. He looked at Baelios, the worry written in his eyes.

"Eve said that taking a nap might help the labor to progress a bit faster and that when it's time, Ezra should wake up on her own," Baelios said gently as he touched Derik's shoulder. "I'll be back in a bit. I need to take Surala to the Nesting Chamber."

Baelios disappeared again, leaving Derik alone. Derik slid into the bed next to his wife, curled up with her and just held her, letting her rest while laying a hand against her belly.

It was wonderous to him as he fell her belly continuing to tighten, then soften with each contraction. How Ezra slept through it, he didn't know but he just stayed with her, holding her, and felt so proud of her.

Ezra, you're the most incredible woman I've ever met, Derik thought as he kissed her shoulder and just waited for Eve to arrive.

Surala looked around at the chaos that was still going on. Healers and others who weren't hurt were bustling about, helping those who were injured.

Suddenly, the Spirit popped in next to her and Felati again.

"Kayla is in your chamber, Your Highness. Surala, please come with me," he said as he turned to walk out into the hallways.

"Sure, but aren't I needed here?" she asked.

"No, but I'm taking you to where you are needed," the Spirit replied. Surala looked at Felati who motioned her to go on.

"Go on, I'll see you later," she said as she hurried into the hallways herself to go to her own private chamber.

Surala shrugged and followed the Spirit then through the winding hallways, in through what looked like a private Mage's work room…and down into the depths of the Castle.

The stairs led down into an open, very warm chamber! In the center was a nest with a single Dragon's Egg.

And the Egg was glowing!

Surala moved towards it, seeing the small cracks developing as the creature inside struggled to hatch.

"The Sorceress is in labor and neither of us know how to take care of a Dragon hatchling," the Spirit explained then as Surala looked the egg over.

It was perfect, well-cared for and the baby Dragon inside was the healthiest she had seen.

"We need to make this chamber a little more humid to soften the egg-shell, Spirit. Can I have a little water and some stones to put into the fire so I can create steam?"

"Of course," the Spirit replied and disappeared. A few moments later, he popped back into existence and began to put the stones into the fire in a little cairn formation to let them heat up. Then, he took a dipper from a water bucket and poured it over the stones, and Surala took in that steam with relief.

"It's been a long time since I've attended a hatching," she told him as she shifted back into her dragon from and gently nudged the egg. "Come on, little one. I know how strong you are…use your teeth and your nose…you can do it," she encouraged gently as she curled about the nest and began to sing a Draconic lullaby to the little one inside its egg.

"How long does it take for a Dragon to hatch?" the Spirit asked out of curiosity.

"Sometimes it's as long as it takes a woman to give birth," Surala replied with a grin. "And sometimes the little one needs help. I'm honored that you trusted me with this, Spirit. Thank you," she said as she settled in for the wait and continued to sing.

"You're welcome. If you need anything else, just ask and I'll hear you," the Spirit said before he disappeared again. Surala chuckled and went back to singing, singing to the little one of the big skies it would soar, the waters it would swim, the fires it would breathe. All of the lore of the Dragons that she remembered from her youth she began to pour forth into her song.

Each Hatchling had a unique song from its mother normally. But this little one was an orphan.

And Surala had no children.

Come on, little one. I won't let you down, I promise, she vowed silently, feeling as much love for this little Dragon as she had ever felt for anyone.

And more.

Eve slipped into the Sorceress' chambers, trying to be as quiet as possible as she moved to check the Sorceress.

Eve was weary, blood-spattered and a bit of a mess, but she wasn't about to let the Sorceress down.

Derik stirred as she came close to the bed and Eve smiled, resting a hand on the Sorceress' belly next to his and used her healer's senses to see what was going on.

Inside, the babe was getting close to its big arrival. It wasn't quite there yet, but it would be very, very soon.

"How is she doing?" Derik whispered to Eve as she lifted her hand away.

"Very well. We'll need to wake her soon, but I'm going to go and get cleaned up a little first. Then we'll get ready for this baby to finally arrive," she whispered back, glad that thus far, this birth seemed to be on track.

"Thank you, Eve," he whispered back as he settled back down. Eve's heart went out to them both. They were both so tired, exhausted, from the battle.

And now they had another about to truly begin. The birth of their baby. Eve slipped back out and went to her own chambers to get cleaned up and smiled as she saw Phyla already in the tub.

"I have wine, I have cheese, bread and fruit…and a nice hot bath," Phyla said as Eve walked over to her lover and leaned in to give her a hot, passionate kiss.

"The Sorceress' baby is coming. I'm going to be up a while yet, but I wanted to get cleaned up before it's time to deliver the little one."

"Oh, well let me help! I'll play assistant to you, and we'll celebrate after," Phyla replied as she helped Eve to get out of her tunic and leggings.

Eve laughed and kicked off her shoes and slipped into the tub with her, nearly flooding it as they spent a few precious moments alone together.

Surala continued to sing. She was beginning to feel tired as the adrenaline from the battle ran out of her veins. She didn't sleep though. The egg was beginning to rock and glow.

It won't be much longer now, Surala thought as she nudged the egg again gently, crooning to it and seeing the cracks getting bigger and bigger along the sides of the shell.

Ezra woke as the contractions got worse! She sat up with a cry of pain and clutched her belly just as the door opened and Eve and Phyla swept into the room.

"Ah, just in time," Eve said as Derik sat up next to Ezra and stroked her hair. "Breathe deep breaths, relax, Sorceress. It isn't going to be very long I think, you were nearly fully dialated when I last checked on you."

"Wait, you checked on me?" Ezra asked, not remembering that at all.

"You were deep asleep, and I wasn't about to wake you. You needed to rest for this moment. And now…you're finally going to get to meet your little one," Eve said as she slipped on some gloves and parted Ezra's legs. The Skirt of Ezra's dress was pushed up and Ezra felt her head dress and the smaller cuff about her neck being removed. She looked up and saw Baelios putting them on her dresser before he settled down on her other side, cradling her as Derik was. "Okay, boys, lift her legs a little bit, give her something to push against. Now, Sorceress…I want you to push, bear down with everything you've got on the next contraction. Take a deep breath in! Now push!"

Ezra took a deep breath as she felt the next contraction hit just then and pushed down hard, as hard as she could! She took another breath and pushed again while Phyla and Eve both encouraged her, even counting to ten to help her. She took a breath, rested as Eve told her to wait for the next contraction and pushed again!

In that moment, there was nothing but a fight, a fight to push this baby out of her at last.

Pain seared through her loins, a burning sensation hitting her as she struggled to push again.

"Come on, don't give up on me now. It's going to hurt, but it'll pass, I promise! Push, Sorceress, push!" Eve exclaimed, and somehow Ezra found the strength to push and to keep pushing!

Surala gasped as she saw the little dragon push out a chunk of eggshell, making its nose appear. It rested, a dark eye looking up at her from the little missing piece in its shell.

"Hello there, little one. Welcome to the world. Come on now…you have this. You can push your way out," she crooned to the little dragon, watching it as it watched her with a tenderness she'd never felt for anyone or anything before.

Is this what a mother feels like for the first time? She wondered.

Ezra screamed briefly before she pushed again! She felt the baby moving out and down—

Then suddenly the baby seemed to just tumble out of her! She lay back, crying out in relief and surprise and looked as the baby began to cry to Eve. Eve was holding the baby cradled in one arm and doing what she had to do to clear the little one's airways.

"It's a girl!" Eve said with a happy smile as the baby began to cry.

Ezra began to sob in relief as she heard those cries, leaning into Baelios and Derik, her lifelines through all of this.

"Congratulations," Phyla said as she took the baby from Eve once Derik had cut the umbilical cord. Phyla turned to go and clean the little one up over at a station she and Eve had set up with warm, damp towels. Diapers and baby clothes sat next to the damp towels and Phyla began to hum soothingly as the baby protested against being cleaned.

"One more push, Sorceress," Eve said then. Ezra looked down at her, surprised. "For the afterbirth," Eve explained, and Ezra whimpered.

"Do I have to push?"

"Just one more big one and then you can rest, I promise," Eve said in a gentle tone. Ezra took one more breath and pushed, feeling something else slide out. "That's it, got it. Nothing's broken, it's perfect," Eve said as she rose to go and wrap it up in a bit of cheese cloth. "I'll have the servants dispose of it later," she promised as she went back to Ezra and began to clean her up.

Shortly after, Ezra was helped out of her bed and two servants came to change the bed sheets. Eve helped her into a clean set of clothes and finally Ezra was allowed to lay down again…

And hold her baby. Ezra looked down at that perfect, tiny face and felt her heart melting as she cradled her in her arms. The baby looked up at her as if she knew her and Ezra kissed her tiny fingers.

"She should nurse then you both need some rest," Eve said and began to explain how to nurse the baby.

Ezra followed her directions, feeling a little awkward but soon the little one was suckling happily away.

"Do you have a name for her?" Phyla asked.

"We haven't discussed it," Derik said as he looked at Ezra, puzzled. Ezra smiled and she kissed him, feeling a surge of love for him. He might not be the child's biological father, but she knew that he would be the best father her child could ever have.

"It's okay, I have one for her already, Derik. It's Angelica," Ezra said as she looked down at her small daughter. "Our little Angelica," she added, feeling so tired and not wanting to close her eyes again just yet.

The baby was nearly out of its shell…and at last it finally broke the last pieces away and crawled awkwardly towards Surala, who picked the baby up in her claw and brought her to her chest.

"Welcome to the world, Little one," she told the hatchling, seeing that it was a female Dragon, healthy and whole and cradled her against her big scaley chest.

The baby hiccuped and a little bit of water vapor blew through the air, making Surala chuckle.

"Spirit, we need some fish or some chicken of some sort, please," Surala said out loud to the empty chamber.

"Cooked or raw, Lady?" the Spirit asked as he appeared again next to her out of thin air.

"Cooked. When they're little, Dragons need cooked meat though later on they can eat raw," Surala replied, completely enraptured by the little one in her arms.

The little dragon was blue-green with streaks of black and beautiful startling Pink eyes. Her wings and her claws were webbed, perfect for swimming and there was a little fluffy tuft at the end of her tail, which would smooth out later to become more rudderlike in the water.

She's a water dragon, Surala realized and felt almost a sense of prophecy. *No wonder she and the Sorceress' baby are bound together. They'll be a good team, able to take things on and face them together.* Surala chuckled as moments later, a platter of cooked fish and game bird appeared next to her. She picked up a bit of fish first in her claws and offered the bit of food to the baby, watching in pride as the little one scarfed it down…

As if she was meant to be her mother all along.

Chapter Eighteen

Derik rose to answer the door as he heard a knock the next morning. Ezra was still asleep as was the baby, Angelica…his daughter. He might not be her biological father, but he already loved the child as if she were his own.

He pulled his robe on and cracked open the door a little to look to see who it was, then slipped out into the hallway when he saw it was Lita.

"Greetings, Lita. What's going on?" he asked as he tied his robe closed and shut the door behind him so their voices wouldn't wake Ezra or the baby.

"Ambassadors Talice and Suidan are asking if we're going to have the tournament now that the danger has passed. It seems their rulers are wanting to stay a few more days and everyone wants to celebrate the birth of the baby and the victory at the Fortress," Lita explained. "But I didn't know if it would be a good time—"

"It might be a good idea. The battle wasn't nearly as bad as the last one, but it could help to eat up everyone's leftover energy. How much time would you need to finish putting it together?" Derik asked as he shifted on the balls of his feet.

"Two days at most. We've got prizes and categories and with this many people here…it'll probably be a big event," Lita replied with a chuckle and a gesture down the hallway, where various people from all over Axrealia were waiting for Lita to tell them whether or not the tournament was back on.

"Then let's get started," Derik replied. "I'll get dressed and I'll come down to help you finish making the arrangements as much as I can—"

"Oh, no need, Derik. Wahya and Tala said they'd both help out. You should rest and help the Sorceress with the baby. And are the two of you ever going to get married?" Lita asked. "Because we could have a priest marry you at the tournament—"

"We did get married, quietly, and only before the Gods, Lita. The Sorceress didn't want a big ceremony and neither did I. We just wanted to do it quietly and without a lot of fanfare. There was just so much going on, we just didn't tell anyone is all," Derik told her, giving her a wistful look as her hopeful face fell.

"Oh…well can we at least pretend—"

"No. We're married and we're happy. We can have a reception if you want after the tournament, but that's it," Derik told her, glad to see her smile brighten again as he promised her that. *Ezra'll kill me later for it, but well this'll kill the protests about not having a big ceremony,* Derik thought with a tinge of regret that he'd have to subject Ezra to a little more fanfare than she had wanted.

"Deal. Are you going to enter the tournament?"

"Of course. I told you I would the first time," Derik laughed, feeling better now that the danger was over…for now anyway.

"Good. I'm going to make sure that everyone has a great time," Lita promised as she turned and briskly walked down the hallway. "Okay, Everyone, we have a lot to do! The tournament is back on! Everyone go to my office down in the city and those who are signing up had better come in and sign up today! Everyone else, come by so we can get this thing put together!" Lita called and the crowd at the end of the hallway cheered!

Derik laughed and went back into his and Ezra's chambers. He was still weary after the battle and wanted to be close to his family. Ezra *had* just given birth, after all.

Wahya and Tala already had their marching orders, so to speak. Tala tackled the arrangements for the party that would be happening after the tournament to celebrate the tournament, the victory, the birth of the Sorceress' baby…and the marriage of the Sorceress and Derik.

"Wonder when they had time to pull that off," Tala muttered as she sat down with the cooks that would be working night and day to feed everyone for this big grand affair. She looked over the inventory list and hoped to the Gods that it would be enough to feed everyone not just for the party but for the next few days.

Next to her, Wahya and Aeryn were going over the last of the plans for building the last section of the stadium where everyone would be watching. Including a nice box for the Sorceress, her family and the more important guests to watch under a nice big pavilion to keep the sun off of them.

Probably best for the baby, otherwise the poor little thing might get sunburned. Don't want that to happen, immortal or not, Tala thought as she picked out the more appropriate solutions for entrees for all of the different people to choose from. Each sort of people tended to have their own specific idea of what was appropriate to eat or were limited by what their bodies could consume. Tala didn't want anyone walking away from this affair complaining of hunger.

Luckily, the cooks agreed with her. They had the menu completed in short order and the cooks and their assistants all got up to begin the preparations for the feast. Until the tournament, everyone would be getting a quick and easy meal for each time—things that could fill everyone up in short order and yet needed no cooking. Pickles, salads, cheeses and of course smoked meats and hard-boiled eggs would all be served for the humans and for most of the rest of the peoples gathered. Everyone else would be getting whatever their customs or bodies demanded so long as it didn't need to be cooked ahead.

As a result, it would give the cooks more time to concentrate on what needed to be made ahead for the feast.

Tala headed out with Wahya and his crew to help them with the last of the construction and was surprised to see a slew of others coming out to help from every party that was currently staying in the Castle.

Jarod looked up as he felt a mental summons and was surprised to see the Spirit of the Council was the one calling from Ammora Castle.

"Greetings, Spirit. What can I do for you today?" Jarod asked as he settled himself down in front of the mirror.

"Greetings, Lord Jarod. Ammora Castle is hosting a tournament in two days if you'd like to attend. The baby is fine and healthy. You have a beautiful new niece," the Spirit informed him.

"Of course, Spirit! I'd love to attend. Is there anything that they need for the baby? And what's her name?" Jarod asked, feeling a surge of pleasure at the news of having a niece to spoil.

"They really don't need anything, Lord Jarod, but I'm sure if you wish to give them something for her, they'll be pleased to receive it," the Spirit replied smoothly. "And of course, they'll be glad that you're coming for the tournament."

"What time do I need to be there by?" Jarod asked.

"The tournament begins just after mid-day, so if you arrive at mid-day that should suffice."

"I'll be there in two days at midday then. Thank you very much, Spirit," Jarod said as he wrote it down so he wouldn't forget. With people needing help and having to replace a lot of troops that had betrayed his people, Jarod knew he still had a lot on his plate.

"We'll see you then, Lord Jarod. I wish you well in the meantime," the Spirit said before the contact was severed. Jarod rose and hurried to begin making his own preparations. After all, a tournament would need fighters and spectators and he knew a lot of his people could use a decent diversion.

Wahya looked to Tala, Aeryn, Bear and the others that were helping him to build the last section of the stadium that needed to be completed.

The sun was already beginning to sink in the horizon, but they were nearly done. Wahya knew if they pushed it, they would be done with this and there was still more to do tomorrow.

"All right, Bras and Sistas! Come on…let's push this Mother up onto her feet! Ready? One….two….THREE! PUSH!" With a roar, Wahya pushed with all his might along with the others in the line.

With a groan of wood, the stadium section rose up and flipped onto its feet into the foundation they had prepared for it. And stayed up. The men and women all looked up at what they had accomplished, panting and sweating.

"Great work! Hit the baths! Get something to eat, we've got more to do tomorrow," Tala, ever the taskmistress, called as she motioned for them all to head back to the city or castle. Wahya took her hand and walked with her, still breathing hard towards the castle. "You all right, Big Daddy?" she asked him as they walked.

"Yeah, just sore and tired, Tala. I'll be all right," he admitted as they made their way into the back entrance of Ammora.

Ezra was amazed at the progress the builders had made so quickly!

Last she knew, the stadium hadn't been ready, nowhere near it! And yet here it stood, completed. Not painted nor treated, but it was built. A feat in and of itself.

Ezra cuddled Angelica against her chest as she settled into the chair that had been made for her to sit in with Derik seated to her right. To her left, Lord Jarod sat in a chair and the Council members sat near them in all of theirs. The Ambassadors and their monarchs from the Dark Elves and the Forest Elves sat with their retinue down before them.

"I'll be fighting in the second half, Sorceress," Derik reassured her as she leaned Angelica against her chest. Behind them, crooning in her Dragon form with the Dragon Hatchling was Surala. Queen

Felati, Princess Kayla and the rest of their guards sat in the row before the Dark Elves and the Forest Elves.

No one was arguing. Everyone had pulled together to work this out. Prizes sat gleaming on the tables for the winners of the tournament.

And the day was beautiful. Sunny and perfect, warm but not hot. A perfect day to hold it, Ezra realized as she looked around.

"All right, but please don't get seriously hurt, Derik," she said, feeling her own worry surge up at the thought of having to watch him fight again so soon after a big battle.

"I'll be fine, Sorceress. Really. I have a little extra nervousness to work off," Derik said with a dry chuckle as Angelica stirred against Ezra's chest. Shifting the baby to her shoulder, she rubbed her back and studied the man she had come to love so fiercely.

He doesn't understand how much I worry about him, being mortal, does he? Ezra thought somberly as she struggled with her own emotions for a moment. Eve had warned her that she was going to be emotional for a while after the pregnancy. But she hadn't expected to feel so so…. human was the only word for it. A feeling she hadn't had for a very long time.

::It's perfectly natural to worry, Ezra. You love him and care for him. And besides, you're a new mother now and new mothers, or mothers in general, tend to worry,:: Baelios soothed her telepathically as she settled in to watch the first of the matches.

::True, Baelios. But I'm immortal and I shouldn't be this worried about him. I know he can take care of himself in a fight,:: she replied, trying to hide just how worried she was from him.

::;Ezra, if you didn't worry, you wouldn't be you,:; Baelios replied, which made Ezra relax. Angelica was stirring against her shoulder again and Ezra rubbed her back, soothing her as she took a breath.

It will be all right, she told herself as she settled in to watch the tournament unfold.

Derik wasn't worried. His bout wasn't until towards the end, but he was enjoying watching the early bouts between insectoids and Orcs, Tribesman against Tribesman. The current fight was between Wahya and an Insectoid.

There was no killing, as per the rules since this wasn't a real battle. But it was all in good fun. The swords were wooden and were dipped in chalk to show the marks on their opponents.

The circles were clearly established with chalk on the ground so the fighters could only go so far from each other during the fight.

Everything had been planned with painstaking detail to keep all of the fighters safe, but also to use up the excess energy that they hadn't used in the battle. The battle had been good and hard fought, but it hadn't been as hard as the first battle a few months ago when they had fought Juktis and his men.

Derik shifted a bit, leaning forward as he saw a particularly good move by Wahya which left an orange chalk mark on the Insectoid's black and tan hide.

"Yeah, Big Daddy, that's how we do it!" Tala called from somewhere nearby. Derik couldn't help but laugh hearing Tala cheer for her husband so loudly.

"Are you going to cheer for me when I'm down there?" Derik asked Ezra with a twinkle in his eye. Ezra gave him a worried look.

"With Angelica asleep? No, but…I'm sure there'll be plenty of cheers from the crowd, Derik. I will be cheering inside for you," she reassured him with a wink and leaned in to kiss his lips briefly before their attention again turned to the fighting down below.

Wahya was in his element. He had once been a feared warlord before he and Tala had been cursed. He had killed hundreds of people back when he was mortal. And while he regretted that now, he couldn't help but enjoy a good fight, even if it was just for a tournament.

These days, I enjoy it more when I know no one's going to die as a result, he thought as he dodged the Insectoid's wooden sword yet again.

Somewhere in the stands, he could hear Tala cheering for him as he came up, giving a surprise attack that the Insectoid had probably never seen before in his short life and Wahya again danced away, bouncing lightly on his toes with his wooden blade in his hand.

The Insectoid, whose name was Serifan, was twice the size of Wayha, and quite agile. Of course, Wahya hadn't aged since he'd been cursed which was when he was around forty years old.

Since then, he'd lived fifteen hundred years at least, possibly more. The years had blended together for Wahya, and while the curse had been horrible at first, these days he counted it as a blessing.

All of his children had inherited his and Tala's curse as well but they all followed their parent's example of trying to help those to turn their lives around before it was too late and trying to soothe those whose time had come.

Serifan struck again and Wahya dodged again, leaving another Mark on Serifan's back as he danced away lightly. Serifan, frustrated, turned on Wahya.

"How are you so damned fast?" the Insectoid asked, his mandibles around his mouth moving in a way that formed the words showing his anger and frustration at not being able to just down Wahya and be over and done with it.

"Years of Practice, Bra. Years of practice," Wahya replied smoothly before he struck with another move that took Serifan by surprise this time and brought an end to the bout. "Well fought, Bra! If you want, before your tribe leaves, I'll show you some counters to some of these moves so you aren't taken by surprise again," Wahya offered as he offered his hand.

Serifan took Wahya's forearm and shook it with a sound that burbled like a brook, the Insectoid's version of laughter.

"I'd like that, Wahya. Well fought," Serifan agreed as they turned to return to the stands to sit and watch the rest of the tournament.

"That was a good fight," Jarod observed to Ezra's left as he clapped for both contestants. "I haven't seen many men able to stand up to an Insectoid's attack."

"It can be done, but you need experience and lots of practice," Ezra replied as she shifted Angelica, who was now asleep, down to rest in the crook of her arms and rested them against the arms of the chair.

"Wahya is immortal, is he not?" Jarod asked with a thoughtful expression on his face.

"Yes. He was cursed with immortality long before I ever met him. I didn't know that until he came to Ammora with Tala to help us take on your brother," Ezra replied, giving Wahya and Tala a big smile and mouthed the words *Well done* to avoid waking the baby.

"Wonder why he was cursed with it. Not very many mages would bother to gift a mortal with immortality. Most would destroy an enemy," Jarod mused as he shifted in his chair.

"He used to be a warlord long before I was born. Some of his old followers continued even after he ended his own reign of terror…the temple where I grew up was taken out by descendants of those followers," Ezra said, remembering that grim day when she had had to hide and listen to the screams, the sound of battle…and had emerged to find those who had raised her and most of her sisters were all dead or taken.

"Yes, but why curse him with immortality? That's a difficult thing to do and something that isn't done easily," Jarod insisted.

"I don't know. I don't even know which Mage cursed him. Perhaps they saw something in him and Tala…something that could be turned around and changed," Ezra said as she thought on it, studying the pair as they settled down to watch Aeryn face off against a Forest Elf.

"Perhaps I can help with that mystery. I know quite a few immortals that are older than you and I. I may be able to find the mage and ask their reasoning."

"Jarod, it's in the past. Wahya and Tala have changed and used their curse to stop others from following in their footsteps. Why not just let it be?" Ezra asked.

"Because sometimes, it's more important to know than not to know," Jarod replied with a smile. "I love a good mystery to unravel and that would be a decent tale to muse over some wine and see why they felt it necessary to do what they did. I'd like to know how they did it also. If they still live."

"If they're immortal, then they would still be alive," Ezra said, puzzled at what Jarod's thoughts were and not reaching out to find out.

"Unless they gifted him and Tala with their immortality. Sometimes, immortals do that and take on the mortality of the person they are gifting."

"Why would they do that?"

"So they could die," Jarod replied. "Not every immortal easily lives forever," he told her with a wistful look. "Sometimes I wonder if Juktis would have done what he did…if he had gifted his immortality to another and become mortal instead."

"You can't know what Juktis was thinking or feeling other than greed. He was evil and sometimes there isn't a reason for being such other than a thirst for power," Ezra told him, remembering the man who had tortured her and raped her when he had managed to defeat her the first time.

"True, but we had everything as a family. He killed my parents…something that I didn't think was possible. Absorbed them like a parasite—"

"There was nothing you could have done to stop him when he did that. You did what you could and what you had to do. We defeated him and now…his power is being absorbed by the Orb of Eithal. He is being punished for his crimes," Ezra told him, reaching with her free hand to touch his arm in an effort to soothe him.

"I should have done more," Jarod said with a look of regret in his eyes. "I—"

"How? He was stronger than you, stronger than I was before we got the Orb. It took the effort of four of us to defeat him," she reminded him gently, wishing she could take this guilt from him.

"We're lucky it didn't take more. As it is, it may take more to defeat Alyra once and for all. How are you going to defeat her? Do you have a plan?" Jarod asked.

"I don't know yet, Jarod. I don't know, but I have to find her first. I know her true name now, and that's an advantage that she doesn't have. Now, it's just a matter of finding her and finding a way to trap her like we did your brother," Ezra replied, remembering the vision of her taunting Alyra within Ammora…and the horrible creatures that Ezra knew was now the source of the screams and cries of those in the cloud the Wizard's Council had foreseen.

Aeryn lost though he fought like hell against his opponent. Match after match and Ezra looked to Derik, wondering when his turn would be next.

Derik finally rose, gave Ezra a wink and headed down to go and face off against Ambassador Talice herself.

With worry about her problem of how to defeat Alyra as well as her worry for Derik, Ezra settled in to watch.

Derik's turn was last in the tournament. He and Ambassador Talice had agreed to face off as the last bout. Granted, Talice was faster, more agile than he was.

But Derik was infinitely more patient. He waited as Talice moved to strike, blocked her with one sword and struck her with his second sword, leaving a long blue mark against her white gown spun of spider silk.

Talice whirled and he ducked and lunged, managing to get a light hit in.

"Light!" Derik called quickly before someone could claim he was trying to cheat, which he wasn't. Light strikes were allowed so long as they were called out. Talice laughed and landed her first strike against his arm before she whirled and landed another against his belly.

"Light," Talice called as he fell back, bouncing on his toes as he studied her. She lunged and he whirled, landing two blows against her back with both swords, one after the other as she hadn't anticipated his dodge.

"Winner, Derik!" Lita announced as he and Talice grasped forearms and congratulated each other on a good fight.

"Before we leave, I'll train more with you," Talice promised with a wink and a smile on her glistening red lips.

"I'd like that!" Derik replied, knowing that it could only be to his benefit if he took her up on it.

After all, he didn't get a chance to train with a Dark Elf every day.

Chapter Nineteen

After the tournament, there was a grand feast inside Ammora Castle. It was a chance for those who had fought in the tournament to eat and share stories with their fellows at the tables. Everywhere Ezra looked, there was a mix of peoples all gathered around food and drink and sharing stories.

Laughter rang through the air as everyone enjoyed themselves. Ezra settled with Angelica into her usual chair and smiled as a plate filled with her favorites whisked itself down in front of her. Picking up some cheese and bread, Ezra nibbled as she cuddled her sweet daughter.

Thus far Angelica had slept most of the day, which meant that Ezra likely had a long night ahead of her. She didn't mind, she felt better now that the baby was finally here.

Jarod had settled next to her as had Derik. Lita, Talice, Suidan, Surala and Felati all had come out as well and were all sitting at her table.

How often does one get a chance to share a meal with this mix of people? Ezra thought in awe as the Insectoid Chieftain settled down with Wahya along with an Ogre chieftain. Ezra nodded to both and listened as the people around her began to share their own stories. Stories of past battles, of past losses and victories. *I can't imagine being without this now, even though it's been noisy and not the most convenient. Baelios was right. I should have allowed others to settle here sooner,* Ezra thought with a tinge of regret.

::I'll remind you of that one day when you're frustrated and tired of the noise,:: Baelios sent telepathically with a mental chuckle.

::Oh hush. This is a beautiful moment and a beautiful time right now,:; Ezra replied, her own mental voice showing her own repressed laughter. :;And it'll all be gone all too soon after this.::

:;Unfortunately, yes. Everyone plans to leave in a few days and Jarod may well leave tonight,:; Baelios replied, his own mental voice showing a tinge of regret at the thought.

:;We were alone for far too long…I should've listened and allowed people to live here sooner. But…I just hope that I don't regret the decision some day…like when Alyra finally does come to strike.::

::Don't let her, Ezra. We'll find her and we'll stop her,:: Baelios sent, his voice echoing with a Draconic timbre again.

Ezra hoped he was right as she settled in to listen and share some stories of her own.

Derik wasn't as uneasy as he had thought he'd be with Jarod sitting to one side of Ezra and he sitting on the other. At the same time, it felt right now. He wasn't flirting or trying to seduce Ezra anymore, but he looked different. More confident in himself perhaps, a bit more worried about the future than he had been when they had first met.

Ezra wasn't as uneasy with Jarod either, she was more relaxed and open than she had been since his first arrival at Ammora. It helped Derik to relax, knowing that if she felt safe enough to let her guard down, she was likely sensing something and no longer so haunted by the man's twin.

Good news all around, so far as Derik was concerned as he and the others took turns sharing stories of past battles, past training and trainers.

It was a good night, filled with stories and laughter.

As it should be.

Chapter Twenty

The days following the tournament were busy. Ezra and Derik scarcely got a chance to sleep as the baby was up much of the night but would sleep quite a bit during the day. Eve assured them both that this was normal for any child, so they just took naps whenever they could.

Jarod had informed Ezra before he returned to the Fortress that every prisoner was rescued and those who had been changed were back to normal. Well, those that were still in his Fortress that is. Those who had come back to Ammora were also normal and the prisoners who had been held as hostages were recovering from their wounds.

Kayla had recovered very quickly with proper food and a chance to exercise her weak body a little each day. She also was showing signs of changing soon, something that Felati seemed very proud of.

There was just one problem.

"Alyra got away," Ezra said softly as she rocked the baby in her arms as she walked through the hallways towards the Entrance Hall.

"I know," Derik said as he walked with her, rubbing the small of her back. "But this isn't the end, Sorceress. We'll get her. There's got to be a way to track her down," he said in a tone that showed her plain as day that he was just as frustrated as she was.

"She's hidden herself for so long…the last time I saw her, I could've sworn that she was mortal," Ezra replied, puzzled and even more frustrated. "I don't even know where to begin looking for her," she admitted.

"I have faith in you, Sorceress. You found her this time, you can find her again," Derik said as they entered the Entrance Hall, where the tribes that Wahya and Tala had sent for, as well as the Hive people, were waiting to depart.

Dark Elves, Forest Elves, humans, Insectoids, Ogres…everyone was milling around and wishing each other well on their journeys home. Even the Dark Elves and the Forest Elves had agreed to send Ambassadors to each other's homes soon to begin discussing a peace treaty.

"If you need any help with that, you can send your Emissaries here to negotiate on neutral ground," Ezra offered with a smile as she lowered the drawbridge to allow those who were ready to begin their journeys. The city had offered everyone supplies so those who were traveling wouldn't have to worry about running short of food.

Thank the Gods Cephra's Farm and the other farms had such a good season this year, Ezra thought as a horn blew and people began to march.

"We may take you up on that offer, Sorceress. Our deepest thanks for all your help and all you have done," Ambassador Talice of the Dark Elves offered before their party turned to leave Ammora at last.

"As shall we and thank you. We could not have found our people without you," Ambassador Suidan of the Forest Elves said before the Forest Elves moved to march beside their Dark Elf Cousins to begin their journey home. Both of their Monarchs and their Consorts had been rescued and Ezra wasn't surprised to see both pairs marching in the middle of the retinue, where they would have the most protection from their own people.

Ezra smiled as she shifted Angelica to rest against her right shoulder and rubbed her daughter's back.

Surala and the baby Dragon came up to stand beside Ezra and Angelica, though Surala was no longer in her Draconic form. The baby however, being a full Dragon, couldn't shape-shift but she was a fully healthy and quite playful baby. The little one looked to Angelica with wide, pink eyes and Ezra looked down as both Angelica and the Dragon Baby began to glow.

"What's happening?" Ezra asked Surala, who chuckled.

"That's their bond. One day, they will be a team and they'll inherit my Dragon's Keep and take over for me. My time is growing short, Sorceress. I have maybe fifty years left before I must have a Successor trained and ready to take over. These two…will take my place one day," Surala said sadly but with pride in her eyes. "I'm glad that we found each other, Sorceress, so the children can grow up together."

"I have no idea how to raise a dragon, so I am very glad that we met, Surala. And yes, we'll have to visit back and forth so they can play and get to know each other…once Angelica is old enough. Eve says it'll be a while before she can travel," Ezra said as the glow faded after a few moments, though both children seemed very content. "When will you and Felati be ready to head for home, Surala?" Ezra asked, in no hurry to see them go but she had a feeling that Surala would wish to return home soon as she had duties of her own to fulfill.

"A few more days, I think. Kayla's nearly ready to travel but…this little one will need a few days more before I'm ready to take her home. Felati said she'll return when I do, though…she said that the chamber here in your Castle is very comfortable for her and Kayla and their retinue," Surala said with a wink to Ezra.

"Good, it'll give the children a little more time together then," Ezra said with a nod. "I'm glad that Felati and Kayla like their chamber. It was designed just for them."

"Oh? Who was your designer? They designed it perfectly for mermaids," Surala said, genuinely interested.

"The Castle did," Ezra replied honestly and couldn't help but chuckle when she saw the surprise on Surala's face. "This is an unusual place, Surala. It's alive…and I am bound to it."

"That explains why you protect this place so fiercely. I wouldn't wish my Keep to fall into the wrong hands, I expect you feel the same. The amount of power here is incredible. I feel almost as if I'm basking in it," Surala admitted.

"The Wizard's Council created a powerbase here and merged into one being. I became the guardian here to protect the powerbase from those who would misuse it. It wasn't exactly my choice," Ezra explained.

"And yet you bear it well. It's not easy living with such a task, particularly if you didn't wish it in the first place," Surala murmured, lightly bouncing the little Dragon against her chest.

"Thank you. So, what's her name?" Ezra asked with a chuckle as the little Dragon suddenly burped and a fine mist of water bloomed forth. Angelica opened her eyes for a moment, smiled a little and resumed napping.

"Etorir. She'll be a fine and strong Water Dragon when she's all grown up, which will be in about ten years. Your daughter won't be grown for ten more beyond that but…that'll give Etorir time to mature and be ready for her new partner."

"That's a beautiful name….Etorir," Ezra said and rubbed Angelica's back. "Etorir and Angelica…sounds like quite a power house to me," she said with a smile as Derik stepped away to speak with another of his friends that was departing.

"It does indeed," Surala agreed as the last of the tribes, clans, ambassadors, entourages and all of the rest who had gathered once again to defend their world departed.

Leaving behind just friends and those who lived here.

Ezra breathed a sigh of relief, hearing the castle quiet down to its normal levels at last for the first time in months.

"So much better," she sighed as she walked with Surala and Derik back to the chambers that Surala was currently sharing with Felati.

Ezra, Surala, Felati, Reanalia, Kayla and Derik spent the afternoon just enjoying each other's company and everyone took a turn with the babies, either holding or changing Angelica's diaper or playing with Etorir to help wear her out for a nap.

It was a peaceful afternoon…one that Ezra had not expected to enjoy.

I failed to catch Alyra. Again, she mused unhappily.

:;There was much going on and you went into labor at the end of it. We're just lucky that you didn't go into labor before the battle, Ezra. We'll find her and we'll stop her. We'll trap her, somehow,:: Baelios whispered encouragingly into her mind.

::And what if we fail, Baelios? What if this was all for nothing?:: she said, worrying at that thought like it was a worn out stocking that she couldn't stop from unraveling.

::Then we will go down fighting to save our world,:: he replied.

::Do you think we can honestly win?::

::Now that we know how she intends to unleash the darkness? Forewarned is fore-armed. We will manage, Ezra…I believe we will,:: Baelios replied into her mind, a soothing presence that reminded her to let go of her worry.

And reminded her to enjoy the little things.

Epilogue

"So, little one, I see you are back," the God of Destruction smiled a grim, almost horrifying smile down at Alyra as she shifted nervously on her feet.

"Yes, I'm back, M'lord. I failed to bring the darkness to the world. I failed in my task," she admitted, her cheeks burning at the embarrassment of her failure. "It was that Sorceress of Ammora. She interfered with my plans again!"

"Placing blame on another. Pitiful. Perhaps your plans were not as foolproof as you thought. How did she find you?"

"I don't know! I don't know how she found me or found out about me. But she told Jarod that I was there…he helped her!" she growled as she looked up at the Destruction God with anger flashing in her eyes.

"Then he should be added to your list of targets. Take them down, one by one, little one. Take time to recover, regain your strength…and when the time is right, truly right…strike."

"Yes, my Lord. I won't fail you again," Alyra said, bowing her head. The Destruction God chuckled and disappeared back into the shadows from whence he came.

Alyra went to the mouth of her cave and looked out at the glowing Castle far in the distance and motioned for the cave door to close.

She was strongest, after all, in the Dark. She was born from the darkness…and right now, she yearned for its dark embrace.

Tomorrow, she would begin to rebuild.

Tonight, she would rest.

A Friend's Heart

By Dawn Wilton

For Meri, Allison and Lynda—I love you all

It was a beautiful sunny day outside in the Mercenary Compound. In the distance, the white marble walls of Ammora Castle gleamed beautifully in the sunlight and glistened like new fallen snow. But it wasn't snow, it was stone. Even so, Lila couldn't help but compare it to the frozen wastelands up in the very far Northern reaches of Axrealia.

Goddess, it reminds me so much of home! Right now, Da and Ma are likely feeding the animals along with my brothers and sisters. Too bad I'm such an odd duck and a disappointment, but...I couldn't pass up the chance to join! Okay it's not the greatest adventure, maybe, but it's far better than working on a farm for the rest of my life! Lila sighed as she began to head for the training courses, determined to better her score.

Only to find that she wasn't alone!

Who is that? She thought as she saw a woman with flowing long blonde hair that was as straight as an arrow, beautiful purple and pink eyes wielding a deadly blade against a set of pells. The woman was dangerously graceful, picking her targets with care and yet striking as easily and as deadly as any of the seasoned Mercenaries.

Lila couldn't help but feel a twinge of jealousy as she picked up her own bow and a practice sword and began to work on the course. In comparison, she felt like a clod! She hadn't met everyone in the Company yet, but she had thought she knew most of the women in it!

Even so, Lila set to her task with a grim purpose, focusing all her might on it. She didn't realize at first that anyone else might be watching her.

"Not bad," a voice rang as Lila finished the course, sweat pouring down her brow, neck and back and feeling at least accomplished if not graceful! "Have you been fighting long?" the other woman asked, the same one that Lila had been watching earlier.

"Oh sorry. Um, only for a year and a half. I joined shortly before the company came here. I'm..Lila. And you are?" Lila asked, feeling awkard and blushing a bit at the praise from the woman that looked as graceful as a dancer and who wielded her weapons with far more skill.

"Sunas. It's nice to meet you, Lila. I've been with the company for a long time, amazing we haven't bumped into each other before now," the other woman replied with a playful grin. "Want some pointers?"

Hope welled up in Lila's chest.

"Please?"

Sunas laughed as she plunked down her tankard on the wooden surface of the table.

"So, then I go to take my drink from the bartender and some idiot grabbed it, threw it against the wall and said because I'm a woman, I can't be good with a sword," Sunas explained, still laughing as she told Lila the tale. "Well, I took my sword out, and dragged him outside by the ear…then proceeded to kick his sorry ass into next week. Afterwards, he paid for a new drink, lodging for the night…and well, let's just say that we ended up spending a very cozy evening together in the baths," Sunas said with a wicked gleam in her eye.

Lila laughed as she plunked her own tankard down.

"Oh Goddess! I think you're even naughtier than I am. Da couldn't stand that I wanted to be a fighter, so he tried to marry me off. When I saw the company passing by, I just grabbed a horse, my sword and a pack. And just filed in with it where Da and Ma couldn't see. One of my brothers saw, but he just waved and gave me a smile. He knew I wasn't happy there. First night out, I found myself in a tent with a big strong man with bad breath and gropey hands. Lost my virginity to him but…he did make it very memorable…and pleasurable," Lila shared, her cheeks flushing as it had been her very first time away from home and what had she done?

"Oh, that's nothing. I've been with dozens of these guys. Not planning on settling on any any time soon. And the women aren't bad in bed either," Sunas shared as she waved her hand dismissively. "Some of them are even better than the men."

"I've…never considered being with a woman."

"You might want to try it. You shacking up with anyone now?"

"Oh no, got my own place and just enjoying the peace and quiet when I'm home. Ugh..I feel all dusty and gritty," Lila said as she scratched an itch on her head, raking her fingertips through her long blood-red tresses. Sunas flipped her long blonde ponytail back over her shoulder and grabbed Lila's hand.

"Well, what're we waiting for? Let's go to the baths. We both tumbled around a lot today, let's go get the dirt and grit off!" Sunas laughed and finished off what was left in her tankard before plunking it down and rising. As usual, the tankard whisked itself off to the kitchen for the kitchen staff to wash. Lila finished her own tankard and rose, laughing a bit.

"Sure, let's go!"

"Race ya!" Sunas turned and took off, running lightly through the crowd, darting around the people as she made her way out of the room. Lila raced to catch up, using the same tactic and laughed as they finally broke free and ran towards the bathing house.

Equally matched in speed, they both arrived breathless and even sweatier and dirtier than they had been before! Grabbing their spare clothes from where they were kept in cubicles at the bath house itself, the pair walked into the steamy, warm atmosphere of the main bathing room. One large deep pool was in the center, nice and hot, and as they stripped and tossed their clothing into the hampers, Sunas and Lila each sank down into the water up to their necks… and sighed in relief.

As most of the mercenaries had seen each other naked more than a time or two, this particular room was unisex. Males and females were both allowed to come and go at their leisure and, at the moment, it was empty except for the two of them.

The pair sat and began to scrub their hair and bodies and then relaxed afterwards, sharing stories. Sunas had had more adventures than Lila had, but Lila was in awe of all the things that Sunas seemed to have seen and done.

"Sounds like you've been all over Axrealia," Lila said as they began to dry off after finally leaving the warm waters of the bath.

Sunas was drying her hair with a towel and flipped it back to smile at her.

"Just about, but you will too. There's always something going on somewhere, unfortunately," Sunas said before reaching over to flick a fingertip over Lila's bare nipple, and that wicked look was back in her eyes. "You'll have plenty of adventures, of that, I am sure."

Over the next few weeks, Sunas and Lila met up every single morning to spar and go over the training course together. Their friendship grew, though it never went beyond that. Over drinks they would chat and laugh over their stories.

Then, one day, it all changed.

"Hey, I thought we were supposed to go over that new move you promised to show me," Lila said as she slid onto the bench in the eating hall across from Sunas. Sunas looked up and gave Lila one of those infectious wicked grins.

"Sorry, I was um...indisposed this morning."

"Oh? Share, woman! Details, details!" Lila said as she began to tuck into her breakfast omelette with fruit on the side, tossing her long braided red hair back over her shoulder again and grinned.

"I was with one of the skirmishers. He and I got to talking last night and well, we kinda ended up in bed together. He's really nice, makes me laugh a lot," Sunas said as one of the men strolled over, looking like he'd conquered the largest mountain in all of Axrealia and plunked down.

Big, broad-shouldered, dark hair, dark beard and piercing blue eyes studied Lila. It was Devlin, one of the best skirmishers in the company. And as Lila raised her brow at him, he put his arm around Sunas possessively.

"Hey, woman, I didn't tell you you could leave my house yet," he said in a tone that made Lila's skin crawl.

"Lila, this is Devlin. And baby, I told you, I was supposed to have been up hours ago," Sunas said with a chuckle that made Lila frown.

"Baby nothin. You don't leave the house until I say so, understand?"

"Um, she's got her own house—"

"No one asked you, skinny. Now, I gotta go and get a tankard and get my ass out on the training field. See you out there, Sunas...I intend to run your ass all over that field today," Devlin laughed, giving Lila a cold look.

Lila had never liked Devlin. She had met him once or twice and knew that he tended to sleep around even when he was in a relationship. He was arrogant and talked down to all of the women in the company as if the sun rose and set in his trousers.

"Him? Are you serious?" she asked Sunas as Devlin strolled away like he owned the world. Why Captain Lita kept him around, Lila had no idea.

"Oh, he's just playing. Meet you out on the field tomorrow?"

"I already did the field this morning...but I could meet you out there—"

"Oh, Devlin wants to show me some new moves but, I'll see you tomorrow at the usual time," Sunas reassured her.

"Oh...Okay, see you tomorrow then," Lila said as Sunas got up and walked out to go and join Devlin outside.

That was only the beginning.

"Hey, where were you this morning?" Sunas asked as she slid onto the bench across from Lila.

"I was pulling guard duty, which you would've known if you'd seen me at all in the past two months," Lila replied, feeling sleep deprived. Over the past two months, she had barely seen Sunas at all. Sunas had become so wrapped up in her relationship with Devlin, she hadn't come to training with Lila or done any of the things they had done together.

Lila had begun to give up on Sunas. She adored her, but she never saw her anymore. And worse, Devlin was spreading all sorts of lies about Sunas all over the city amongst the men. Lila had heard some of it in passing and all of it was slowly starting to damage Sunas' reputation.

Every time Lila tried to get close to Sunas, she had an excuse to be somewhere else.

"I can't seem to get any time with her anymore," Lila had told one of their other friends, Max, with concern just the other day. Max and Sunas had once been lovers, but now they were just really good friends.

"I heard a rumor. Devlin likes to restrict his lovers so they only spend time with him when they're off-duty," Max said with a worried look in his own eyes. "His last woman told me he treated her really badly. Had her feeling so low, that she couldn't face being near anyone else.

"Then why was she with him?"

"He made her feel like the only person she deserved to be with was him. He's charming at first, but the longer it goes on, the worse it gets," Max explained. They had been repairing the Company's stash of armor from the last battle. With odd shadows showing up at night, both Max and Lila had been spending a lot of time on guard duty and keeping armor repaired so that they wouldn't get hurt if it came to a fight. The rest of the Company all kept their armor in one place, and everyone took turns repairing it. This week, it was Max and Lila's turn.

All of that was still on Lila's mind as she looked across the table to Sunas.

"I'm sorry, Devlin and I have been—"

"Busy. I know. You're always busy. He has you doting on him hand and foot, cleaning his house—which isn't even your house—"

"It is…now," Sunas said wistfully. "I was going to tell you, it was kinda sudden—"

"Bullshit! Bull shit! Do you know what Devlin is saying behind your back?" Lila asked, her voice dropping to a whisper.

Just then, Devlin strolled up and plunked right down, ceasing the entire conversation.

"I didn't tell you to come here to eat, Woman! What are you doing with this riff raff?" Devlin growled, giving Lila a glare that made Lila's blood boil.

"Her name isn't woman. It's Sunas! And she and I are friends…or do you not remember that there's more to the world than your cock being inside of her."

"She's whatever I call her, Cunt! She's my hole to fuck, my maid to clean my house. She is Mine," Devlin growled back, leaning forward.

Sunas looked at Devlin, then at Lila.

"Sunas, you can do so much better than this asshole!" Lila said point blank, letting her voice rise loud enough that the entire mess hall suddenly went very quiet.

Even Max looked over and suddenly half of the room stood up, hands on their swords. Lila and Devlin both rose as Devlin looked around, flashing a smile.

"Go back to eating! Who cares what this wench thinks? She's an uneducated barbarian, a nobody! Has she saved half of your asses?"

"No, but neither have you, Devlin. Everyone knows you're in it for the money and for what you can get out of it. You have acted shamefully these past two years and I've turned a blind eye to it because you are really good—" Captain Lita started as she walked over, a furious look in her eyes.

"Oh really, Captain? I could run this company better than you ever could!" Devlin roared back, raising his fist to attempt to hit the Captain.

Max grabbed one wrist, Bear suddenly grabbed the other and Lita glared.

"Devlin, you have one hour to get out of the city. You are no longer part of this company. You think you're so good? Good luck coming up with the coin to begin your own. Knowing you, you'll be back in the shit, throw-together companies with the rest of your peers…and sooner or later, I might get the chance to kill your ass. Get him out of the Castle, NOW!" Lita barked. Max and Bear began to drag Devlin off, with Devlin shouting insults at the Captain the entire way.

"Shit! Oh shit! Now what am I going to do?" Sunas asked as she got up. Lila grabbed her shoulder.

"Do? He's an asshole! Let him leave, you're better off without him! He's spreading all sorts of lies about you—"

"Let him leave? He makes me happy! How dare you, Lila—"

"Happy? How can he make you happy? He treats you like a slave and like you don't even have half a brain! Lila, wake up! You don't mean a thing to him—"

"You don't know him—"

"I wouldn't want to know him! What little I do know is that he treats women like garbage. Ask Max if you don't believe me!" Lila snapped back, losing her temper and storming off herself.

She looked back once only to see tears streaming down Sunas' face.

Sunas stormed back into the home she had shared with Devlin for the past three days. He had out his packs and was deep in the middle of packing.

"Maybe if you apologize—"

"For what? To that cunt? No, I don't bow to a woman! Never should've joined up with this shit-show in the first place. Start packing, woman! We're heading to a better company, a REAL company!" Devlin roared back.

"What? You want me with you?"

"Of course I do. You're Mine. Now, come on, get ready. We're leaving in thirty minutes, got it?"

Sunas looked at their belongings and saw that he hadn't just been packing up his stuff, but hers too. And in a very shitty way.

"All right, let me repack everything though—"

"It's good enough! Get the rest and hurry, we're getting outta here," Devlin roared before he stormed out. "I'm getting' my weapons from the shed."

Sunas sighed but she couldn't bear to be away from him. Other than Lila, he was the best thing that had ever happened to her. She dug into packing, repacking everything quickly and got done with the last of their things just as he returned, lugging his weapons.

"Get yer weapons and yer armor, let's go, Woman!" Devlin roared.

"Okay, okay, I'm going!" Sunas said back, hurrying to go to the armory.

Lila was fuming. Max didn't look happy. Lita looked even more grimly at the two of them from over her desk.

"Sunas just walked in and resigned. I know she's friends with both of you. Would you know why she would do this?"

"It's gotta be Devlin, Captain. Ever since she met him, he's been taking all of her time and energy. If she's not with him, she has to be on duty. She doesn't train with me anymore, she hasn't for two months now," Lila explained.

"I haven't hardly seen her either and Sunas and I used to play games when we weren't busy to keep our minds sharp. We also generally do a lot of the same things together as Lila does but…lately it's just me and Lila and Sunas is either on duty or at home doting on Devlin or keeping his house clean. It's not a healthy relationship, Captain. He's been saying awful things about her to anyone who'll listen and none of it is true," Max added.

"I've heard the same and I know this. Both of you should go and tell her goodbye…she is leaving with Devlin and…if she doesn't see that he is abusive to her, it may be a while before we see her again, if ever.

"I don't want to tell her goodbye—" Lila started. "I want to kill Devlin—"

"Do so and you'll be out of a position. We don't kill off of the battlefield unless that person has committed a crime. As disgusting as it is, Devlin hasn't committed one yet," Lita pointed out calmly. "Just be here for her for when it's over. I have known Sunas for a long time. Sooner or later, she'll realize what's happening…and she'll return. I promise. She has a lot of friends here… and we are all a family. One that'll be stronger without Devlin around," Lita said as she walked around to lay a hand on Lila's shoulder and gave her a sympathetic look. "Sunas will remain on the roster…for when she's ready to come home."

Lila didn't like it…not at all. But Lita was right.

"Yes, Captain."

"You're both dismissed. I'll see you outside," Lita said as she swept out of the room, leaving Lila and Max all alone.

"What can we do?" Lila asked Max.

"Remind her that we're here for her. It's all we can do," Max replied. In real anguish, Lila turned to follow him out.

Their goodbyes were short and sweet, thanks to Devlin. He was practically dragging Sunas out the gate as Lila, Max and Lita all arrived.

"Get your hands off of her," Captain Lita snapped, making Devlin and Sunas pause.

"Shut yer hole, Woman! I don't take orders from you anymore," Devlin snarled, not releasing Sunas. His white knuckled grip tightened on Sunas' arm and Lila saw her friend wince in real pain.

"Sunas, you don't have to go with him—" Lila started.

"Oh shut it! I know you don't like him! I know you've never liked him! But he makes me happy so yes I'm going to go—" Sunas started.

"Sunas, you always have a place with us. Devlin, come anywhere near this place again, and your head will be on a pike," Captain Lita said, her tone gentle when she addressed Sunas but turning cold as she addressed Devlin.

"Thank you, Captain. Love you, Max and Lila!" Sunas called over her shoulder as the pair walked out of the gate.

Max put a hand on Lila's shoulder and Lila sighed, somehow feeling all alone.

Life wasn't the same anymore. Lila just went about her schedule robotically, feeling no joy in anything she did. She missed Sunas greatly but was surprised whenever she got a letter from her friend once a moon.

Naturally every single one seemed to sing Devlin's praises at first. They had joined one of the less ethical companies, but Sunas had managed to fit in and make herself well liked, as usual. Everyone adored her.

I just don't understand why no one likes Devlin. He's a great fighter, a good lover, and I love him so much—

Lila couldn't bear to read the rest. She crumpled up the letter and tossed it in the fire, not wanting to read the rest.

Then she began to write back. Telling Sunas of the things happening here at the city and castle, letting her know all the gossip.

This went on for two long years. In that time, their company had gone to the Fortress and battled the creatures that the mages and healers managed, in the end, to turn back to normal. Every moon, Lila would get a letter from Sunas. Every moon, Lila would send one back.

Lila, I know you don't like Devlin, but I can't just leave him. Okay, he's been ignoring me lately and some of the others here are claiming he's sleeping around. But he really, really loves me.

Sunas, I know that you think he loves you, but he's slept around whenever he was in a relationship here too. Just ask Max, Inas, Tala and a few others. They've all heard him brag about it. This isn't healthy, love—

Lila, I can't just come back! He says that Lita was talking out of her ass—

Sunas, I asked the Captain Again. Here's her letter. Read it for yourself. You will always have a home with us. Come home. I miss you. Please.

That last letter left Sunas in tears. For two years, she had traveled all over with this shit show of a company that Devlin had claimed was the best.

The best for the men maybe. She barely got enough to keep clothes on her back and food in her belly. And naturally, this company didn't feed its soldiers.

Devlin came storming in with a look of rage in his eyes as he took the letter out of her hand and read it.

"She's lying to you. You have nowhere else to go—"

"How was Inas? And better yet how was Flaka last night?" Sunas asked as she got up, grabbed her pack and started to fill it with just her belongings.

"Where the hell do you think you're going?" Devlin roared, grabbing her arm.

"Home! I quit! You don't love me! If you loved me, you wouldn't be sleeping around. If you loved me, you wouldn't say that I suck in bed or that I'm not good enough for you to make babies with! I've heard it, that's right! Get away from me, I am LEAVING!"

Sunas snapped back, putting the last of her few belongings left as Devlin had broken most of her stuff, or thrown it away claiming she didn't need it. She grabbed her weapons.

"If you leave me, you'll have nowhere else to go, Woman!"

"My NAME is Sunas! And anywhere is better than here! Captain, I quit!" she roared as she stormed out of their shared tent, went to the auxillary supply tent and grabbed one of the many spares she knew was around here. She figured they owed her anyway.

After that, she got on the first horse she saw…and headed for home.

Lila was outside in the sunshine, practicing against the pells. She wasn't as graceful as she remembered Sunas being…but she was better than she had been two years ago.

She turned, hearing a commotion and gasped as she saw who was coming in the gate.

On a horse, looking weary and forlorn, Sunas rode in. Max ran over to get the horse while Lila ran over to help Sunas down and put her arms around her, hugging her tightly! She felt thin even to Lila, even with clothes and armor on. And her face looked wan.

"You were right, Lila. How…how come I didn't see it?"

"Because you didn't want to. Welcome home, my friend—"

"Can you forgive me?"

"Of course, for what?"

"For leaving as I did. I should never have gone—" Sunas started. Max came around and put his arms around them both.

"I'm sorry too, but I couldn't tell you what I knew you wanted to hear. I had to tell you the truth. Even if you didn't want to hear it," Lila replied, hugging her two best friends to her, and nearly crying with joy at Sunas' return.

"Welcome home, Sunas. Lila, can Sunas stay with you for a few days until we can get her house back in order?" Captain Lita asked as she walked up.

"Of course! What're friends for?" Lila took Sunas' bag and snagged her by the elbow, steering her towards her own home just a small walk away. That first night, they spent quite a bit of time just talking and catching up and everything felt as right as rain.

A few weeks later, Sunas and Lila were once more facing off on the training grounds.

"You've improved while I was gone," Sunas remarked as she dodged. "And I'm really rusty!"

"You're not that rusty," Lila replied as she dodged and parried before pulling a new move that Max had taught her. "And well keep practicing with me and you'll be back to being a bad ass warrior in no time," she teased, flipping her red hair out of her eyes.

Sunas flipped her loose ponytail of long flowing blonde back again and laughed.

"I hope so, I'd hate to think I'm busting my ass out here for nothing! By the way… thank you."

"For what?"

"For being my friend, Lila. For still being there for me, even…when I wasn't wise enough to see what was going on right in front of me."

"I love you, Sunas. You're part of my family. I have your back, even if you make a bad choice."

"I love you too," Sunas said with a genuine smile. Lila smiled back, hoping that her friend would take the time to truly heal inside. She saw the signs though that her friend would be all right. Lila said a small prayer to the Goddess, hoping it would help.

As the two headed for their ritual bath together, Sunas paused, looking up and pointed up in the sky.

"Wonder who said a prayer?" she said as Lila saw the falcon circling overhead. Lila smiled, feeling relieved. The Goddess herself had sent a sign.

Everything would be all right.

Note from the Author

Thank you so much to everyone who has supported me, laughed with me, cried with me and reminded me that I am only one human being. Thank you so much to my husband of now 20 years, John, whom I love and adore and so so glad that you are still with me after all this time.

Thank you to Mrs. Faucett, who encouraged me to make my short story that eventually became my first book, Vision of Darkness, into a book! It took me a while, but it was worth the effort.

Thank you to my kids! I love you all so much!

Thank you to my friends, Gretchen, Aimee and Brenda. You guys have always told me if you like my work or not and I hope you enjoy this one.

Thank you to Allison—Alley Cat, I so appreciate the help that you gave me with this one and the kind words that you gave me after you read my work for the first time. I hope to continue to make you proud.

Thank you to Meri and Lynda. You two keep me grounded at times when I need it most! Thank you for all the support and encouragement.

Thank you to Pat who sent word via a mutual friend that she really liked my first book. I hope you enjoy the second!

About the Author

Dawn Wilton grew up in Colorado Springs, Colorado. She went to High School at Mitchell High and attended college at the University of Southern Colorado in Pueblo where she got a BA in Music and in Mass Communications. She lives with her husband and her three children in New York State.

www.ingramcontent.com/pod-product-compliance
Lightning Source LLC
Chambersburg PA
CBHW071427200726
48294CB00002B/548